Readers love the Desires Entwined series by TEMPESTE O'RILEY

Designs of Desire

"*Designs of Desire* is a tough realistic book that is touched by violence countered by the growing love between the two heroes."
—Sensual Reads

"The characters of Seth and James were very well rounded and believable… I would be more than happy to read more books by this author…"
—The Novel Approach

"I found it a beautiful tale of unhappiness changed to romance and then love with a happy ending."
—Rainbow Book Reviews

Bound by Desire

"I'd like to say 'thank you' for this little extra snippet of Seth and James."
—Hearts on Fire

Desires' Guardian

"It's a great book to fall into and enjoy some really good characters."
—Love Bytes

"This is my favorite in this series so far. I love seeing how these characters are growing, all of them. As individuals, as couples, as friends, and as a family."
—MM Good Book Reviews

"I had a lot of fun reading this one, and I really CANNOT wait for the next one!"
—The Blogger Girls

By Tempeste O'Riley

Caged Sanctuary
Grand Adventures (Dreamspinner Anthology)
Whiskers of a Chance

DESIRES ENTWINED
Designs of Desire
Bound by Desire
Desires' Guardian • Desires' Pride
Temptations of Desire
Truth in Lace
Signs of Desire

Published by DREAMSPINNER PRESS
www.dreamspinnerpress.com

SIGNS *of* DESIRE

TEMPESTE O'RILEY

DREAMSPINNER PRESS

Published by
DREAMSPINNER PRESS

5032 Capital Circle SW, Suite 2, PMB# 279, Tallahassee, FL 32305-7886 USA
www.dreamspinnerpress.com

Signs of Desire
© 2015 Tempeste O'Riley.

Cover Art
© 2015 Reese Dante.
http://www.reesedante.com
Cover content is for illustrative purposes only and any person depicted on the cover is a model.

ISBN: 978-1-63476-582-4
Digital ISBN: 978-1-63476-583-1
Library of Congress Control Number: 2015949570
First Edition November 2015

Printed in the United States of America
(∞)
This paper meets the requirements of
ANSI/NISO Z39.48-1992 (Permanence of Paper).

To Grace and Peter—for never giving up on me, or allowing me to give up on me. Thank you for all the love, shoves, and cheering!

This story is for all those who believe in love, just not for themselves. You are worth loving! Period.

author's note

This story takes place after *Desires' Guardian* and *Temptations of Desire*, but in the spring and summer of 2014. This becomes important near the end of the story, as certain events unfold. Thank you so much for again taking the time to read along with my characters' lives and loves.

The Drag Ball mentioned later in this story, as well as the program the money raised through the ball, are very real and sadly needed. If you are a youth in the greater Milwaukee Area and in need of help, Pathfinders (http://pathfindersmke.org/) is there to help.

The other place of import mentioned here and in both *Desires' Guardian* and *Temptations of Desire* is the MKE LGBT Community Center (http://www.mkelgbt.org/). They also provide services for teens, adults, and older members in the LGBTQ community.

In my stories the Center is a combination of the MKE LGBT Center and Pathfinders.

chapter one

THE DARKNESS of the parking lot stretched out in front of Adrian Keys, and the door to the Mexican restaurant spilled light onto the pavement every time someone opened it to exit or enter. *Stupid.* He regretted letting his friend talk him into going out with "the guys." By the time he reached the door, he had almost talked himself out of going in, but no such luck. A gentle tap to his shoulder broke him out of his paralysis. When he turned, he was face-to-face with Chase, his one-time date turned friend.

Distracted by his concerns, he barely noticed Chase was dressed in a light blue button-down shirt that conformed to his lean and lithe chest. He wore low-rise black jeans that were faded on the thighs, chunky biker boots, and a platinum wrist cuff on one wrist—Adrian knew the cuff was new. When they'd met, Chase had worn a double-buckle black leather one instead. The thing that caught his attention, as it always did, was Chase's eyes. They were one part amber, one part blue, and another part green, with the most beautiful flecks of gold in them.

Shaking off his inappropriate distraction, he tried to smile, and said and signed, "Hi."

"Hi, Adrian. You're not leaving already, are you?" Chase signed. Adrian loved how hard Chase worked to improve his ASL and how he always used it with him now. Even though he could read lips quite well, communicating in his native language and style was more fluid and comfortable for him.

"No." Adrian bit his bottom lip, looking away from Chase. He glanced at the restaurant a moment, not sure his worries would make sense to anyone Hearing before returning his gaze to his friend. "I'm worried

1

your friends will be uncomfortable with me or that I won't be able to keep up with the conversation."

The grin that spread across Chase's face was both endearing and unnerving. "There's only a few of us, and it's really good food. Promise." He winked. "Tonight is a night for fun!" Before Adrian realized what was happening, Chase draped his arm around Adrian's shoulders and pulled him in for a hug.

Adrian allowed Chase to drag him inside, and before he knew it, he sat at a long, curved booth with six others, including Chase. Warmth blanketed him on all sides thanks both to the warm bodies and the heater that valiantly fought off the frigid temperatures outside. Milwaukee in the early spring was cold, icy, and just plain miserable to be out in, though he would take cold over heat any day of the week—you can always put more on, after all.

"Adrian, you know Rhys, and these guys are Dale, Simon, Jamie, and Grayson," Chase explained, signing as he spoke, making sure to gesture to each man in turn. "We're only missing Vaughn, but he's still overseas doing his teacher-swap thing. Boys, this is Adrian."

He worked hard to smile and waved. "Hello."

They all replied with *hey*s and *hi*s as he looked between the men.

A pretty little waitress stopped by the table but didn't face him, so Adrian had no idea what she said. When she finally turned to him, she stared at him expectantly, but he wasn't certain what she wanted. Chase smiled at him and signed, *"Soda pop, tea, beer?"*

"Coke, please," he said, hoping she could hear him well enough. This was one of the reasons he hated going out, especially in a Hearing group. Nevertheless, he had promised Chase, and honestly, he did need to get out for something other than work or family.

Chase said something to the woman that made her blush. As he watched, she apologized repeatedly before hastily retreating. *"Sorry about that."*

Waving the words away, Adrian smiled. "It's okay, Chase. Hearing people expect everyone to be hearing, and since I don't wear hearing aids, she had no way to know any better." He looked around at the other men at the table, recognizing Chase's partner, Rhys. "It's good to finally meet you," he said, wondering how the man would take his presence. They had never officially met, though he had seen him on his and Chase's one and only date.

"And you," the large, muscular man said. Adrian took a moment to look him over again; yep, Rhys made Adrian's own six-two seem small, and the shoulder-length ginger hair reminded him of some Celtic God from the storybooks his mother gave him as a boy. "I'd say I was sorry for messing up your date with Chase, but I'm not," Rhys added with a wide grin.

"Brat," Chase teased as he cuddled into Rhys's side more. "Seriously, I'm glad I took Adrian out that night, even if things didn't work out for us. He's a great friend," Chase said, head tilted up but still visible.

They all debated what to eat and chatted for a little, Adrian mostly staying quiet and watching the others. He noticed one of the other men seemed just as out of it as he was, the one Chase had called Grayson. He was handsome, tall, and powerful like Rhys, but he had long black hair, deeply tanned skin, and light brown eyes that were almost amber. He was a little thinner than Chase's partner, though just as intimidating a presence.

The other man who caught his attention was named Simon. Adrian knew a little more about him because Chase spoke of his closest friends often, and Adrian loved meeting Chase's friends even if the outing was nerve-racking. Simon had light brown hair, big puppy brown eyes, and a slender body. The longer Adrian looked, the more he wondered how Simon would look when dressed in something a little less bulky.

A tap to his shoulder pulled Adrian out of his musings. He turned and realized the server was back with their dinners and blushed at how entranced he'd been. He didn't usually stare, hating when others did that to him. *"Sorry."*

"No sorrys." Chase hugged Adrian, then dug into his bowl of chicken and dumplings.

Simon waved to get Adrian's attention and smiled when he looked up from his country-fried steak and mashed potatoes with white gravy. "Chase said you were his teacher before and are now a friend." Adrian nodded. "How'd he convince you to go out with his skinny butt?"

Heat infused Adrian's face as he laughed. "Chase was very sweet and asked nicely."

"I love your laugh, by the way. It's deep like your voice, kind of carefree." Simon looked slightly sad. Adrian knew he'd had a hard time lately. Chase said he'd been cheated on a year ago and had refused to date since. Adrian knew the feeling, though he pushed the thought away, hoping not to dwell on why he was alone.

He ducked his head slightly. "Thanks? I don't know how anyone sounds, even myself, so it's always weird to get comments like that."

"I said the same when we went out," Chase commented. "But don't let him fool you. He's an excellent teacher and speaks in all his classes. He knows his voice is good."

"No, I know it's clear enough for you to understand. That's something I work hard to make true, but I have never heard my voice, so I have no idea how I sound. And well…. Chase was the first person to ever say something like that."

He worked regularly with various computer programs to improve and maintain his speech, knowing if he didn't it could cost him his position at the college. He had always struggled to make sure he spoke well for Hearing people, considering his family's opinion of his Deafness. His dad knew sign language, but his mom refused to learn, insisting he learn to be "normal." Adrian had always thought that was extremely unfair, especially as a child. Considering his hatred of being dependent on others for his communication, he was thankful he could read lips and speak as well as he did.

"Then you know the wrong people, 'cause he's right." Simon nodded to emphasize his point, confusing Adrian more. Why would he be so determined with his compliments?

Shrugging off his curiosity, Adrian tried to push past the topic. "What do you do?"

Simon's eyes tightened at the edges slightly, his shoulders drooping a little more. "I'm a writer."

"He's a romance author, and a damn good one," Jamie, or James as he knew the guy's actual name was, said. Chase talked about his best friend often, though this was the first they'd met. "Don't let him talk down about what he does."

"James, hush. He's not interested in what kind of writing I do."

"Yes, I am. I love to read. Would I know any of your work?" Adrian didn't have a large collection of romances, but he had read some. He couldn't think of any authors named Simon, though.

"You're an author?" Grayson asked, turning to join their conversation.

The nod seemed reluctant, but the smile on Simon's face, while small, looked genuine. "Yeah, I write under the name Tyler Jacobs, a pseudonym, but I have a few books out. But, um, I thought we were trying to get to know Adrian and Grayson, not more about boring ol' me."

4

Adrian looked to Grayson and back, then shrugged. "I thought it was so we could all get to know each other."

"Actually, I think Chase was trying to play matchmaker," Rhys said, shoving Chase playfully.

"Matchmaker?" Adrian asked. Whom was he trying to set up with whom? And why?

Chase scowled and swatted Rhys. "I was hoping to introduce a few new friends and hoped everyone got on well, brat." Chase reached out and patted Adrian's hand, confusing him further. "I swear, I'm not trying to push you if you don't want to date anyone right now."

"Just who were you hoping to match up?" Dale asked, smirking as he stared at Chase.

Honestly, Adrian wanted to know that as well. It was obvious Chase meant to fix him up with one of his other friends, but he couldn't imagine which one. James was married, Chase was happily with Rhys, and he didn't know Simon, Dale, or Grayson beyond what he'd learned of them since he'd arrived, really.

Only two of the people at the table even interested him, truth be told, but he couldn't figure out why anyone would try to set him up with either man. In Adrian's experience, most Hearing people didn't overly like dealing with having a Deaf partner. His few exes certainly hadn't, no matter what he did to seem more "normal."

Chase shook his head, clamping his lips closed as he glared at Rhys.

"Chase?" Adrian said and signed. *"Who were you hoping to set me up with and why?"*

Their eyes locked for a few moments before Chase looked away, his shoulders drooping. After a moment, Chase turned back to face Adrian and replied, *"Grayson. He's in IT, like you and I are, he's super loyal and really cute in that quiet reserved-guy kind of way."*

"Grayson?" Well, he was handsome and seemed nice, if a little stoic. Adrian didn't know how to feel about Chase trying to set him up with one of his friends, though. *"I can get my own dates, Chase."*

"I know that. It.... Grayson is really nice, and I'd love to see Rhys's buddy happy. And I like you, but we're not right for each other, either. I thought of you two, though. You'd make a beautiful couple. His Native American features and your slightly Asian ones...."

He couldn't help it, Adrian chuckled, amused at Chase's logic. The man was sweet and a total flirt, but it seemed he was a bit of a ditz when it came to understanding his friends. Chase frowned, folding his arms across his chest as he stared at Adrian—more a glare really. *"Sorry, sorry."*

"What are you two saying and why is Chase pouting?" Simon asked.

"Considering Chase pointed at me more than once, I think it's obvious who his other intended victim is," Grayson said, his lips almost curling into a smile—more the hint of an attempt than an actual smile.

Adrian nodded. "Said we'd look pretty together," he explained, barely suppressing the laughter threatening again.

Simon glanced between Adrian and Grayson and frowned. "Well, I can see that, sorta, but no. Grayson needs someone outgoing and loud to compliment the whole stoic-intimidation thing he's got going on. Adrian, though, he needs someone more… hmm… fun and playful but less, I don't know. Less party, more cuddly."

Chase's pout morphed into something more confused, then curious. "Huh. You think?"

A sharp nod was all Simon gave.

"Don't we get a say in this matchmaking game of yours?" Grayson asked, his eyes dancing with humor, though the smile still wasn't quite there.

"Well, of course," Chase said, then stuck his bottom lip out in an adorable fake pout. "But I like my friends happy and all. *And* I'd really like for you to stay, Grayson. This thing of you only visiting Rhys and me now that I'm safe bites. Not that my ex is behind bars, but that you're hardly ever here."

"Just 'cause you're all domestic now doesn't mean we all need to be," Dale interjected. He didn't seem as amused with the matchmaking as the others. Adrian wondered if Dale was against the idea of Grayson and him as a couple or if Dale was against couples in general for some reason.

He watched as the others ate and playfully argued back and forth. It was hard to focus on so many people talking at once, so he kept quiet. They'd been good about facing him for the most part, but even so, it was tiring trying to keep up as his focus, by necessity, bounced around the table.

As the server cleared the dinner dishes and offered dessert, Adrian continued to observe, amused with what he noticed. *So that's why Dale was annoyed....* Dale watched Grayson, interest clear in his eyes, though he seemed to work hard not to show it. That part confused Adrian, but he filed his observation away to ask Chase about later.

Grayson was handsome, and he did seem nice, but the only one who truly caught Adrian's attention was Simon. He knew Simon wasn't a good bet to ask out, though. Not if he was still as hurt as Chase claimed, which his body language backed up. While Simon chatted and smiled, it seemed forced at times, and he held his body tighter than someone hanging out with friends ought to. There was also an air of sadness around Simon that worried Adrian; one bad breakup shouldn't make Simon seem so lonely while surrounded by friends, he didn't think.

"Your order?" Simon asked, catching him watching him again.

"Just coffee, thanks." Adrian didn't have any room left for sweets right then, but coffee was always welcome.

A few minutes later, cream and sugar added, Adrian sipped his warm drink between chuckles as he watched the others tease and pick on each other. It wasn't unusual for him to people watch, he did that all the time, but it was more fun observing his new friends than he had expected.

"Hey," Chase signed. *"Are we too much for you? You're being so quiet, even quieter than James."*

"No, I'm having fun. Hard to follow everything, but glad I came."

Chase grinned, that wide, open smile that had won Adrian over when he'd asked him out to dinner the first time. *"Cool!"* Chase fidgeted, not meeting Adrian's eyes for a moment, then asked, *"You mad about me wanting to set you up?"*

Adrian thought about that for a moment, but the fact Chase wanted him happy warmed him more than he expected. He rarely dated, and no one had tried to set him up in ages. Well, ignoring his mother and her insistence he should settle down with a wife and make little baby Keys. Kids... maybe. A wife.... No! Women were lovely creatures, great for friends, but never once in his thirty-three years had one ever enticed him even a little. Not that she listened.

Shaking off the morose thoughts, he turned back to Chase. *"No. It's cute. Thank you for caring, but I think you need to pay better attention to your friends. Watch Dale."*

Chase's brows scrunched together as he blinked repeatedly. *"Dale?"*

He nodded, then laughed at Chase's confused look. Before he could add more, Dale stood and grinned. "Who wants to hit the clubs with me? Come on, Si, I know you do."

Simon shook his head. "No, I'm going to call it a night when everyone's done."

"Spoilsport. Fine." Dale turned to Chase and Rhys next. "You two will come out with me, right? You love to dance, Chase."

Chase and Rhys talked, but Adrian couldn't make out what they said, though Chase clearly wanted to go and Rhys didn't.

"I need to get home to Seth and Danni," James said while Chase and Rhys were still debating. "I'll catch you all later, and Adrian?"

At his name and the direct gaze, Adrian started. "Yes?"

"It was really nice meeting you. I hope you'll come around more often. Maybe I can introduce my husband and our daughter to you soon."

Adrian nodded and smiled. "I would like that."

"Great."

Hugs and handshakes were passed around as everyone said their good-byes. Adrian noticed Dale sidled up beside Grayson, flashing a killer grin up at him as he spoke. Adrian didn't need to hear to know what Dale was up to, or rather, who he would be with later, if Grayson said yes.

After Adrian paid his bill, he gave one last wave to the group, then stepped to the front of the restaurant before he pulled out his cell and started typing.

He hit Send just as someone tapped him on the shoulder. When he turned, he found Simon standing there, a shy smile on his lips—and what lips they were. Pink, plump on the bottom, and just made for nibbling. Pulling his gaze away from temptation, he met Simon's eyes and asked, "Yes?"

"I. Um." Simon looked down, shifting from one foot to the other, though he kept his head up enough Adrian could still make out his words. "I wondered if I could catch a ride with you? I rode with Dale, but he, Chase, Rhys, and Grayson are going to the club, and I don't really feel up to it. I don't want to delay James getting home, either." His eyes went wide as he suddenly looked up. "Do you even drive? I'm sorry if not."

Unable to restrain his amusement, he laughed, the sound seeming to cause more embarrassment and confusion for Simon. "I do drive. My TA texted me just a moment ago that he has some tests ready, so I need to stop and pick them up. If you don't mind riding with a Deaf guy and a short delay, I don't mind driving you."

Adrian waited, wondering if Simon would still want the ride after reminding him of his lack of hearing. He was a good driver; never a speeding ticket or any form of citation, but he also knew many Hearing people didn't understand that hearing was not required to be a good driver.

"I'm not worried," Simon replied, that shy smile back on his handsome, if too thin, face.

"Great. Then let's go. I will stop at Kelley's and then drop you off at home." They walked out together, and he turned toward his little graphite blue Nissan Rogue SL.

Once inside, he turned and showed Simon his GPS. "After I stop at Kelley's, punch in your address, okay? I can't read lips and drive at the same time, so you can't give me directions after I pull out."

Simon agreed, and they buckled up. Moments later Adrian pulled out into traffic, both confused and a touch excited to have the cute guy he'd been admiring all night alone with him, even though he knew nothing would come of it. He still liked having Simon near for a little longer.

chapter two

SIMON STEPPED out of the shower and grabbed the hunter green towel off the hook next to the frosted shower door before beginning to dry off. He didn't pay much attention, not caring if he was completely dry; he simply didn't want to get his lounge pants wet or get too cold. Spring in Wisconsin, even indoors with a decent heater, was still no time to stay damp.

As usual, his mind turned to things other than what he was doing; this time it wandered to the night before, to when he'd been in the car with Adrian. He'd focused on Adrian as Adrian drove. They hadn't spoken during the drive, though Simon had caught a glimpse of the TA, Kelley, when Adrian stopped at the man's home. Kelley was cute enough but seemed a little cocky, and right then that was not an endearing trait. Simon's last boyfriend had been cocky, self-assured, and sexy in a boy-next-door kind of way. The problem, other than the constant insults the last few months they'd been together and the lying and the bordering-on-brutal sex, was the cheating. Had it been once and an honest oops, Simon believed he could have forgiven him, but not when he'd found out about the cheating because his now-ex had been caught with another guy having sex in public. Right after that bombshell, Simon had learned that Kris had been sleeping around for virtually their entire relationship. He'd never been so glad to have insisted on always using condoms in his life.

Pushing away the hurt and memories threatening to overwhelm him, he pulled up the image of Adrian as he'd looked when he'd shyly told Simon good night and waited until Simon was inside before pulling away. The man was sexy and cute at the same time. He was a little over six feet, probably six two or so, with black hair so dark it was almost blue, almond-shaped, vibrant green eyes, and lightly tanned skin. He had to agree with Chase; Adrian did look sort of Asian—Japanese, he thought—but that didn't seem quite right either. It didn't matter to Simon, though. No matter what his heritage was, Adrian was just plain yum.

The thought brought on a long sigh as he reminded himself that Adrian wasn't the right guy for him. The trouble was, Simon wasn't sure he believed everyone had a Mr. or Mrs. Right anymore—a dangerous concept for a romance author, in his opinion. Trying to shake off the morose thoughts, he focused on dressing, though simple cotton pajama bottoms in blue with little dancing books on them didn't take much thought to put on.

By the time he was dry, dressed, and had dumped his dirty clothes in the hamper, he wanted a nap. Since it was only nine in the morning, he knew that wasn't an option. Instead, Simon padded into the small kitchen and pushed the button to start the coffeemaker after adding the filter pack and water to the machine. He wasn't hungry, but Chase and James both had mentioned his weight loss the night before—thankfully each man had spoken to him alone—so while he waited, he popped a bagel into the toaster and pulled out the strawberry-blackberry preserves. He finished smearing a nice thick layer of the fruit on the toasted bagel as the coffeepot gurgled, letting him know it was ready.

Minutes later he stood in the room next to his bedroom, working through his list of work for the day. He'd converted the second bedroom in his home into an office shortly after he'd moved in. Against one wall was the antique mahogany roll-top desk he and James had found years ago while out window-shopping. It was large, beautiful, and he loved all the drawers and cubbyholes it had. In direct opposition to the elegant nature of the desk sat the ergonomic balance-ball chair he always used when writing. The only thing sitting out on the desk right then was his large-screen laptop. The same laptop he had failed to use for the most part in over a month.

Looking around, he again took in the far wall that was nothing but bookshelves, the window with the sheer curtains over blinds, and the other odds and ends he'd tucked away in various nooks and crannies around the room. On the wall over his desk hung framed posters of his different book covers—each of which he was profoundly proud of, even if he couldn't seem to write lately.

When his cell beeped, alerting him of a text, he pulled his thoughts back to the present and checked to see who was texting him. Chase. It was only then that he realized he'd been standing in the open doorway to his office for a half hour. Forcing himself to focus, Simon stuffed the last of his bagel into his mouth as he stepped over to his desk, setting his coffee mug—the huge one that kept the drink hot for hours (a gift from James that he loved)—down before he read the text and turned on his computer. He snorted at the words, glad he wasn't drinking his hot coffee right then. Yeah, of *course* Chase wanted to know how last night had gone. *Ugh!*

»Adrian drove me home. He was very nice but quiet. That's it. «

He set the cell down beside his laptop, shaking his head. Sometimes he wondered how he and not Chase was the romance author. The man was a hopeless romantic, though only his close friends knew that. Simon settled on the ball, then opened Microsoft Word, knowing he had to work through his latest round of edits. The story was angstier than his usual, the characters' journey a little rougher than his normal style. He knew the tone had changed thanks to his own love life being dead. Still, he thought it a good story, if a little painful before the characters got their happily ever after. Even in his current mood, he couldn't make himself write a romance with a sad or painful ending. He knew authors who wrote that way, many he even loved, but it just wasn't in him to do that to his characters—they deserved love too, dammit, even if he didn't seem to.

By the time he had the current manuscript open to where he'd left off, Chase had already texted him again, twice, demanding more details. Why Chase thought anything had happened between him and Adrian was beyond him. Simon used to love to dance and party as much as Chase, but just like Chase, he was a long-term kind of guy. Unlike Dale. Now he'd probably gotten some the night before—from Grayson if he got his way, or from some other cutie at the club—but that had never been Simon's thing. Dancing with all the sexy boys, oh yes! Taking them to the back rooms or home, no.

»I have work to do. So do you, ya nosy brat! *kisses*«

»Be that way. HUFF«

»Love you too. Now be good! TTFN«

After hitting Send again, Simon set the phone to the side and dove into the world of his characters and the list of comments and edits scribbled across his digital pages.

Three more chapters in, Simon's cell rang, pulling him out of his work and the world he'd created. He blinked hard, trying to get his eyes to focus on something other than the text on the page, as he scooped up his phone. He hit the Answer button before checking the display, but as soon as the voice of his caller came through, he groaned.

"Simon!" The yell did nothing for his headache, but he resigned himself to another painful chat.

"Yes, Zoey?"

"Don't you 'yes, Zoey' me, Simon." He loved his sister, really, but since he came out shortly after graduation, he'd rarely spoken to her—she'd sided with his parents, claiming he was only playing gay to hurt them. A concept that never had made any sense to him. "Mom and Dad's anniversary is coming up soon, and I want you there. It's in the ballroom at The Pfister. It's time you stop all this nonsense and come back to your family! They need you."

"You know full well I can't go to their party, Zoey. I'm not welcome there."

"You would be if you'd do the right thing and act like a normal person instead of continuing this gay nonsense." Her tone dripped disgust, though that was normal for her as well as his parents, on the odd occasion they all spoke. The last time he'd spoken with his mother, she'd tried to set him up on a date with a girl *and* told him his father would help him get a nice, normal job with good people at the construction site he owned. God, he hated the word *normal*!

"I'm not *acting* gay, Sissy. I *am* gay. I *like* being who I am. *And* I do not need their approval to live my life. So thanks for the reminder, but I'll have to pass on the party. I will send them a present, though, as I do every year." Simon always sent his parents a gift card for Red Lobster—even though many of their friends thought Red Lobster too common, he knew how much his mother loved their food—flowers for his mom, and a gift certificate for the pro shop at his father's country club. He wasn't even certain they used the cards, such things probably being beneath them. He never received the same in return, but that never stopped him from trying.

The sigh she let out was as loud as it was annoying. "Fine! Don't say we didn't try to include you in the family." With that said, she hung up.

Simon shook his head as he set the phone down again. *Why do I bother answering her calls?* He knew the answer but didn't want to think about her, or them, any longer.

Stretching both arms above his head until his back popped felt good, but he knew he needed to get more work done—not that he would be able to focus after Zoey's interruption. Simon took a sip of coffee, then realized it was the bottom of the cup and frowned. Annoyed with himself for still caring what his family thought, he made sure his work was saved, then stood. Moments later, empty mug in hand, Simon entered his kitchen. When he looked around, he noticed the clock on the wall said it was after one. *Huh, no wonder my eyes are hurting.*

Instead of fixing lunch as he ought to, he poured the rest of the pot into his coffee cup and closed the lid tight. He debated making another pot of coffee but chose to clean the machine for the next morning instead. He lived on coffee most days, but he hoped to wean himself down sufficiently that maybe he could actually sleep later. The next day would be long anyway without his usual lack of sleep—driving was tiring enough without starting the trip sleepy—but he'd promised to go with Dale to Chicago. Well, he was going to help drive, not that it was that far from Milwaukee. Once Dale was at his vet convention at the hotel, Simon hoped to hang out with Dal Sayer and Dal's partner, soon to be hubby, Alex Noble. He missed Dal now that the two lived in Chicago, and while he didn't know Alex all that well, the sweetie was fun to be around. Besides, he wanted to pick Dal's brain for a character for a story he was planning to write soon.

Simon collected his mug and started back to his office but then thought better of it. He looked down at himself, taking in the sleep pants he still wore, and frowned. Detouring to his bedroom, he decided he should at least get dressed.

He rummaged through his dresser before pulling out a pair of well-worn, faded blue jeans, a long-sleeved, lavender Henley, and a pair of black boxer-briefs. Once he dug out a pair of clean socks, he stripped and re-dressed. On his way to the living room—he'd even spent the time to fix his hair and brush his teeth—his thoughts were derailed by another text from Chase.

»Did you eat? «

Seriously? Simon knew his friend worried about him, but he wasn't that thin, he didn't think. His jeans were a bit looser than normal, but it's not like he was anorexic or something. Giving up, he sent a quick note back saying he was going out right then to eat, hoping that would calm Chase down. He doubted it would work but figured it was worth a try.

14

After pulling on a pair of Sketchers Flex Advantage shoes, Simon grabbed his wallet, keys, and distressed leather jacket before locking up and jogging down the stairs to the parking area. Instead of getting in his Toyota Avalon in Sizzling Crimson Mica—he loved the name of the paint almost as much as the color itself—he turned left once he hit the sidewalk, deciding to walk to the Indian place a couple of blocks over rather than wasting the gas by driving.

By the time Simon was done eating—he'd even taken a picture with his cell and sent it to Chase to prove he'd eaten—he'd had text conversations with Chase, James, and Dale, as well as his editor, and was tired of talking to people. Well, tired of people who wanted to bug him about his eating, his love life or lack thereof, or wanted to set him up on dates. He knew they were just worried about him, but sometimes it was all simply too much.

As for his love life, well, that was a much harder issue. In the last five years, Simon had been cheated on, lied to, stolen from, and told he was a lousy lay because he refused to role-play in bed. His faith in love was more than a bit shaky lately, and the only man to pique his interest in ages wouldn't be interested in him, he was certain. Adrian was sexy, smart, successful, and interested in guys like Chase, not him. But God, when those piercing green eyes had looked at him the night before, Simon had had to fight the need to squirm. And then when Dale decided to ditch him to chase Grayson, he'd ended up asking Adrian for a ride home… except he hadn't wanted the man to leave.

Knowing it was pointless to fixate on the hot professor, Simon took the long way home, hoping to walk off some of his funk before he had to return to work.

SIMON SAT in front of his computer, trying, vainly, to focus on his editing. Unfortunately, his mind refused to focus on the story in front of him. He still had two days to finish and return the edits—he knew that—but he wanted them done and over with. With only two chapters and an epilogue left, he knew it wouldn't take long, if he could just settle his scattered thoughts.

When his doorbell rang moments later, he was thrilled at the excuse to stop working. Hopping up from the ball chair, he padded to the front room. After checking the peephole, Simon pasted on a smile and opened the door.

There stood James, one of his best friends, along with his husband, Seth. It took a moment for what Seth held in his hands to sink in.

"Hey, James. Seth. Um, what's all this?"

"I know you hate cooking and well…." James gave him the same shy smile that always melted Simon. No one could ever say no when he looked at them that way. "I thought it might be nice for you to have a delish, home-cooked meal once in a while."

"Come in." Simon stepped aside, careful to stay out of the way of James's forearm crutches—he had his rainbow ones this time. Simon always loved how James's crutch choices changed day to day, event to event. He wasn't certain, but at last count, he thought James had at least a dozen sets, not that he knew why anyone needed that many.

"Thank you," Seth said, stepping past and heading directly for Simon's kitchen. They'd all spent time at each other's homes, so there was no formality left, not even with Seth, James's doting, if dominant, lover.

"You really didn't have to cook for me, James. I told you I ate," Simon grumbled. He didn't need to be mothered!

"I know you did, but I also know how little you like to cook and thought you would like something other than fast food and microwave meals." James took his right crutch with his left hand, freeing the one arm, and gave Simon a hug, holding on longer than Simon thought necessary, though he found himself sinking into the contact quickly.

"Thank you," Simon whispered, unable to make himself any louder. He hated how needy he felt some days, but since throwing out his ex, his closest friends were the only people who touched him at all. It was weird, but he'd never realized just how tactile a person he was until recently.

"We're always here for you, Si, you know that."

When Simon finally managed to disentangle himself from James, he turned and noticed Seth standing in the doorway between the kitchen and the living room, a soft smile on his face. What he wouldn't give to have someone look at him with the same love and devotion.

"Thanks. I promise to eat everything and return the dish."

"We know." The grin in James's voice made Simon smile. "But we can't stay long. Danni's with our housekeeper, waiting for us to take them to the movies. She's already seen the dolphin movie five times—that I know of, but no, that's her special outing request. Anyway, I just wanted to drop off the food and wish you a good trip tomorrow."

"Thanks." He gave each man a hug.

"Oh, and have fun in Chicago. And try to keep Dale from getting too wild in Boystown."

Yeah, right. Like Dale ever listened when there were easy, cute boys to pounce. Simon watched as the two men left, locking up again after them, before going to see what yum James had left him—James was an excellent cook, almost as good as he was an artist. But whatever it was, Simon was certain he'd love it, and well, it was about dinnertime. Then maybe he'd kill things playing his latest addition to the *Assassin's Creed* series before he tried to sleep.

chapter three

"*WHY AM I here?*" Adrian signed to Chase, not sure why he was over at Chase and Rhys's home. It was only the second or third time he'd been up to their third-floor loft. The building had been a large home, but Rhys had bought it with his best friend Mark and converted the first floor into offices for the Coiled Dragon, their PI agency. Mark lived on the second floor, and Chase's IT consulting business was now located in the back half of the old home.

"*Because I invited you over for dinner and you love me.*" Chase's grin was infectious, and Adrian did adore his friend. Their one date had led to their friendship, not a relationship, but he didn't mind.

Unable to stop himself, Adrian smiled back. "*I do. But there are four settings, not three.*" He knew Chase was up to something, figuring it was another blind date attempt, but as he hadn't seen anyone but Chase and Rhys so far, he was at a total loss for who the other victim was.

Chase smirked before his face smoothed into a look of pure innocence. "*I have other friends than just you. Why?*"

Uh-huh…. Deciding to just play along and humor Chase, Adrian dropped the questions right then. "*Whatever,*" he signed with as much attitude as he could manage, using his entire body to show his lack of interest. He ruined it a moment later when he wound up laughing at the fake pout Chase gave him. "*OK. OK. What's for dinner? That OK to ask?*"

Instead of answering, Chase stuck his tongue out, then grinned.

"*Brat!*"

"*Always. We're having lasagna, garlic bread, the works. Oh, and I have fresh-made peach ice cream and a crumb cake for dessert.*"

God! He was going to gain twenty pounds from the one meal. Adrian couldn't imagine how Chase and Rhys stayed so fit with how Chase cooked, but they both were. He made an exaggerated show of how fat he would be after he ate all that, which pulled laughter from Chase—one of the few sounds he truly wished he could hear.

By the time they had both stopped laughing and sobered, mostly, Rhys thumped into the room. Adrian turned as Chase lit up and ran over to Rhys and wrapped his arms around his huge partner.

Rhys looked down and smiled at Adrian. "How are you?" he asked, thankfully facing Adrian so he could understand. Adrian was lucky, he read lips well enough that he could mostly fake it if need be. It made things like teaching at the university much easier as he could give his own lectures and everyone understood him fine. He worked at it, though, practicing with a computer program that he had tweaked and modified until it was barely the original program anymore. Chase had helped him with the last few modifications; his hearing had been needed for some of the sound corrections.

"Good. Thanks for inviting me, though Chase still won't tell me what's up with the fourth place setting."

"Really?" Rhys asked, turning to face Chase more, though thankfully he didn't turn too far. "What are you up to?"

"Nothing. Now go answer the door, and be good, Rhys."

The puzzled look that crossed Rhys's face made Adrian curious until Rhys shrugged and turned. "Seems someone is at the door, though I don't hear anything. Be right back."

"He can't hear the doorbell? Is something wrong with Rhys's hearing?"

Chase grinned again. *"No, I just told him someone needed to be let in before the buzzer sounded. He hates when I do that."*

Adrian thought about that, but as he had no hearing, the concept made little sense to him. Chalking it up to Chase being playful, he nodded and turned, intending to find out who else was there.

When he entered the living room, Simon was standing there. He couldn't pull his gaze away, but then he noticed Simon seemed to be staring at him just as much. Swallowing his nerves down again, Adrian managed to paste a smile on his face. "Hello."

"Hi." Simon fidgeted and broke eye contact but didn't turn away, so Adrian could still read his lips. Lips he still wanted to taste. "It's nice to see you again."

"Thank you. Are you here for dinner too?" Was Chase playing matchmaker again, or was he simply trying to get others to spend time with Simon? He knew Chase was worried about Simon, but he wasn't sure blind-dating was the best answer to Simon's pain.

Simon looked around but nodded. "Yeah, Chase said I had to come eat. Something about making too much food or some such nonsense." He suddenly smiled. "Not that I mind eating his cooking. Has he cooked for you yet?"

"Yeah, he has, and it's always wonderful."

"You, um, you want to sit with me while they play in the kitchen?" Simon asked. Only then did Adrian realize Chase and Rhys were both missing.

"I would."

Once Simon sat on the couch, Adrian chose to sit there as well but left space between them so they could face each other to talk. He didn't want to crowd Simon, though Adrian would love to get to know him better, if Simon was open to that.

Simon leaned in slightly once they were both settled. "You know this is a setup, right?"

He dipped his head in agreement. "Yes. I had that feeling as well. Do you mind? I can go if you don't want to put up with Chase's machinations."

"I-I don't mind."

Adrian took in how Simon's hands fluttered, how he nibbled on his bottom lip slightly, the shy but hopeful look in his eyes, and wondered if that was really all for him. Could Simon actually like him, as more than just Chase's friend? "You sure?"

"No, I would like to get know you."

It took Adrian a moment to decipher what Simon said, and he'd assumed Simon mumbled the words. Whatever it was, it was hard to understand the words, but he hoped he got it right. "Then I'll stay. Thanks."

"Oh, I should probably apologize for messing your date with Chase up, but we all knew Rhys was who he needed, even when he didn't."

He'd gotten the story from Chase after the fact, but on their one and only date, Rhys had shown up at the same restaurant, with a bubbly, very handsy twink on his arm. Chase had been so upset and distracted, it was obvious to Adrian that Chase wasn't over Rhys. He'd later learned that Simon and James had told Rhys where and when to be to deliberately derail their date. He thought it adorable that Chase's friends were so determined to be there for him, and while he hadn't ended up with a boyfriend, he had gained a sweet and loyal friend. So it wasn't such a bad night in his opinion after all.

"I like having Chase as a friend, so it's okay. And I understand why you did that. I would have done the same if I were you. So apology not needed but accepted."

"Glad. So, um, Chase said you were his professor at one point, and I know we stopped at your TA's house the other night. What do you teach?"

Basic get-to-know-you questions. Okay, this I can do. "I teach a couple of different IT courses at UW Milwaukee, and I work freelance for a couple of places doing IT work. Computer forensics and networking work, mainly. Kelley is my TA and a great help when dealing with the amount of paperwork that comes with teaching. He's also a friend, but that's all," Adrian added, having noted the little tensing around Simon's eyes when he mentioned Kelley.

"That sounds fun. Do you have trouble teaching Hearing students?" Simon flushed so red it was closer to purple. "I mean, I know you speak well, and your voice is a touch flat in spots but deep and sexy"—at which point Simon's blush went lower than his shirt collar and up to his ear tips—"but do-don't your students ever try to use your lack of hearing against you?"

"Yeah, once in a while. They learn fast that I pay attention to what's going on around me, though, and usually quit quickly. Kelley hears perfectly, so even if I don't catch them, he does, so it's not a problem. Honestly, most of my students are not the freshmen that are still learning the rules of college, so I don't usually get more than one or two that act up the first class." Taking a deep breath, Adrian decided to add one more thing, dipping his head slightly as his nerves ramped up again. "And thank you. I don't know what I sound like, but I'm glad you like it."

Simon looked away and said something, though Adrian couldn't see what. When he turned back, he held out his hand. Adrian looked at it, confused. "What?"

"It's time for dinner. I, um…." Simon started to pull his hand back, but Adrian caught it before he could move too far. The warmth and softness of Simon's hand felt wonderful. The heat and electricity that shot through him at the touch, though, aroused him. It had been ages since he'd felt excited by something so simple as holding hands. Not letting go, Adrian stood and tugged Simon to standing, smiling as he did.

"Then let's go eat."

He didn't let go of Simon's hand until they were at the table, but instead of just sitting, he pulled out Simon's chair and waited for him to sit down. Adrian then took the chair next to Simon and looked to where Chase and Rhys were entering the dining room.

The scents from the large pan Rhys carried made Adrian's stomach rumble and his mouth water. Chase carried a basket of bread and a large bowl of salad. Once they set down their dishes, Chase looked from Adrian to Simon and back before flashing a bright smile. "Food is served. Enjoy."

They all settled and passed the wonderful foods around. Adrian hated trying to follow group conversations when no one was signing, especially because it was hard to know who to look at next, so he simply enjoyed his food and the warmth of the company as they chatted.

When Rhys reached one big hand into Adrian's peripheral and waved slightly, Adrian looked over. "Yes?"

"I was just wondering if you're okay. You've not said a thing since telling Chase thank you for the food." The concern on Rhys's face was easy to see, and he hated that he'd worried the gentle giant.

Adrian took a sip of the wine, then smiled, hoping to make Rhys relax. "It's just hard to follow the conversation. The only one here that signs is Chase, and it's really hard to sign and use a fork." He could still vividly remember his dad accidentally launching pasta across the dining room table once when he was little. His dad had been so involved in telling Adrian a story, he had forgotten he still held a forkful of spaghetti. His mother wasn't amused, but Adrian had loved it!

"Oh, I didn't think of that. I don't know ASL or anything or I would try to include you."

"It's okay, Rhys. I don't take it personally. It simply is what it is."

As the conversation picked up again, Adrian felt a gentle tap to his shoulder. When he looked up, Simon was looking at him, sadness clear in his deep brown eyes. They reminded him of a lonely puppy's, though he would never tell Simon that. "Hi."

"Hey. I wanted to talk to you some more. Earlier was nice."

"It was. What did you want to know?"

Simon shrugged. "I don't know. I just liked talking to you."

"I like talking to you too. Why don't you tell me about you? You asked me what I did, but all I remember is from the other night and from Chase. You're an author—romance, right?"

"Yeah. I write gay romances. Well, they aren't just romances, but that is the main thing to them." Simon paused, looking toward Chase for a moment before he returned his focus to Adrian, a slight flush on his cheeks. "Okay, Chase says I shouldn't call them 'gay romances' since I do have a couple of bi characters and am planning to write a character based on Dal's partner, Alex."

"Alex is gender fluid, right?" Adrian had met Alex and Dal and thought Alex was adorable—and downright edible in the strappy little sundress he'd had on. It had taken him a moment to figure out what was behind Alex's nervous fidgeting. Dal had explained that Alex was gender fluid and was still shy about going out and meeting people when in nonmale clothing. Alex was cute, sweet, and obviously made Dal extremely happy.

"Yeah. That's the reason I want to write about a character like him. I think more people need to be open to others and need to understand that differences aren't a bad thing. Same reason I added my first bi character. I had a good friend in college that was bi and got crap from straights and gays for it. I hated seeing him get rejected because of who he was."

"So you write stories to show love and give the people you care about happy endings? I like that." The more he learned about Simon, the more he wanted to know.

"I… I guess so. I never thought of it that way, but why not write the story so love wins instead of hate or bigotry or mistakes?"

"I think it's a great way to live, Simon. It's cool that you can make a living doing something like writing and that you get to teach and right wrongs with a pen, or keyboard as the case may be." *God!* If Simon didn't stop blushing, Adrian was going to have to kiss him.

They continued to eat, Simon talking to him off and on. When Chase served dessert, Adrian's taste buds rejoiced. The food was delicious, the coffee perfect with the ice cream and cake. By the time they were done, Adrian didn't think he'd be able to eat again for a week. Since Chase had cooked, he stood and started gathering dishes, determined to help. Chase wouldn't let him, though, taking the plates from Adrian's hands and then shooing him back into the living room, promising to send in more coffee.

Giving up, Adrian did as he was told. He settled again on the couch, and a moment later, Simon came in and flopped down beside him. "I was kicked out too."

"I think they are trying to get us to spend more time together." Adrian had caught the smirks and knowing looks Chase threw their way throughout the meal. For once, he had to appreciate having a friend willing to meddle, especially if Simon returned his interest.

"I do too." Simon nibbled on his lip again, and Adrian worried he might draw blood considering how often he'd bitten it that evening. "While they are busy, I wanted to ask you something."

Adrian scooted a little closer to Simon and took his hand again, careful not to startle him. When they'd touched earlier, the heat and connection had surprised him, but touching Simon now was just the same. The warmth and rightness was there, as was the excitement. "What was that?" When Simon didn't say anything, just stared down at their joined hands, Adrian tried again. "Simon? What did you want to ask?"

"Oh, sorry." Simon lifted his gaze to Adrian's, hope and fear mixed in his expression. "I wanted to, um, ask if you'd like to go out to dinner with me sometime. I mean, like a real date, not where we're being pushed together and monitored."

"I'd love to." Adrian smiled, trying to put as much of his joy at being asked into it as possible. "How about I pick you up Friday about five? I'll take you someplace quiet where we can eat and chat without our nosy friends hovering behind the door," Adrian added, forcing his voice louder to make sure Chase could hear him. "Or would you rather drive?"

"No, I don't mind. Here, give me your phone. Please," Simon quickly added, looking away enough that Adrian wasn't certain if he said any more or not. When Simon pulled out his own cell and presented it to Adrian, he realized Simon had turned away to get it out.

After swapping cell phones and numbers, Adrian took his back and repocketed it. "I'll text you tomorrow and we can work out the details. Plus, I'd kind of like to chat with you more."

"Me too."

Shortly after they were done, Simon announced he needed to head home. When Adrian noticed the time, he thought he should get home and to sleep as well. After giving hugs and promises to text all around, Adrian walked Simon to his Audi, Simon's hand in his. He bent and kissed Simon's knuckles briefly before saying his good nights and headed to his Rogue, happier and more hopeful that he had been in a very long time.

chapter four

"I BROUGHT *Call of Duty: Modern Warfare 2*," Dale singsonged as he flounced through the open door of Simon's office. "I thought we could play tonight and then go hit the clubs tomorrow after work."

Simon looked up from his laptop and blinked. "Huh?" He had been working on a new story—having finally finished the edits the night before—so hard he hadn't heard Dale, hadn't realized he'd even arrived until right then.

Dale glowered down at Simon. "Gaming tonight, flirting and chasing cute guys tomorrow night. What's with you?"

"In case you can't tell, I'm writing. I was in the middle of a scene when you came in yelling about playing."

"What?" Dale pouted, shoulders drooping as he continued to stare. "I thought we could hang out and play. I have *Call of Duty*. Come on.... *Modern Warfare 2*," he added, his voice higher than normal as he waggled the game case at Simon. "You know you wanna play."

"Sorry, didn't mean to snap at ya. I was just really focused on the new story I started late last night. Don't mind me." It had been a while since Simon had felt the driving spark to write, and while he was always happy to see his friends, interrupting his word flow was one thing he truly hated. "And yeah, *CoD* sounds like fun."

"It's okay." Dale shrugged and then smiled. "How long do you need now? I'll go play with your PS4 until you're ready for me to kick your ass."

"Uh...." Simon looked back at the screen, thinking about the scene in question. "Give me like an hour, tops, and I should be ready to stop. 'Kay?"

Simon barely heard Dale agree and bounce out of the room, immediately drawn back into his manuscript and the characters within it.

By the time he was done with the scene and hit Save, he was ready for a break. He often wrote in thought dumps, as he thought of them, but still, he was shocked when he checked his word count and realized he'd finished just over eight thousand words. He hadn't managed more than about a thousand words or so at a sitting since his breakup over a year before.

He checked it over quickly to make sure the save was uploaded to his Dropbox before shutting everything down. Simon looked around, noticing how many coffee cups were scattered around his desk, and groaned. "Really gotta stop doing that," he grumbled as he collected them, hoping Dale had missed that there were no plates sitting around. He really didn't feel up to another lecture about his eating habits, or the lack of eating, in his case. It wasn't deliberate most of the time. He wasn't hungry, so he didn't eat. Often, the stories flowed and he got so caught up in his writing he managed to forget to eat. Unfortunately Dale didn't listen to that logic. Neither did Chase or James, for that matter.

After a quick stop in the kitchen to rinse the cups and add them to his dishwasher, he poked his head into the living room and smiled when he saw Dale sprawled out on the floor, having a blast playing *Destiny*. Instead of announcing his presence, he backed out and headed back to his bedroom. He felt grungy and stiff—he always did after a long writing jag.

Deciding on comfort over looks, knowing Dale didn't care, Simon grabbed a pair of sleep pants and a long-sleeved T-shirt—that coordinated; he wouldn't go that far and not match, even if it was just jammies—and went to the bathroom to shower and shave.

Once clean and dressed, Simon looked at himself in the mirror and winced. The shadows under his brown eyes were more pronounced than he liked, his eyes seemed duller than before, and his skin, while clear, was paler than he remembered. "No wonder they're so worried."

Quickly putting in his eye drops, he took one last look at himself before he turned away and padded back into his room. There he dumped his dirty clothes into the hamper bag, then scooped the whole thing up. He made it as far as sorting and loading the clothes into the washer before Dale found him.

"What *are* you doing?"

Simon looked up from adding the soap pod, curious what Dale thought he was doing because it was perfectly obvious he was doing laundry. "It's a strange thing we humans do once in a while called washing clothes." Cocking his head to the side and widening his eyes, he added, "Haven't you ever heard of it?"

"Ass!" Dale lasted to the count of two before he started giggling. "Fine, I know what you're doing," he managed once they both calmed and caught their breath. "But why? You're supposed to be in the other room getting your butt kicked on the PlayStation!"

"You were playing, and I realized my dirty clothes were overflowing. Didn't think you'd even notice, honestly. So who won?" he asked as they reentered the living room and settled on the floor just in front of the couch. Simon couldn't explain it, but when playing video games, he always sat on the floor.

"I did, of course. Are you done with being the happy homemaker now? Can we kill shit now?"

"Always so eloquent, Dale. Yeah, we can. Oh hey, do you have to be back at the clinic tonight?" Simon knew how Dale was about the animals at his vet clinic. He rotated shifts with his vet techs so the animals staying overnight were never alone too long.

"Nope. I'm off tonight and tomorrow night." Dale grinned wide. "So there's no getting out of games or dancing."

"Actually," Simon started and looked away, more nervous than he would have expected. "I, um… I have a date tomorrow night."

"Like a *date*, date? Like as in a 'going out with a real boy' kind of date?"

"Your tone is not lost on me, dickhead." He nudged Dale hard with his shoulder as he got up to switch out the game disk. "Yes, like a real date with a sweet guy."

Dale didn't say anything, and when Simon turned to go back to his spot beside his friend, he paused at the annoying sight before him. Dale was gaping, his eyes wide. "Who are you going out with, and why didn't I know already?" he snapped.

"Adrian. He asked me the other night when Chase dragged me over to his place for dinner. Honestly, I figured Chase would have told you as I know he heard. He is so not subtle in his matchmaking."

The snort from Dale made Simon smile. "Yeah, bat to the head would be about as subtle as Chase, but seriously? You're going out with the Deaf guy Chase dated?" Dale's brows scrunched up as he frowned. "Wait, isn't that like against the friend code or something? No dating your friends' exes?"

"First off, Adrian is *not* 'the Deaf guy.' Adrian happens to be Deaf, but that's not all there is to him!"

"Sorry." Dale raised his hands in surrender. "Sorry. I didn't mean it the way it came out. You know me and my mouth."

"Yeah, okay, but be nice. Oh, and secondly, yes, I'm going out with Adrian. Since Chase is who set up the dinner-party-date thing, I'm pretty sure he isn't going to be weird about it. And really, what are we? Fifteen-year-old girls or something? I didn't poach, and they didn't really even date!"

"Wow, you must really like this guy if you're being so defensive already. And stop scowling at me. I think it's a good thing, as long as he's really as nice as Chase thinks he is."

Slightly mollified, Simon sat back and turned on the controller. "He was so sweet and nice, and well, I don't know, he seemed to like me for me, not for what he might be able to get from me. Ya know?"

"Yeah, I do." Dale knew how many losers Simon had dealt with over the years. He seemed to attract the ones who wanted him for his wallet, not for who he was. Sometimes he'd even gone so far as to play down the money he had, hoping to find someone decent, but that never seemed to work either. Here he was, a trust-fund baby who wrote romance, but he couldn't find a guy who wanted him, not really.

"Come on, I don't wanna talk about exes or dating. Let's go kill things." That said, Simon pushed Play and they spent the next couple of hours killing things and yelling at the TV, each other, and the characters before Simon ordered a large veggie lover's plus pineapple and jalapeños.

By the time they'd eaten all the food, gone through all the soda, and were too tired to play, Dale was half-asleep, resting against Simon's shoulder.

"Hey, Dale? Come on, I'll walk you to the spare bedroom and you can crash, okay?"

"Mm-hmm. Was fun."

It took two tries to get Dale off the floor, but eventually they both made it to their respective beds. Even though Simon was exhausted, he couldn't fall asleep. The realization that he was going on a date, with Adrian no less, kept his thoughts pinging too much to doze off. He'd spent time wondering how the date would go, promising himself that no matter how good it was or how hot the man himself might be, he would not go to bed with him that night. Jumping into relationships too fast was never a good idea, as time had proven to him again and again.

Eventually Simon drifted off, an image of Adrian's jade-green eyes floating in his mind until he remembered nothing more.

AFTER WAKING Dale up and sending him home to get ready for work—not the easiest thing to do on the best of mornings—Simon tried to go back to sleep. Tried but failed. Too many thoughts and worries ran through his head, making rest impossible. Eventually he gave in and got up, deciding that writing would be a much better use of his time than staring at the ceiling and walls of his bedroom, no matter how much he loved the blue-and-cream décor. He paused long enough to look at the mantle and fireplace across the room and sigh. He'd had so many hopes for that area when he'd bought the place, but that was just before the asshole's betrayal. *Maybe Adrian will be the one?* He immediately shook off the thought, both not wanting to jinx the date later and not wanting to get his hopes up again.

Twenty minutes and a cup of coffee later, Simon was back at his laptop, typing away, trying to focus on the confusion of the main characters and angst of his story. Unfortunately every little thing distracted him: faint sounds of cars passing, the hum of his refrigerator cycling, the fact his friends kept texting him about his date later. The only texts he hadn't minded were the ones from Adrian. They'd chatted for almost two hours that way, Simon never setting his cell down, waiting for the next time it chimed with a new message. After Adrian had to go, something about a class and then office hours, Simon had decided to find out a little more about ASL and sign language in general. However, he managed to get entranced on the ASLPro website. He was fascinated by how ASL worked and tried to learn at least a couple of signs to use when he saw Adrian later.

When Simon's cell alarm went off at 3:00 p.m., hours and hours after he'd started working, he was beyond annoyed that he had made little progress on the story arc. He had lots of notes but little in the way of actual writing.

Disgusted but excited at the same time, he saved everything, double-checked that his work had been saved to his backup as well as to the computer itself, and then shut it all down.

The problem as he saw it was that even though he'd been the one to ask Adrian out, Adrian would be doing the driving and the planning. He still wasn't sure how that happened, but at the time, Adrian planning the date rather than him seemed the most natural and logical thing. Now, however, he had the issue of deciding what to wear.

After standing there staring at his closet, berating himself for acting like his mom about how to dress—a place he really didn't want his mind going to—he gave up and grabbed his cell, shooting Adrian a text asking if he should dress up or if casual clothes would be more appropriate to their dinner venue. The immediate response startled him enough he dropped his phone. Thankful no one was there to see his idiotic behavior, Simon got down and picked it up from just under the edge of his large four-poster bed. *Casual-dressy? What the hell does that mean?*

Okay, he could do this. He knew what most thought of casual-dressy and how he tended to dress. After a few moments, he managed to finally calm down enough to actually gather his clothing and get ready for his date. His shower wouldn't have taken half as long had he not been so worried that he washed his body and hair twice thoroughly, and shaved carefully while worrying about nicking himself, before finally turning off the hot water and drying off. Fixing his light brown hair didn't take but a few minutes, but that was part of the reason he paid good money to have it cut as he did, with the gold and copper highlights put in. It always looked good, even if he didn't bother with it much. He debated using his kohl but worried that might be too much, especially with how dark his eyes were already and because he didn't know where they were going.

When he was finished dressing, Simon looked himself over in the full-length mirror in his large walk-in closet and nodded. The gray polished wool Korean slim-style peacoat with mini lapels and a Mandarin collar over a thin maroon faux turtleneck sweater and a pair of lightweight gray dress slacks worked well in his opinion. The slight tapering at the waist accentuated his lean but slightly muscular form without making him look too thin, he hoped.

Simon stepped back from the mirror and took a quick selfie, sending to Chase, Dale, and James, asking their opinion on his outfit. When he quickly received three positive responses, he finally calmed some. Now he just had to hope Adrian liked the way he looked as much as his friends did.

He slipped the jacket off again, not wanting to get hot as he waited for Adrian to arrive. Back in the living room, Simon draped it over one of the large overstuffed chairs before checking his watch, again. When he realized he still had half an hour, he started pacing, his nerves and racing thoughts increasing as he moved. *What if he doesn't like me once he gets to know me? What if he wants a different kind of guy? What if I'm just not the kind of guy anyone will ever love and want to keep?*

When the doorbell rang, Simon was so tangled in doubts and worries he jumped and gasped. "Just a minute," he called out before he remembered Adrian couldn't hear him. Shaking his head at his stupidity, he hurried to open the door.

"Hello." Adrian stood before him dressed simply. *But wow*! The dark smoky-gray V-neck pullover cashmere sweater, layered over what appeared to be a bright green silk T-shirt, hugged his fit body well. On his lower half he wore a fitted pair of gray straight-leg jeans and—he blinked hard, startled but enchanted—a pair of Chuck Taylor All Stars. The outer area was green, the inner canvas a dark gray, and the laces were half and half—the opposite color to the side they were coming from.

It took a moment for Simon's brain to kick in. When he managed to pull his gaze from Adrian's clothes, he smiled, thoroughly enjoying the light blush on the sexy man's cheeks. "Hi. You want to come in while I get my jacket?"

"Thank you," Adrian spoke, his voice softer but still clear, though Simon also noted his hands twitched at the same time.

Simon wondered idly if Adrian was trying not to sign to make him more comfortable and frowned as he retrieved his jacket and slipped it on. "I don't know where you picked. Is this okay?" he asked, holding his arms out for approval. He knew it was a bad habit, but his last two boyfriends had harped on him regularly about his "odd sense of fashion."

"Edible," Adrian replied, the blush that hadn't completely gone away suddenly getting much more pronounced.

Simon grinned, not caring if Adrian thought him silly. "Thank you," he said and tried out the sign he'd picked up from the website earlier. "Shall we?" he added without signing.

Adrian signed something, but he had no idea what.

"I—" He paused, fidgeting as he continued "—I only remember a couple of the signs I looked up. What…. What did you say?"

Adrian laughed, a carefree, almost childish sound, completely at odds with the rich deepness of his voice. "I said, 'You're welcome and yes.' As in 'Let's go.' I'm eager to get you started on our date."

Moments later they were down the stairs and on their way.

chapter five

ADRIAN EXITED his blue Rogue, nervous but eager to begin his date with Simon. He had planned and considered and reconsidered what he wanted to do, where to take Simon. He just hoped Simon liked it as well.

As he stepped up to Simon's front door, he again took in Simon's home. It wasn't huge, but it was bigger than he would have expected Simon to have, though he couldn't put his finger on why. It was a cute little one-and-a-half-story brick-and-stone bungalow where the oak door was set on the side of a bay-style front room. Adrian paused to take in the beveled glass center of the door, surrounded by pale gray textured glass that complimented the gray of the exterior.

Wiping his hands down the legs of his jeans, again, he held his breath a moment before letting it out in a controlled exhale. When he thought he could appear calm, Adrian pasted on his best smile and rang the doorbell. He hoped it worked, knowing if it didn't, Simon would have no way to know he was there. That had happened once or twice when he was younger. He quickly learned to knock if no one answered the bell.

Before he could worry too much, a shadow crossed the glass panel in the door, and then the door opened, revealing Simon. Adrian nearly swallowed his tongue as he stared, unable to take his eyes off the perfectly fitted clothing and the body beneath. He knew he shouldn't stare, but Simon seemed to be doing the same to him, so he didn't feel too bad.

He swallowed hard before forcing out, "Hello." God, he hoped it was loud enough. Adrian didn't usually worry, knowing how different levels of sound felt, but his mind was on Simon, not his speech.

After a long moment, Simon raised his eyes to meet Adrian's, a small smile on his sensual lips. "Hi. You want to come in while I get my jacket?"

Adrian nodded and said a quick "thank you" before stepping inside into an octagonal foyer. The room was larger than he'd thought it would be from the outside and housed plants and a set of chairs. A small table between them made Adrian think of lazy afternoons spent reading and holding hands. Shoving the ridiculous thought away, he focused on where Simon had gone, following him into a large front living room. One wall housed a large fireplace, another a floor-to-ceiling bookshelf, overflowing with all kinds and sizes of books. The dark leather furniture looked both comfortable and expensive. The long couch faced an immense entertainment center.

Before he could peek more, Simon was back with a light gray jacket on, the likes of which he'd never seen. It resembled a pea coat but only in a vague sense. More like a souped-up, cooler version where when buttoned, it still looked as though one side was pulled back and a vest was exposed, despite being all the one jacket. "I don't know where you picked. Is this okay?" he asked, holding his arms out for approval, Adrian assumed.

"Edible," he replied, heat rushing up his cheeks and down his neck when he realized he'd said the word, not simply thought it.

Simon grinned. "Thank you," he signed and said, startling Adrian. "Shall we?" he added without signing.

"You're welcome. Yes." He waited to see what Simon would do.

"I—" He paused, fidgeting as he continued "—I only remember a couple of the signs I looked up. What? What did you say?"

Adrian laughed, pleased Simon would go to such trouble for him. "I said, 'You're welcome and yes.' As in 'Let's go.' I'm eager to get you started on our date."

As they walked to his car, Adrian smiled when Simon reached out, slipping his hand into Adrian's. When they reached the Nissan, he opened Simon's door. "Don't forget, I cannot read lips while driving, so tell me now if you need something."

"I'm fine and thanks." Simon quickly settled in the car, pulling his door shut as Adrian walked around the front of the vehicle. Once he was situated and certain Simon was ready, Adrian started the car and backed out, pointing them toward downtown.

About halfway to the restaurant, Simon slowly moved his left hand over, and eventually Adrian looked down for a moment as Simon laced his fingers with Adrian's. The tingle and warmth seeped into him and settled in his stomach, finally calming the jittery butterflies that had taken up residence since the night at Chase's. Adrian gave a gentle squeeze, hopeful that things would go well this time. His last date had ended abruptly when the man he'd gone out with had decided having to look at Adrian while speaking was too much trouble. He didn't think Simon would be like that, but he hadn't thought his last date would, or he wouldn't have gone in the first place.

When they pulled up to Sake Tumi downtown, he parked and turned to Simon. "This okay?"

Simon nodded, a bright smile on his beatific face. "Very. I love their maki."

Thrilled he'd picked right and that Chase's suggestions of places and food types had also been right, Adrian got out and stepped around to Simon, placing his hand on Simon's lower back as he had the other night.

They didn't have to wait long to be seated, and while Adrian had only been there once, he was still impressed with how the place looked. But more impressive than the tables and the decorations was the food he saw on the various tables as they followed the server to a small table along one wall. Many of the dishes appeared to be laid out to resemble dragons or fish. One even looked a lot like a raging fire spread out along a long, thin plate. The scents made his mouth water and his stomach demand attention.

Once they were seated, the waiter gave them a few minutes to decide on drinks and appetizers—he had peeked at the menu online, wanting to have some idea of what to order before sitting down to dinner. The gentle touch to the back of his hand pulled Adrian out of his musings over his food choices.

"Want to split a Buddha Pouch? There's two in an order."

Adrian looked to see what was in that one and nodded. He loved shiitake mushrooms and carrots and had tried the curried cream sauce that came with it the last time he'd been there. "Yes."

He watched as Simon ordered for them, and the server was polite and quick. Once the man stepped away, Simon looked up at Adrian again. "You like the food here too?"

"I've only been once, but it was very good." Adrian hoped he was speaking loud enough but not too loudly. Simon didn't show any signs that Adrian wasn't speaking correctly, so he settled back and relaxed some as they discussed which dishes to order for their main course. Once the food arrived and they began eating, conversation would become harder for him, though one-on-one meals like this were easier to follow.

By the time they'd decided on their main entrees, the server had returned with sodas and their appetizer. Simon ordered the Firefly Maki, surprising Adrian. He liked spicy food, but he was pretty certain that the Firefly was hotter than he could eat. He chose the Sexy Scallops, amused at the smirk and light pinking to Simon's cheeks when he told him what he wanted to order. He'd found letting his date order was often easier. That way he didn't need to worry if the server could hear or understand him. Adrian often went out alone and didn't worry too much then—there was no one to impress—but he'd learned that Hearing people often were annoyed with his speech in loud, or presumably loud, places like restaurants. The last thing he wanted to do on their first real date was bother or embarrass Simon.

"You ordered that just to make me say 'sexy' to the cute waiter, didn't you?"

Adrian needed a moment to figure out what Simon said, but when he did, he smirked. "No, that was a nice side benefit, though."

"Brat."

Adrian shrugged one shoulder, happy he'd put a smile on Simon's face. He knew it was a rare thing over the last year, even if he hadn't met Simon until recently. One of the benefits—or drawbacks, he still wasn't sure—of being friends with Chase was knowing a great deal about Chase's friends, even if his knowledge of their faces was a new phenomenon. "I like scallops. If you like, you can try mine." He knew many people would order dishes and share, but he wasn't certain of Simon's intentions.

"Sounds good. I've never had the scallops here. So." He paused and looked down a moment before he raised his gaze again. "You want to tell me more about what you do while we wait? I'd like to know more about you."

Adrian spent the next couple of hours lost in conversation, then eating, and then talking again as they finished their drinks. When the check arrived, Simon reached for it, but Adrian snatched it, checked it carefully, then gave it and his credit card to the server.

"I should have paid for dinner," Simon said, the corners of his pink lips turned down and a deep V between his brows. "I asked you out."

"But I brought you, so I pay. You can pay next time." He hoped there would be a next time for them. The sudden bright grin and how straight and tall Simon sat reassured Adrian more than any words Simon could have offered. "Now would you like to walk a little and maybe stop for coffee and dessert?"

Simon agreed, and a short time later, hand in hand, they wandered downtown toward the Third Ward District. When he found Grace's Cafe, he tugged Simon to the door. They had, as their sign said, exceptional espressos and divine desserts. Inside they also had standard tables near the counter, and closer to the walls were couches and large chairs with short tables between them with various games set out. One wall was nothing but books; people brought books in and took others with them, so you never quite knew what you would find. He hoped the place would appeal to the author in Simon as well as keep them communicating.

Adrian didn't want their date to come to an end yet, but he also wasn't ready for anything that might lead to an intimate end to their evening, either. He'd been teased, sometimes playfully, sometimes painfully, for his attitudes about sex. He wasn't a prude, he just wanted there to be more than physical attraction and need. He thought he and Simon had a chance, but he wasn't willing to push things too far too fast and wind up alone the morning after.

This late there wasn't a long line, as he'd hoped. "What do you want?"

"A cafe au lait with a shot of caramel and a shot of cinnamon."

Simon's eyes lit up when he stared into the dessert case. By the way Simon's animated face moved, his lips pressing together or suddenly gaping slightly, Adrian assumed he was making "happy noises," though he wasn't sure what kind and having never heard such, just hoped they were all good noises. Simon said something, but he was turned to the case still, so Adrian could only tell that his lips were moving.

Annoyed, Adrian thought about how best to word his request. After a moment, he leaned forward and touched Simon's cheek gently. Hoping not to sound too frustrated, he asked, "Please face me when you speak. I can't understand otherwise."

Simon turned bright red and stared at the ground for a minute before he looked up again. "I'm so sorry, Adrian. I didn't think. What I said was, 'Turtle cheesecake. Need a slice of that.'"

"Hey." He made sure his smile was in place and tried to regulate his tone to be kind. "I'm not mad, no need to be upset. I just couldn't understand.

That's all." Adrian touched Simon's cheek again, cupping it. "I like looking at your face, even when you're not talking. Okay?"

"I...." Simon swallowed hard, drawing Adrian's eyes to his bobbing Adam's apple. "Thank you. I kinda like yours too."

Just then Adrian noticed the barista saying something, but he couldn't understand her. He did note that there was no one in front of them, though. "Simon, I think you're next."

"Oh." He turned and spoke to the woman before facing to Adrian again. "Your turn."

"A chai latte, please."

After receiving their treats, Adrian led Simon over to a set of plush chairs with a short table between them. "We can sit and drink, eat, and maybe play a little."

Brows scrunched, Simon tilted his head to the side and stared at Adrian. "Play?"

"Do you play chess?" he asked, motioning to the chess set already laid out on the table. "If not, we can just chat more."

"Oh." Simon beamed at Adrian. "I love chess."

"Wonderful."

Instead of starting a game right away, they sipped their drinks. After a little time, Simon cut a bite of his cheesecake with his fork and scooped it up before he held it out to Adrian. "Would you like some?"

Adrian's gaze locked with Simon's as he bent forward and carefully wrapped his lips around the morsel. When he pulled back enough to separate from the fork, he quickly flicked his tongue out to caress the tines, catching the traces of chocolate and caramel still there. He noted how Simon's eyes dilated as he said, "Delicious."

Simon's hand trembled slightly as he put the fork down. "You, sir, are evil."

He shrugged, enjoying the heated look Simon gave him. "I was simply enjoying your sweetness."

The next bite Simon took left a small bit of chocolate at the edge of his lips. Adrian started to let him know but changed his mind at the last moment. Instead he reached out and traced Simon's bottom lip, catching the drip. Before he could pull his hand back, Simon turned his head, looked at the thumb hovering there, then took the tip into his mouth, licking and swirling his tongue around the pad, pulling a groan from Adrian.

As soon as he realized he'd made the sound, he clamped down on his reaction, worried he would be too loud and draw attention to them. Adrian quickly pulled his hand back and swallowed hard as he glanced up to Simon's eyes. "You missed a spot," he said, no longer interested in his drink or the planned game.

"So I did. You want—" Simon stopped midsentence and frowned. "Stupid," he said, shaking his head, not meeting Adrian's eyes.

"What's stupid?" Adrian didn't like the idea of Simon unhappy, but what was he calling stupid? And why?

"Me," Simon replied.

More confused than before, Adrian took Simon's free hand. "No, you are not. What's wrong?"

"Thanks, but I kind of am. Look, I really like you, but I don't want things to move too fast. You're worth more. I'm worth more than that."

Adrian agreed, both with the sentiment and the speed. He hadn't meant to upset Simon with his touching. It was Simon that took his thumb into his mouth, and Adrian was still half-hard from the light touch. "I can keep my hands to myself. I'm sorry. Would you still like to play?" he asked, hoping Simon didn't ask to be taken home right then.

"I'd like that and—" Simon looked down at his hands as he picked at one cuticle. "—it's not you. You didn't do anything wrong. I just don't want… I want to date, not just fall into bed or anything. Do you mind?"

Adrian considered what he knew about Simon's past and the way Simon held his body as he spoke, how he bit his lip, the tightening around his eyes, the ghost of pain in his gaze, and wondered just how messed up the man's past relationships had been. Shaking his head, Adrian pasted on a soft smile. "No, I like that plan. I want a boyfriend, not just a night. Let's play a game and sip our drinks."

"Agreed." Adrian took the first move on the board and smiled as they sank into the game.

By the time they left, things were back to how they'd been before the aborted teasing: light and fun. The ride to Simon's home was comfortable, and Adrian thrilled a little when Simon slipped his hand back into Adrian's as he drove.

Not ready to leave Simon quite yet, Adrian got out of the car after parking in the driveway to walk Simon to the door. "I had a nice time tonight. Would you like to go out again?"

"I'd like that, but it's my turn this time. I'll text tomorrow and we can set things up. Okay?"

"Thank you."

They stood there on Simon's steps, looking at each other until Simon moved forward to cup Adrian's face in his long-fingered hands. Adrian held his breath, wondering if Simon would actually kiss him after the issue earlier. He was almost surprised when Simon leaned in and tilted his face up before brushing his lips lightly over Adrian's. It was more an intention of touch than an actual press of lips, but the heat and want that shot through Adrian was more than he could ever remember feeling with anyone, much less someone he'd never been with sexually.

When Simon did it again before pulling back, Adrian sighed, certain there was something truly special about Simon. He couldn't wait for their next date!

Minutes later he was back in his car, heading home, happier than he'd ever been after a first date. Adrian just hoped it had meant as much to Simon as it did to him.

chapter six

SIMON'S CELL chimed, alerting him to a new text. He and Adrian had been texting off and on for the last three days, and he was getting antsy. He really wanted to see Adrian again, but Adrian had been slammed at the university with grading and student conferences or some such. Simon knew how university worked—he had his degrees in business and finance, after all—but that didn't make it any less frustrating to have to put off their second date.

»What about this weekend?«

Patience was never one of Simon's specialties.

»Dinner at my house and a movie. Wednesday night?«

Adrian had told Simon Wednesday was his short day as he only had morning classes that day.

About ten minutes passed as he continued to stare at the phone that was rudely not showing Adrian's reply. When it came, he grinned wide and whooped, not caring there was no one to hear.

»OK. 6 ish? «

»Done. Can't wait to see you again. «

Simon hit Send, then thought better of it. *Did that sound too needy? Screw it, too late now to worry about it.*

They chatted for a little longer before Adrian had another student stop by, effectively cutting their conversation off.

Simon sat the cell down beside his laptop, determined to focus on his newest story. It was flowing well now, and he was certain that if he kept writing as he was, he would be done by the end of the month. He loved when the stories flowed, something that hadn't happened in a long time.

Later that night Chase dropped by with James in tow. "Hey, Si! How are you?" Chase asked when Simon let the two men inside. Chase immediately hugged him, as usual.

"Not bad. Writing again, finally, and I have a date Wednesday." Simon knew he was grinning like a fool but didn't care. "Thank you so much for dumping Adrian."

"Uh, I didn't exactly dump him, Si."

"Yeah, yeah, whatever."

"I take it that means the date Friday went well?" James asked once they settled in the living room—James and Simon on the couch, Chase on the chair closest to the couch.

"Very. I really like him; I just hope he's as good a guy as you say, Chase."

Chase stared at Simon hard, and the look made him a little uncomfortable. "He's a sweetie that deserves someone that will accept him and love him."

"Be nice, Chase. I'm sure Simon thinks the same about Adrian or he wouldn't be going out with him again. Right?"

James's tone and the arched-brow look he gave Simon had him nodding before he thought of what to say. "No, I really like him. He's smart, sweet, and even when I screwed up and turned away while talking to him, he was nice. The good kind of nice."

"While talking? What did you do?" Chase asked as he sat forward. Thankfully, he seemed to have calmed down; his tone was no longer accusatory or irritated.

"I just looked away while talking. It wasn't deliberate. I was checking out the desserts at the coffee shop he took me to after dinner and didn't think about his hearing. I mean, he speaks so well and never seemed not to understand, other than when the server didn't face him," he explained and shrugged. The way Adrian had touched his face and how soft his voice had been when he'd turned Simon back to him brought another smile to his lips, he was sure.

Chase sighed and flopped back on the couch. "Yeah, that was the one thing I worried about trying to set you two up. You don't know sign language."

"But he could learn," James interjected. "If I can learn to be subish for Seth, I'm sure Simon could learn a new language."

Simon couldn't help it, he snorted as he tried to suppress a laugh before the chuckle; then a full belly laugh broke through. Both James and Chase laughed right along with him. "Subish? That's not even a word," he managed to get out once he calmed. "And you did *not* learn to be submissive for Seth. You were always that! You just learned to do things the way he wanted you to, let him push you past your hang-ups and fears."

"Since when do you know so much about Dom/sub things?" James asked, his smile still firmly in place.

"I have known at least a little about BDSM since I was probably eighteen or nineteen. I'm not into the lifestyle, but I had a roommate in college that was, and when you write romance, you research all sorts of things." Simon shrugged. It was one of the reasons he'd never worried about Seth and James, especially once he'd known what kind of Dom Seth was.

Both men stared at him for a moment before shrugging nearly in unison. "Who knew?" James fidgeted a moment with the ornate choker Seth had given him—Simon knew it was actually a collar, but none of them made a thing of it, knowing it would likely unnerve James—before looking back to Simon. "The point is still the same. If it's an issue, take a class in ASL or join a Hearing and Deaf alliance or go to one of the Silent Suppers they have around the area. You've never let anything stop you before. I can't imagine you'd let little things like language or hearing stop you if you really like this guy."

"I've actually already thought of that. The classes, I mean. I'm going to start a beginners' ASL class soon, and I've been spending time on a website called ASLPro. I tried a couple of signs the other night with him, and he seemed pleased." He had loved the happy look on Adrian's face; he just wished he'd known more signs. James was right, though, if he wanted this to work out—and he did—then learning Adrian's language would be important.

"Then what's got you so worried?" Chase asked, hopping up from the chair before sauntering into the kitchen.

Simon raised his voice to make sure Chase could hear him with the noise he was making. *Seriously, how loud do you need to be to get more soda?* "I don't know."

"Bullshit. Try again." Chase came back in, three Mountain Dews in his arms "You know what's bothering you, and I bet James and I can even guess, but us telling you won't help you. So spill. What's got you all twitchy?"

Damn friends think they know everything! "He doesn't know about the money or my stuck-up, money-hungry family. What if that matters to him like it did to Carl or Dan or well, damn near all my exes? Soon as people find out I'm one of 'those' Tylers, I lose their interest in me in favor of my checkbook."

James reached over and grasped Simon's hand. "We didn't and still don't care. I never cared about Seth's money or Chase about Rhys's—not that most would even realize how much Rhys has, but you know what I mean. None of us are like that, so why assume Adrian is?"

"I know, but… you're my friends, that's different. If how you act had anything to do with how my love life went, I wouldn't still be single." And he hated being single!

"True," James said, giving Simon's hand a gentle squeeze. "But not everyone out there is going to be a gold digger, Si. You know that."

"I do. Well, I do up here," he said, pointing to his head. "But here"—he pointed to his chest—"I'm not so sure."

"Did your family call and start crap with you again?" Chase asked, his normally happy, open face suddenly looking sober and focused. "Is that why you're worried about the money thing again?"

The sigh that slipped out answered for him before he could get out any words. He hated how they made him feel, always had. He was never going to be the kind of man they would be proud of, not unless he completely submerged who he truly was and pretended to be the proper gentleman by day and the rich playboy at night. "Yeah. Zoey called to demand I grow up and go to my parents' anniversary party at The Pfister. It's always *so* much fun to be reminded how far from grace I am with my own family."

Chase snorted. "You're not going, are you? I mean, I know they're your family and all, but—"

"No, no, I understand. Moreover, no, I'm not going. I'd love to, but I know I wouldn't really be welcome. Well, maybe if I had some brainless but rich bimbo on my arm. Then I'd be welcome, I'm sure."

"Sorry." James set his drink down on the coffee table, then shifted to face Simon more. "I know how that goes, but you have a family, even if not by blood, as you pointed out to me many times over the years, so don't let them upset you or make you paranoid about Adrian."

"Yeah, I promise I wouldn't have encouraged you two going out if I wasn't 100 percent sure he would be good to you. I mean, come on. He didn't even get upset when I lost it during our date when Rhys and that tramp showed up. Besides," Chase added, his smirk wicked. "He's a great kisser."

Simon grumbled, not appreciating the reminder that Chase had kissed Adrian all those months ago—and no, the fact Adrian kissed Chase first did not help. Simon and Adrian hadn't even had a full-on kiss yet and they'd known each other longer. "You better not kiss him again."

Chase giggled. "Oh please, the only guy I kiss now is Rhys and you know it." He waved his hand as if shooing away the thought. "Besides, Adrian is a total top. What the hell would I do with him?"

Simon's head snapped up as he stared at Chase. "How the hell do you know, and are you sure?" He hadn't thought Adrian and Chase had done more than eat dinner and share one kiss, which had proved to them that they were friends and nothing more.

"Oh, I'm certain, but not because we did anything, hon. But even if we had, you know I don't kiss and tell. Well, okay, so I sorta do, but you know my point. Anyway, I know because he told me once when we were talking about guys and such. I said something about being a top and finding it annoying how everyone always assumes I'm not because of how I look, and Adrian mentioned he'd thought the same. During that conversation, he also said he was glad we hadn't gone any farther than that first date. Two confirmed tops do not a good relationship make."

Huh. Well, that worked for Simon, as he could top but didn't like to. Not that he hadn't ever—most men he knew were switches, after all—it just wasn't what did it for him. The problem came with being able to trust the person enough to let them inside his body.

"Well, okay. I guess."

"No pouting, Si, that's Chase's job," James teased. "But I'm sure you can handle Adrian. You just have to meet him partway, which it sounds like you're working on doing."

"Brat," Chase fake groused. "Seriously, though, James is right. Just let things happen and go with it. Learn ASL—I'll even help if you like—but try not to let your worries get in the way of you actually being happy."

"I'll try." When he saw Chase wind up again, he quickly added, "Honestly, I will try, it's just hard to trust sometimes."

"And you have every reason for your worries," James replied before Chase could say anything, thankfully. "I get it, but I think you need to relax and let Adrian show you the kind of man he is."

He knew Chase and James were right, but he couldn't simply turn off his concerns. "I promise to try." In a bid to get them off his love life and on to something that wouldn't upset him, Simon quirked a smile. "Now, who wants to help me plan what to make for dinner?" James and Chase were both excellent cooks and were the go-to-guys for all their friends if they had to make a dinner to impress parents or new partners.

They spent the next while discussing foods, tastes, and personal likes and dislikes of various foods and dishes. Eventually, they had the dinner planned and decided to simply hang out, playing games and having fun.

ADRIAN LOOKED up from the papers he was grading when the lights flickered. Since he couldn't hear, he had his office set up like his home: instead of a person knocking, which he wouldn't know about, he had a doorbell that caused the lights to blink a moment. That was one of the modifications he used, and the university had been great about the accommodations he needed, as were his students. When he looked up, his TA Kelley stood in the doorway, smirking.

"What are you doing?" Kelley never used the bell; he just sauntered in, even if there was a student already in the office.

"Tormenting you."

Adrian rolled his eyes and pointed at the empty chair across from him. *"Sit and tell me what's on your mind."*

"Spoilsport. Fine. What's up with you lately? Meet someone?"

Adrian thought about it a moment and realized he hadn't told Kelley yet about his date the other night. Even though Kelley was his teaching assistant and a university student technically, they were also friends and usually shared such things. *"Sorry. You remember the man in the car with me the other night? The night I stopped by your home?"* When Kelley nodded, he continued. *"We went out last Friday. He's... I like him."*

"Yay!"

Adrian scowled at Kelley. He knew he didn't go out all that often, but the overdone exclamation, whole-body yay was a bit much!

47

"Sorry, but you have only gone out once since that Chase guy, and that was a total bust. You know it, I know it."

Kelley was right, but still. *"How's Ty?"*

If the glower Kelley turned on him could have been any darker, he wasn't sure how. *"Fine! I will butt out. Happy?"*

"No. I know you worry, I thank you for that, but Simon is nothing like my last date or your last ex. Promise."

"OK. Oh, I want to take your Ethical Hacker class this summer."

"You will do great in it."

"Cool! Now, let's talk dates and boyfriends...."

No matter how hard he tried to dissuade the topic, Adrian actually enjoyed discussing their first date and his plans for more. Kelley even made a few good suggestions on where Adrian might take Simon in the future.

"Movies."

"Can't hear, remember?"

Kelley shrugged as only he could, his whole body part of the movement. *"So take him to one of the theaters that has the closed captioning setup. Movies are a normal date thing, and he is hearing."*

Huh. Well, he could try it. He watched movies at home, or at friends' houses, but he'd just never gone out to one. Deciding he would look into it, he pulled out his cell and typed a quick line to remind himself to look up what was playing and which theaters had the CC device he would need to follow along.

That decided, Kelley pulled out a stack of papers he had graded already and turned them over to Adrian before leaving. Adrian spent the next hour or so dealing with students who had questions or needed advice. On top of his own students, he also helped some of the Deaf students on campus acclimate to the university environment and acted as a go-between occasionally if they had an issue with a professor. It didn't happen often anymore, but sometimes things popped up. Luckily, nothing catastrophic happened, and he was able to leave on time.

By the time he got home, he was exhausted. He still had a couple of hours of reading to do and a computer forensic project he needed to start, but neither gave him more than the feeling of "meh" when he looked them over. What he really wanted was more time with Simon.

Thinking of him, he pulled out his phone and sent a little note telling Simon he was home and thinking of him. That he had work to do still, but he hoped Simon's writing was going well and that he looked forward to Wednesday.

The smiley face and "do you still like lasagna?" made *him* smile. After he sent back his yes, Adrian forced himself to focus and get his work done; otherwise he wouldn't be able to go to Simon's. And that was not an acceptable trade-off for slacking.

chapter seven

ADRIAN LOOKED down at his wrist, checking the time, wishing the day would move faster. His second date—unsupervised date, at least—was later that night, and he both couldn't wait and was tied in knots over it. He liked Simon, more than he expected to, but Simon's weird shying away after being more provocative at the coffee shop had him worried. He still wasn't certain what that had been about, but Adrian didn't want to call Chase and ask, either. Knowing Simon had been hurt by his previous boyfriend, but not knowing the details, left a lot to the imagination, as did the fact Simon had kept a lot of himself closed off when they were talking about their pasts and childhoods.

Noting he still had a couple of hours, Adrian tidied up his home and then ran out to pick up a bottle of wine—red to go with the Italian dish he knew Simon was serving for dinner. He was curious to see if Simon cooked or if he conned Chase or James into making the dinner for him. Adrian hadn't had the pleasure of James's cooking, though he'd heard about it from Chase, but he had tasted Chase's more than once since they became friends.

In a way he hoped for Chase's cooking—because it was that good!— and in a way he hoped Simon had gone to the effort to cook for him. It was probably childish of him, but Adrian liked the thought of Simon doing it himself. The whole personal-touch thing had always appealed to him, though he'd had exes tell him it smacked of a misogynistic attitude—a concept he never had understood, as he didn't date women and he didn't expect his dates to cook and clean for him like some fifties housewife.

As he entered the liquor store, his cell vibrated with a new text. Adrian stepped to the side, just inside the doors, and pulled out his phone to check. *Dad?*

»Son, come over for dinner 2night? «

Ha! Perfect timing. Adrian loved his father, but no way was he putting Simon off to go eat with him.

»Have a date. Rain check? Tomorrow maybe? «

»Date? Who with? Do I know him? «

»LOL Nosy old man. No, you don't. I'll tell you about it at dinner another night. Getting wine now. «

He knew his father would approve of Simon, but no way was he getting into a long conversation about his dating and love life via text before his date. He'd still be standing there instead of at Simon's if he did.

»OK :(«

Really? Sixty-year-old men should not be allowed to use frowny faces in their texts!

»Great. TTYL Dad «

He waited a moment to see if his father would ask what the letters were for—he did about half the time. Adrian was certain he only did that to be ornery. How hard was *talk to you later* to remember, after all?

When the smiley face came through, Adrian grinned. Yeah, his dad always put a smile on his face. After pocketing the device, he quickly moved through the store, intent on getting a nice bottle of wine and then returning home. He still had to shower and dress, but as he had already laid out his clothes, he knew it wouldn't take him too long.

Standing in the wine aisle, he debated between a nice bottle of cabernet sauvignon and another of Roussillon red. The tap to his shoulder startled him; he'd been so focused he had failed to notice anyone getting that close to him. When Adrian turned his head, he found Simon's friend Dale standing there, a huge grin on his face. "Hi."

"Hello. How are you tonight?"

"Not too bad. What are you shopping for?" Dale asked, looking from Adrian to the wine in front of them.

"Simon's lasagna. Don't suppose you know which would work best?" *Please know!* He wanted to impress Simon, not bring something that wouldn't work with the dish. Adrian wasn't even certain if it was a red lasagna. *What if it's a vegetable or white or....*

"Simon's cooking for you?" Dale's eyes widened as he stared at Adrian. "Really?"

What was with Dale's weird reaction? "Well, I assume he is. He said he was making dinner."

"Well, what are you leaning toward for choices? I know what he likes, usually, but he probably bought wine already."

"Oh." He should have thought of that. Frowning, Adrian racked his brain for what he should bring if not wine. He didn't know Simon well enough to know what he liked. Not yet anyway.

"Hey, don't look so sad, man. Why don't you get him some of that imported beer he likes? Or.... No, you don't have...." Dale turned away from Adrian, so he had no idea how the sentences finished.

"Dale." When the man turned back to face him he explained, "I'm Deaf, remember. I have no idea what you said after you turned."

He flushed red and looked down. After a moment Dale raised his head. "Sorry. I know better than that. Really. I was just thinking out loud that taking him something a writer would like would likely impress him more than wine anyway. I mean, he could buy and sell this store ten times over, probably."

Adrian filed the comment for later thought. He knew Simon had money, but the way Dale worded it made it sound like a lot more than Adrian had already assumed. Pushing the curiosity away, he thought about something for a writer. That could work, but he didn't really have time right then, not considering how long he'd spent at the store already. "I'll try that for another date, maybe, but I don't want to be late. What beer would you suggest?"

"Easy. Get him a pack of peach meal cads and he'll be thrilled. It's a bit of a weird beer, in my opinion, but he loves it."

"Peach meal cans?" *What that hell is that?*

Dale laughed and shook his head. "No, no, peach—never mind. Here, let me show you. It's a Belgium beer, a peach beer no less, so it's probably hard to understand even with how well you read lips."

Dale grabbed Adrian's hand and tugged, leading him across the store to a different area, this one labeled for foreign beers and ales. Adrian wasn't used to others being so touchy with him, but he'd noticed Chase, Dale, and Simon seemed to be handsy people, so it didn't bother him. It would have if anyone else had led him around that way. His mother had had an annoying habit of doing things like that when he was young, as if being Deaf somehow impaired his intelligence.

The four-pack Dale handed him said Pêche Mel'Scaldis. *Oh, that makes more sense.* Though he had no idea how one would say the name. When he looked at the price beneath where the box had sat, he was surprised. He didn't mind spending money to get something Simon would like, but he'd never paid that much for beer before.

"He loves sweet beer, sweet coffee. Well, he just likes sweet things, period. If you don't, you might take a second thing of beer so you have something you like too."

"No, I'm sure this will be fine. Thank you. I—" He checked the time again and frowned "—I really have to go or I will be late."

"Yeah, being late is never a good idea for a date. Not if you want to actually keep the guy." With that odd statement, Dale waved and practically bounced back across the store, leaving Adrian confused.

Deciding Simon's weird friend would have to be figured out later, he took his pack of beer to the register and a few minutes later was back in his car, driving home, excitement making his stomach flutter and roll as it hadn't in ages. He just hoped that was a good sign for his possible relationship and future with Simon.

WHEN HE entered his home again, he quickly put the beer in the fridge, hoping it was one that tasted better cold, before he hurried into the shower. The water felt fantastic after having been out in the evening chill, but he refused to give in to his body's desire for fun. His dick perked up when he lathered up, but he ignored it in favor of being fast. He wanted to get to his date! They'd just seen each other on the previous Friday, but he was already pretty addicted to Simon and his sweet, shy ways.

Stepping out of the shower, he dried off, then hung his towel up before going to put his clothes on. He had his black briefs on and his slacks pulled up but not buttoned or zipped yet when he noticed his cell flash as it sat on the comforter beside his shirt. He picked it up and ran his thumb up the screen to open the text. He noticed it was from Simon and his breath stopped. Why was he texting right before Adrian was to leave? He wouldn't cancel, would he?

»Looking forward to seeing you tonight :c) «

Okay, yeah, that was actually kind of cute.

»Be there soon! «

Hurrying, he finished dressing, fixed his hair, and collected his wallet, phone, jacket, and keys. In his rush to go, he nearly forgot to grab the beer out of the fridge. Soon, though, Adrian was back in his car, driving toward Simon and, he hoped, an evening filled with fun for them both.

Adrian was certain he hit every red light along the way, which only served to ramp up his nerves. He hated being late, and he was going to be if something didn't give soon. Every light, slow driver, and idiot on the road seemed to find his or her way in front of him.

By the time he arrived at Simon's, he needed a moment to breathe and calm down. Looking up at the house, seeing the warm glow of lights, knowing Simon was inside, something in him calmed. He wasn't sure why, but he felt... settled—that was the only word he could think of—when he thought of going into the house with Simon there already.

With a sigh, Adrian opened the car door and stood before retrieving his gift. After closing and locking up the car, he hurried up the walkway and practically hopped up the steps to the door. Before he could push the doorbell, the door opened, revealing Simon standing there with a soft, shy smile on his lips—lips he hoped to feel a little more thoroughly before the night was over.

"Hi."

"Hi, Simon." Adrian held out the beer and smiled. "A little birdie told me you like this kind."

He watched as Simon laughed as he took the four-pack from Adrian's hand. Before he could pull away too far, Adrian leaned in and gave Simon a brief peck on the lips, hoping if it wasn't heavy, it wouldn't freak Simon out too much. He still wasn't completely clear what had upset Simon back at the coffee shop. Whatever it was, Adrian wanted to get Simon past it so they could move forward in their—hopefully developing—relationship.

Simon's eyes were huge when he pulled away, but the happy look on his face belayed Adrian's worries. As he turned, Adrian caught the way Simon's empty hand raised, his fingers brushing his own lips. *Yes*, he decided, *I'll have to surprise kiss Simon more often.*

He followed Simon in, making sure the front door was closed and the lock flipped. Simon lived in a good area, but he didn't relish the idea of surprise visitors. Especially the uninvited kind.

The house was warm inside, and the scents of meat, tomatoes, garlic, and cheese cooking had his stomach hoping dinner was served soon. The smell of fresh bread wafting through the room only made his hunger stronger. No matter who'd cooked, the food would be wonderful, he was sure.

He trailed along behind Simon until they were both standing in the kitchen. It was bigger than Adrian expected, though he didn't know why that fact surprised him any. Simon's home was beautiful inside, comfortable yet classy, yet it was still a little confusing simply because of the size. It seemed more like a home for a family, but only Simon lived there.

"I like your home, and God, that smells good," Adrian said, gesturing to the stove, where the luscious scents seemed to be coming from.

"Thanks," Simon said and signed, his brows pulled together as if in deep concentration. "I cooked lasagna and garlic bread."

Adrian smiled, pleased that Simon was trying signs again. He didn't get the finger spelling of garlic quite right, but just the knowledge that he attempted it thrilled Adrian. Adrian gently corrected his finger shapes, then thanked Simon both with sign and a hug. "It smells wonderful, and I'm sure I'll love it," he signed and said.

"I'm trying to learn some ASL, to make it easier for you. I wanted to ask—" Simon flushed pink to the tips of his ears, but he didn't turn away. "I wanted to ask if you would sign with me, so I can see and maybe get used to it? I want to learn more about your language and, well...." He shrugged. "Is that okay?"

Is that okay? Did he really just ask that? "It's more than okay, Simon, and thank you. I'm happy to help you learn if you want, and yes, I'll sign and speak instead of only speaking with you." It was easier for him to sign all the time anyway, as he usually had to remind himself that Hearing people often didn't like the hand motions when they were speaking. He'd been told many times it was distracting, and not only by his mother. Grinning he added, "What made you decide to learn?"

"It seemed only fair to learn your language. I mean, I know you lip-read well, but why should you have to all the time, especially when with a friend?"

He thought about that a moment but didn't like the word *friend* when applied to Simon. "What about with a boyfriend?" Adrian signed and spoke.

Simon swallowed hard, his eyes widening slightly as he slowly nodded. "Especially with that."

"Good! How about we eat now, and then you can show me what movie you chose?"

"I picked a couple for you to narrow down. All have captioning, and I made sure I knew how to turn it on on the TV. I've left it on, in fact, for the last few days."

Simon had kept the closed captioning on even when Adrian wasn't around? Simon was trying to kill him with his thoughtfulness. "Thank you. That means a lot." He thought about it a moment, then added, "Simon?"

Simon turned to face the oven instead of answering. He held up a finger, indicating he needed a second, before he picked up the two potholders sitting on the counter. Moments later he set a large baking dish on top of the stove, then closed the door. When Adrian looked over Simon's shoulder, he saw the lasagna, the cheese bubbling around the edges slowly.

"Smells so good!"

Simon turned, so close now Adrian could feel Simon's heat and smell his cologne. Without thinking first, Adrian slipped his hands over Simon's hips, resting them there as he waited.

"It-it just needs to set now. Everything else is d-done." Simon looked down to where Adrian's hands rested, then back up, his gaze locking with Adrian's. "I—you—I like your hands there."

"They like being there too." He couldn't sign the words, but he figured Simon would understand, because he didn't want to let go yet.

Adrian watched, entranced, as Simon slowly lifted his hands to rest on Adrian's before carefully gliding along Adrian's forearms, biceps, eventually stopping at his shoulders. Adrian couldn't help it; he shivered under Simon's light touch, heat ripping through him faster and harder than he could remember ever feeling. Instinct took over, and before he knew it, his lips were pressed against Simon's and moving gently. After a moment, though it felt an eternity to him, Simon's lips moved and finally parted, his tongue tentatively touching Adrian's.

He raised his hands from Simon's hips and cupped Simon's face with one hand, slipping the fingers of his other into Simon's light brown hair, tangling them in the silky locks as the kiss deepened. He relished the little trembles and the vibrations against his lips as he continued to kiss, not pushing to deepen any further than Simon chose.

An eternity later, when Simon finally pulled back, he was flush and panting. "We really should eat now."

Adrian reluctantly released Simon so he could sign with his words. "Now is good." He thought about it a moment before he asked the thing he'd been wanting to but hadn't yet. Adrian had seen Simon's friends call him Si, but he wasn't sure if it was okay for him to or not. "Can I call you Si, like Chase, James, and Dale do?"

Simon nodded. "Yeah." He signed *yes* as he spoke. "You're more than a friend, but you are that too, so please?"

"Thank you, Si. Can I help you with anything?" He motioned to the food as he asked.

"Sure. You take the bread basket in, and I'll bring the salad while the lasagna finishes settling."

He couldn't help it. He grinned as Simon signed the few words he knew. He'd never dated a Hearing guy, one who didn't already know sign, who tried so hard for him. Happier than ever, Adrian picked up the basket once Simon retrieved it from the second oven—one Adrian had been too distracted to notice before—then followed Simon's pointing to the large dining room, where he discovered unlit taper candles, a low floral arrangement of early-spring flowers, and dishes already set out.

Adrian set the basket down, and moments later Simon entered carrying a large cut-glass bowl filled with salad. Once they were both seated, Simon reached over, lit the candles with the small lighter he pulled out of his pocket, and then gave Adrian's hand a gentle squeeze. "I hope you enjoy."

chapter eight

WATCHING ADRIAN eat never failed to delight Simon. He was so expressive, but even more so, Simon had never before been envious of silverware. The way Adrian's lips moved over the tines, how his tongue flicked out to catch a dribble of sauce or cheese, the way his Adam's apple moved as he swallowed all served to keep Simon half-hard and completely entranced.

They didn't talk a lot while eating. He knew Adrian had a hard time focusing on his lipreading while he ate. In a way, Simon rather liked the gentle quiet of eating with him like that. It wasn't a strained or sterile quiet—unlike the rare times he sat at a table with his family—but rather a comfortable one. One he could imagine as a regular part of his life. Pushing that thought away, Simon focused on the last bite of his dessert, not wanting to let his hopes build. Too many disappointments and losses had taught Simon that hope was for other people, not him. Well, and his characters— they all got happy endings.

When Simon looked up after setting his fork down, he realized Adrian was watching him. "Um, am I wearing my food on my face?"

He'd quickly picked up his napkin, intending to fix the issue, when Adrian smiled, reached over, and cupped Simon's face in his big hand before pulling back to sign and say, "No, Si. I simply like looking at you. Is that all right?"

He swallowed hard but smiled. "Of course. I…. Don't mind me."

"What if I want to?"

Want to what? Simon felt as though he'd missed part of the conversation, though he knew he hadn't. "Um…."

Adrian smiled softly, his gaze gentle yet warm, as he leaned forward once more. "You really need to relax, Si. Why don't I help you clear the table and then we can move into the living room and pick a movie like you suggested?"

That decided, they made quick work of the dishes. Before Simon knew it, they'd settled on the large comfortable couch, close enough Simon could feel the heat radiate off Adrian, each breath filling him with the intoxicating blend of some musky cologne Simon didn't recognize and Adrian's natural scent.

"Which movie did you pick?" Simon made certain Adrian could see his face. He dimmed the lights some with the remote, though not as much as he normally would have, once he'd asked.

"*Ferris Bueller's Day Off*. It's funny, bizarre, and I seriously love the Ferrari."

Simon laughed at how serious Adrian was as he mentioned the car. "It's a true classic, though I didn't see it the first time until I was away at college."

"Why not? I thought it was a requirement for Hearing teens. I mean, I wasn't able to understand it until I got ahold of a copy with captioning, but why did you wait so long?"

"It's wasn't appropriate entertainment for— Let's just say my parents didn't approve."

Adrian frowned but didn't say anything, something Simon was thankful for, even though he was certain Adrian would ask again. Everyone asked eventually.

As the movie began, Simon tried to focus on Ferris and his insane shenanigans, but all he could manage was to notice how good Adrian felt against him. Eventually he scooted so they touched from shoulder to leg. When Adrian lifted his arm and wrapped it around Simon's shoulders, Simon sighed and snuggled against Adrian's side more. He rested his head on Adrian's shoulder and smiled, though he knew Adrian couldn't see.

Adrian's fingers toying with his nape as the movie continued was the highlight of the night as far as he was concerned until Adrian kissed Simon's hair. Simon raised his head, intending to admire his…. Was Adrian his date for the night, or were they moving into boyfriend territory? He wasn't sure how much Adrian felt for him, but was hopeful it was the latter, not the former. Instead, Adrian leaned forward and took Simon's lips in a deep, plundering kiss. Unlike any kiss they'd shared before—from anyone before, really—Simon found himself pushing into the kiss, reveling in the slide of Adrian's tongue, the sweet taste of his lips, how his teeth scraped against Simon's bottom lip as he nibbled before diving back in. It was hot yet tender, and Simon could feel Adrian's want as much as his care—a confusing mixture, but one he quickly sank into.

When he pulled away, the need for air trumping the desire for the sexy man in his arms, Simon panted as he took in how flushed Adrian's skin was, how the color of his eyes seemed swallowed by the black of his pupils. "I...."

Simon squeaked, glad Adrian couldn't hear the *un*manly sound he made when Adrian tugged him over his lap until Simon straddled him. Adrian pulled him into another mind-numbing kiss, his hands caressing down Simon's back, cupping his butt, pulling his body forward until their groins met.

The rather pronounced bulge in Adrian's pants matched Simon's own, and before he thought better of it, he started shifting, rocking into Adrian as the kiss continued. Their bodies aligned, the friction better than he would have imagined. Simon felt like a teenager, frotting on the couch like they were. Not that he'd ever done such a thing as a teen—not in his family.

Adrian's fingers tugged at Simon's hips as he thrust up against Simon, increasing the friction to an almost unbearable point. The little moans and whimpers falling from Adrian's lips were the sweetest thing he'd ever heard, even more so because he knew they weren't thought-out sounds, not ones the man beneath him made for Simon's benefit.

Moments later Simon found himself scooped up then laid out on the couch, Adrian slipping between his thighs before resuming the frantic rubbing and thrusting against Simon. When he felt a gentle pinch to his left nipple, Simon shuddered and pushed his chest up into Adrian's ministrations even as he continued to rut against Adrian's rather impressive length.

The fire that licked up his spine and across his skin, the tightening in his belly, and the absolute need in his veins rose until his mind shorted out, and the world narrowed down to Adrian and the pure bliss shooting into his boxer-briefs.

He collapsed back into the couch as Adrian frotted a few more moments, then yelled and shook before toppling down on top of him. Normally, Simon hated when lovers pinned him like that. With Adrian, however, everything was so different. Instead of feeling squished, he felt sheltered.

Simon raised his arms until he held Adrian tight against him as they both panted and calmed. Eventually Adrian raised himself up to hover over Simon, and he immediately missed the warmth and closeness. "I'm sorry. I have to be heavy, but you just…. You…. Amazing."

Adrian stole another kiss before pushing the rest of the way up and off Simon. Once he'd settled upright, Adrian took Simon's hand and pulled him up until he was sitting. Simon leaned into Adrian's hands as they caressed his face, holding him still as Adrian seemed to attempt to peer into his soul.

Simon fidgeted, uncomfortable from the cooling come in his pants and from the intensity of Adrian's gaze. "What are you looking at me so hard for?" he mumbled but knew Adrian could still see his lips well enough—or hoped so, at least.

"Just making sure you're okay, Si. I know you wanted to go slow, but you just felt and tasted so good. I couldn't help myself." Adrian stared at him as if he was afraid of Simon's reaction, though right then he couldn't figure out why. They'd both enjoyed themselves and had participated fully, so why did Adrian look so nervous?

It suddenly clicked; Adrian was worried he hadn't been ready. "I'm perfect, Adrian. Well, almost," he said, tugging at his slacks, unamused with the cold, sticky mess within. "Maybe rinsing off and changing might be in order." Simon paused a moment to look Adrian over. "You're close enough, I think, to my size. I have some sweat pants if you'd like to clean up too."

The room was dark enough he couldn't see the pink of Adrian's blush, but he could see how Adrian's skin darkened as he grinned sheepishly. "That would be nice. Thank you."

Twenty minutes and two quick cleanups later, Simon again sat on the couch near Adrian. "I think we missed the movie." He clicked the TV off and set the remote down.

"I liked what we did instead better," Adrian countered, signing and speaking at the same time, as promised. "But I also know you had issues on our first date about things moving too fast." He scooted closer and cupped Simon's cheek a moment before continuing. "You sure you're okay?"

Simon thought about how to explain. He knew others saw his hang-ups as stupid for a grown man to have, but he wanted a relationship where he was loved and valued, not used or tolerated. He got enough of that from his family and men he'd dated. "I am, I promise. I know I probably seemed like a scared little girl or something, but I don't want to just be another notch or trick. I know you said you weren't like that, Chase says you aren't, and you don't act it, but…."

"But your past lovers have treated you that way," Adrian said, a statement not a question. "For us to work, you have to learn that I am not your exes. I'm willing to take the time to prove that, though, so relax," he teased and nudged Simon. "And I'm well aware you are no girl." He winked.

Grinning, Simon laughed. Yeah, he guessed they both knew the other was definitely *all* male. "So you want to try this again sometime soon?"

Adrian leaned in before taking Simon's lips in a sweet, soft kiss. "I would like that," he said, his lips brushing against Simon's as he spoke. The sensation, how low Adrian's voice was, the need clear in the tone, shot straight to Simon's heart, settling there like a warm blanket on a chilly night.

"Me too."

Adrian sat back some, looking curious as he stared at Simon. "What?"

Right! He can whisper to me, but he can't read lips with his own, he thought, then laughed at the idiocy of it. "I'm sorry, Adrian. I said, 'Me too.' As in, I'd really like to see you again. Soon."

"I'm glad. How about I pick you up Saturday and take you out? I like spending time like this with you, but I'd like to take you out too."

Adrian nibbled on his bottom lip, then smiled wide when Simon spoke again. "When on Saturday?"

"Noon?" Adrian looked Simon up and down again, his brows pinched together as he stared. "Do you ever go to the mall?"

Simon stared, trying to figure out if Adrian was serious. *The mall?* "Um, I have been to a couple of them around town, mainly to Southridge Mall for the GameStop there. Why?"

"There's a Silent Supper going on this Saturday. Well, I guess Silent Lunch would be more correct, but you get the point. Yes?"

Silent Supper? "I've never been to anything called that. Chase mentioned something about it once. What is it?"

"It's what the words imply. It's an event, unofficial usually, where the Deaf in a community come together along with the Hearing to sort of…." His one hand rolled as he seemed to consider his words. "Mingle? The colleges around here often give the ASL students projects that the suppers help with. Like wearing earplugs to block sound then going to the mall to see how hard it is to deal with the Hearing world, or the events like the supper to practice with actual Deaf people, to improve their signing and comprehension."

Simon's heart raced at the thought. He'd not started the formal classes yet, though he had already signed up for the next session, and he had been working on his own via a couple of good websites, but would he make a fool of himself and in doing so, embarrass Adrian? And for that, he had no answer. "I...." He struggled to find a way to express his worry, but before he could, Adrian's face clouded over.

"Never mind. We can do something more comfortable for you."

The flat look in Adrian's eyes and the sour note to his tone had Simon scrambling to fix the situation, knowing Adrian had jumped to the wrong conclusion. "No, it's not that!" Adrian looked down, but Simon gently raised his chin, hoping Adrian would pay attention to his words. "I don't know many signs, and I know how fast you and Chase sign together. I can't do it that fast. I don't want to embarrass you. The others there, they're people you know and probably some friends of yours, right?" When Adrian nodded, Simon continued. "I don't want to—"

"What do you think I would think if you have to ask for help or for someone to slow down? It's expected that most of the Hearing people that attend are learning. Things like 'slow down' and 'again please' are a pretty common thing to see. We don't expect perfection from any Hearing, well, other than an interpreter maybe, and certainly not from someone so new to the language. It's not a trick to pick on the Hearing, I promise."

Simon nodded and swallowed, trying to make his thoughts calm and ordered. Maybe if he didn't already feel like a failure in so many things, this might be easier, but he wasn't sure. His family thought him an embarrassment. His exes thought him stupid for demanding fidelity—his last one had even said that was something only "stupid breeders" asked for. That no real man, gay man at least, would ever expect something like that. Again pushing his thoughts down, he shook his head slowly. "No, I don't want to embarrass you." *Or make you give up on me so soon.*

"You could never embarrass me by simply being you. I can take you somewhere else, if you'd rather. I know the mall is probably not really your thing."

"No. I'd like to go and see this supper thing. Get to really see how you would normally communicate and be if you didn't have to make up for my lack of language."

"It's that attitude right there that makes me happy and want to take you."

That made no sense to Simon. Why would pointing out he didn't know the language make Adrian happy? "Why?"

"Simple. You said 'lack of language,' referring to your ability with ASL." Confused, Simon motioned for Adrian to keep going, hoping to understand soon. "You didn't say it was my lack of hearing but that it was your own lack of knowing my native language. Most Hearing people treat Deafness as a disability and often misjudge us as slow or ignorant. Simon, you act like it's no different than if I was from a non-English-speaking country and you're just trying to learn my native tongue. That makes you special in my opinion. Very special."

"But you're not disabled. I mean, I guess medically you would be classified that way, but not really. You drive, work, take care of yourself, live, love, teach. Oh wait, I guess a lot of disabled people do that too." Simon shifted and flushed again. "Um, what I meant was that being Deaf doesn't make you less, basically you just speak a different language."

"Hey, Si, calm down," Adrian said and pulled Simon into his arms again. He started to pet Simon with one hand as he held on tight with the other. "I didn't say you thought that way. I know you don't."

They sat together, Adrian not stopping his soothing motions the entire time. Eventually he pulled back enough to meet Simon's gaze. "Would you come with me so you can see and learn more about my culture and language? Please."

"I'd like that. Besides, it could be fun. I haven't met any of your friends yet, even though you know my closest friends already." His family really, if one didn't count the blood relations who only wanted him around if he would conform to their version of proper and normal.

"I will make sure at least a couple of my closer friends attend so you can meet them, unless you would rather meet them in a less populated setting?"

"No, I'd like that. I mean, if we're going to date, we should meet those closest to the other, right?"

Adrian grinned and nodded. "Thank you." Before Simon could respond, Adrian took his lips in a deep and crushing kiss, shorting out his thoughts and leaving only passion and heat in its wake. By the time he pulled back, Simon was struggling to remember why them going to bed *now* wasn't a good idea.

"It's late, so I should probably go home. I have work in the morning, and you have a story you said you were working on. So walk me out?"

Simon got up from the couch, reluctantly, retrieved Adrian's clothes, and stuffed them in a tote bag, then walked him to the door. He took Adrian's jacket from the coatrack and held it out, waiting for Adrian to slip it on. Once he had, Simon handed over the bag and then tilted his head up for another kiss before standing in the open doorway as he watched Adrian get in his car and pull away. He didn't return inside until he could no longer see Adrian's taillights.

Once alone again, he tidied up, then got ready for bed, but instead of lying down, he wandered into his office and debated writing more. The characters were clamoring to get their story out, but he was both tired and excited.

Giving in, he woke his laptop and let the story flow from his fingers to the electronic page before him. Hours later he finally went to bed, and dreams of Adrian, not his characters, kept him company for the rest of the night.

chapter nine

ADRIAN LOOKED up when his cell vibrated on the desk next to him as he worked on grading tests. It was the part he least enjoyed about his job, but he understood why it was necessary. He set the red pen down, then picked up the phone and tapped the screen.

»What'cha doin this weekend? «

Airy! Airy—Airell Romero, though no one called him that, not if they valued their life—had been one of Adrian's best friends since middle school, but he hadn't heard from the man in almost a month. Airy had been traveling overseas for work.

»You're back? «

»Yeah, back on Wednesday. Answer the ??? «

»Taking Simon to the Silent Supper on Sat. Want to come and meet? «

As soon as he tapped Send, he realized that Airy didn't even know about his dating Si yet. He waited, counting in his head to see how long it took for Airy to react.

Nearly four minutes passed before the cell lit up again.

»WHO IS SIMON?! «

»Friend of Chase's. We started dating recently. I like him. «

Ten, nine, eight, seven... the screen flashed with Airy's response.

»Dating? As in boyfriend? Of course I'll b there! «

Adrian could just imagine the indignant face Airy was probably making as he typed, and smiled.

»Glad. Be nice to him. Oh, he's hearing. «

»But knows sign right? You are NOT dating someone that doesn't know ASL. RIGHT? «

Yeah, he expected that, and to be fair, the couple of times he had dated guys who didn't know sign it hadn't gone well. Simon was different, he was certain of it! Adrian just hoped his friends would give Si a chance.

»He's trying to learn. Promise to be nice. «

»Grrr…. You deserve someone that will accept you as is, Adrian. Hearing guys never do. «

He frowned at the text, hating how jaded Airy had become, but knowing he'd had his share of men who thought him damaged or broken because of being Deaf. Still…

»Meet him before you judge. «

»Fine. I'll bring Teague with me. «

»Good«

Teague Dillon was another of his friends from school, one of the few who had gone all through school with him and Airy—most Deaf kids were sent to the Milwaukee School for the Deaf, but since Adrian's mother had refused to accept his lack of hearing, Adrian had gone to the Hearing school. The fact he could lip-read was the only thing that made it where he could do well in school. Well, and having faculty and administrators who cared enough to make sure he kept up and knew what he needed to do every day.

Teague wasn't biased against Hearing people like Airy, not that he blamed Airy for feeling that way. Adrian just wanted them to give Simon a fair chance. If they worked out—and he was going to make sure they did!—his friends would have to accept Simon.

Deciding to shift Airy's focus away from Simon, he typed, »So… how was Europe? «

They spent the next while texting about all the places Airy had gone and how much fun he'd had. Airy invited him over Sunday to see pictures and to just hang out. Adrian agreed but still worried about how his friends would react to Simon. More specifically, how Simon would react to them. He knew Simon was still nervous, and if Airy was too pushy, that might scare Simon off; something he did not want to have happen.

After they stopped talking, Adrian tried to focus on the last few tests, but his concern over how Airy would behave when he met Simon kept distracting him. Frustrated, he packed up the last few papers and the rest of his things before putting the trash can outside his office door and locking up.

When he was almost to his car, his phone vibrated in his pocket. He shifted his shoulder pack and pulled out his cell again as he kept walking. *Teague? Should have figured it wouldn't take long before Airy tattled.* To be fair, he had agreed to Airy bringing Teague, but still.

»I see I'm going to the Silent Supper tomorrow. Who's Simon? «

No all caps, no fussing. Yep, that was Teague. Adrian smiled as he replied.

»Yeah. I want him to see what it's really like to deal with the Deaf. I speak so well he forgets sometimes. I want to make sure he understands and can be comfy. As to who… hopefully my boyfriend. «

»Nice tactic and I'm happy for you. You really like this guy? «

»:D Very! I think you will too when you meet. «

»That says a lot there. There've been a couple of guys you didn't want us meeting. Glad this Simon guy isn't like that. You checked on him yet? Made sure he's safe? «

Adrian's smile fell as he read. No, he hadn't done a background check on Simon. He hadn't felt the need to, not this time. Simon wasn't like his last couple of boyfriends, he was certain, and Chase vouched for Simon. Still…

»No. «

»Not to be rude, but why the hell not? You do not want to go through another situation like with Tay or Lee! «

No, no he didn't, but it felt wrong to dig into Simon's past. He was curious, though. Simon never gave him much information about his childhood. Most stories he told centered around college and since.

»I'll think on it. Deal? «

»Now I have to meet this guy :-) See what's so special about him. «

»See you Sat then. Need to drive so have to go for now. Be there about noon, btw. «

»OK C'ya! «

That settled, Adrian sent his OK back to Teague, then tossed the cell onto the passenger seat before he slid into his Rogue. He pushed the idea of checking up on Simon out of his head to think about later. Once he started the engine, he headed home, thoughts of Simon swirling around his mind.

He stopped at the Woodman's on the way, still debating what he planned for dinner that night and what they'd do for dinner after the Supper— hoping Simon stayed with him that long. Adrian worried how Simon would feel after the event the next day but chose to ignore the knot in his stomach, instead focusing on making them a nice dinner instead.

He wandered the wide aisles of the huge warehouse-like grocery story, pushing the cart—one with a wobbly front left wheel, like he always seemed to wind up with—hoping something would jump out at him that would be the perfect meal for them. He really wished he knew more about Simon's likes and dislikes.

When he turned another corner, he noticed Chase and Rhys coming toward him, Chase bouncing along as Rhys pushed their rather full cart. Adrian assumed it took a lot of food to fuel a physique like Rhys's. The man was huge and ripped, after all.

Chase looked down the aisle, his lips turning up as he hurried toward Adrian. *"Hi!"*

"Hi," he managed before he was swallowed up in a huge hug from Chase. He held on tight for a moment before he pulled back and turned to look at Rhys. He was glad to see no change in the man's demeanor—he wasn't certain hugging Chase wouldn't bother him if things had been the other way around, but he was glad Rhys didn't see him as a threat.

"Hi, Rhys."

Rhys dipped his chin as he ran one hand down Chase's back. "Hey." He looked to Chase and added, "You want to catch up? I know you two probably have tons to discuss, but I'm on a tight schedule today."

"No, that's fine. I'll be there in a few."

Rhys said his good-byes and continued along, Chase staying where he was.

"I heard Si's going to the Silent Supper tomorrow."

Adrian nodded. *"I want him to understand and be comfortable in my world, and this way he won't be the only Hearing person in the room."*

"Good plan."

"Airy and Teague will be there too."

"Oh…. Wait." Chase frowned, and when he signed again, his motions were agitated and sharp. *"Make Airy be nice to Si. He didn't like me when we met the first time and I sign."*

He loved how protective and loyal Simon's friends were. It spoke well of them and of Simon, to inspire such in everyone who knew him. Everyone he'd met so far, at the very least. *"That's half the reason for Teague to be there too. Airy promised to be nice."*

Chase didn't seem mollified, but Adrian didn't know what else to tell him. He wouldn't let Airy be mean to Simon. Adrian had taken Airy to task when he'd been rude to Chase, so he really ought to know better.

"OK. Sorry, I don't want either of you hurt."

"I know. Thank you." Adrian considered a moment, then added, *"Any suggestions for what I should make Saturday night. For Si?"*

Adrian watched as Chase looked around as if he could see the whole store from there, brows scrunched, his tongue flicking out to toy with the silver hoop through his bottom lip. *"Seared tuna steaks with grilled asparagus over jasmine rice or quinoa with almonds and shredded carrots would work well. Mango chutney or salsa for the fish and some black sesame seeds on the vegetables. Or stuffed portabellas instead of the rice dish. I know he likes all of that, and it's all easy to make but looks fancy when plated."*

He blinked at the long list of foods, knowing he could make it but not sure Simon would like it all. When Si cooked for him, it was simple but delicious comfort-type foods. *"You sure?"*

"He likes fine food, but he freaks trying to make it himself. I think it's because he wasn't allowed in the kitchen until he moved out on his own. The dishes really aren't hard. I can help you find everything and e-mail you recipes later if you need."

"OK." If anyone would know how to cook or would know what Simon enjoyed, it would be Chase. The man was a wonderful cook, even if he was an IT consultant and not a chef. *"Tuna steaks, then."*

By the time he left the store, Adrian had everything he would need for the next day, including wine and dessert. Chase waved as he and Rhys pulled out, having parked only a couple of cars over from his. After he returned home and put away the groceries, he sat down at his computer, intent on running a few search programs to find out a little bit about Simon. He wouldn't do a full background check, not the detailed and in-depth kind he would on others. The nagging curiosity hadn't lessened any, and so he decided to give in to it and find out a little more about his would-be boyfriend. He just hoped Simon would forgive him for prying.

THE LIGHTS flickered, indicating someone was at the door, not that Adrian could imagine who would be there at nine on a Saturday morning. Frowning as he set his spoon down, he gave a last look at his cereal before he stood and went to answer the door. The lights blinked again, making him want to go smack the person's hands. Whoever it was needed to calm down and gain a little patience.

Adrian retied the belt of his house robe, making certain nothing was exposed. Once satisfied, he pulled the door open and was shocked to find Teague and Airy standing there, both grinning widely.

"Hi. You're early."

Teague had the decency to look embarrassed. Airy simply shrugged and barged inside.

"Sorry," Teague signed and shrugged as well, following Airy inside. Thankfully waiting until Adrian moved, instead of acting like a bull... or like Airy.

Shaking his head, Adrian shut the door and followed them to the kitchen. *"Hungry?"*

"Always." Both men grabbed bowls and joined Adrian at the nook with the open box of Multigrain Cheerios and the half-gallon of rice milk from his fridge.

Airy frowned at the milk, then shrugged and poured it over the little O's in his bowl. *"You drink real milk, you eat cheese, so why do you only have rice milk?"*

"Because I like rice milk. Why are you here so early?" he asked, then pointedly looked at the wall clock. *"Meeting at noon. At the mall. So you can meet Simon."*

"We can't want to hang out?" Airy countered.

Teague added, *"He was hoping to catch your boyfriend here, I think."*

"He's at home. Probably asleep still. And if he was here, you'd be dead for interrupting." Adrian knew he was scowling but didn't care. Airy's actions didn't surprise him, though he was still a bit annoyed. The fact Teague was going along with the early wake-up call stood out. *"Why are you here?"* he asked, staring at Teague. *"Airy I expect this crap from, but you?"*

Teague took another spoonful of cereal and chewed slowly before swallowing. Finally he set his spoon down and replied. *"I know. I want to meet him, Simon too."* Teague glowered at Airy, who proceeded to ignore them both in favor of eating. *"I'm here to keep Airy under control."*

Adrian focused on his breakfast, trying to think through how to deal with the ambush attempt. He knew his friends would want to know Simon, and he did want them to all meet. The surprise visit frustrated him more than he thought it should. By the time they had all eaten and rinsed the dishes, Adrian was resigned to having them with him all day.

"Have you run a check on him yet?" Airy asked. For the first time since their arrival, neither man was smiling. *"Is he what you thought?"*

No, he hadn't. Adrian had sat at his computer, the one he'd designed and built himself, but hadn't been able to input the information he had on Simon. *"No."*

"Why not?" Teague asked. *"You said he's a good guy, but you need to make sure."*

"I agree. If he's 'good'"—Adrian didn't appreciate the leer on Airy's striking but insufferable face—*"then he has nothing to hide."*

Before he knew it, Adrian found himself in his office, being pushed down into his computer chair.

"Type," Airy added, brows furrowed, motions sharp.

"It's none of my business yet," he tried, knowing it wouldn't work. When both men stood over him, arms folded across chests, frowns matching, Adrian gave up. *"Fine, but when it shows he's not a criminal, you both promise to be nice and helpful to Simon."*

Both signed yes.

Adrian turned on his system, logged in, and started inputting the basic information he had on Simon: physical description, address, phone number, license plate number—it stuck out to him, WRT LUV—birthday…. After keying it all in, he set the system to do the searching and digging. He had multiple sites and methods, but was startled when he immediately got hits listing some huge publications and events. *People, Time Magazine, Business Week.* Link after link to lifestyle sections of various magazines and newspapers—some small, some national.

As he sifted through the information pouring across his screen, he was dumbfounded. He knew Simon was a full-time author, so either he made decent money from that or had money elsewhere, but….

"He's rich!" Airy signed, his motions erratic. *"Why would you keep that a secret?"*

He shook his head, confused and a little overwhelmed. He couldn't make sense of any of what he read. Simon was Simon Jacob Tyler, the only son of Theodore Francis Tyler and Alana Marie Winston Tyler. He had a sister, Zoey; married with kids. The family was ultraconservative and outspoken against LGBTQ rights, the poor, Medicaid, and more.

Showing them the last bit, articles where Si's family supported gay-to-straight conversion camps and called for support to reverse gay rights everywhere, Adrian fought the desire to either hunt them down or go find Simon early and hug him. *"That is why he didn't tell me!"*

Adrian stood so fast he sent his chair rolling across the room and started pacing. He couldn't believe his sweet, gentle, downright shy Simon could be openly gay and related to monsters like *that*. His heart hurt for Simon the more he thought about what living with such people had to have been like.

The argument between Airy and Teague caught his attention eventually. He paused to see what they were saying, but both men stopped and stared at him. Adrian glared as he signed, *"What?"*

Finally Teague stepped forward. *"Are you certain it's safe to date him? Wait!"* he continued when Adrian started to sign back, in defense of Simon. *"Safe because his family could hurt you."*

"His best friends, Chase, James, and Dale, are very out. Chase would have warned me if there was a danger. I know he would!" But Chase hadn't warned him about Simon's past. *No*, he trusted Simon, even with the new information. Some of the little things about Si suddenly made more sense, though; the nervousness when childhood or blood families were brought up especially.

"Truth?" Teague asked.

"Truth."

Teague and Airy stared at Adrian's reply. A moment later he found himself wrapped in the arms of his friends. Though it was only a quick embrace, Adrian felt better. He knew that meant both men would be there for him and would support his being with Simon.

Airy grinned when he stepped back. *"Get dressed and let's go meet your boyfriend."*

chapter ten

SIMON CRUISED down South 76th Street, tapping his fingers on the steering wheel in time to the music coming from his stereo system. He'd paid good money to have the quality he did and loved it. Music was one of the things that always seemed to feed his soul, no matter how upset or frustrated his life made him. He'd plugged in his iPod and keyed in his "driving music" shuffle.

"Undisclosed Desires" by Muse came on as he turned into the large parking area that surrounded the Southridge Mall. He had been to it a few times, but malls had never been his thing, even as a teen. He hoped Adrian wouldn't mind if he ran upstairs for a few once the dinner thing was over so he could stop at GameStop. He hated buying the games online, much preferring to be able to play them right after buying them. Besides, he had fun just browsing the games, seeing what others were raving about.

Adrian had texted him to meet at the main entrance near Sears, because the food court was just inside, next to the department store. As he searched for a decent parking place, he saw Adrian's blue Rogue and turned down the same aisle. It still took him a few minutes to find a spot, but eventually he did.

He looked at the cars on either side and frowned. His shiny black Audi S8—the dealer called it Phantom Black pearl, but he just liked the deep, rich color—with the silver leather inside, stood out like a sore thumb with the little Focus on one side and the even smaller Geo Metro on the other. Shrugging, Simon grabbed his sunglasses and got out. After locking the car, he jogged up to where he'd seen Adrian.

Adrian waved, smile wide and eyes bright as he waited for Simon to reach him. "Hi," he signed and said.

Simon was thankful Adrian was so willing to be patient with him on the language issue. He had been practicing and studying hard since Adrian had sprung this outing on him Wednesday night. Simon knew he'd have little hope of understanding much of what was said, or rather signed, around him. However, he was determined to learn and show Adrian that he was serious about them dating. "Hi!"

Moments later his arms were full of Adrian, his cologne and personal musk filling Simon as much as the touch soothed him. Adrian's lips pressed his lightly in a chaste kiss before Adrian stepped back. "Glad you made it. Oh—" Two men stepped up next to Adrian. Simon had been so distracted with seeing Adrian, he hadn't noticed them until then. "—these are my friends. Airy and Teague," Adrian explained, gesturing to each man in turn. "Airy," he repeated, finger-spelling the name and then giving a separate sign Simon thought was a variation of *wind*—the sign done near the upper part of Adrian's head—but he wasn't positive. "And this is Teague." Again, he finger-spelled the name and then gave an extra sign. It looked like a *T* that started at Adrian's sternum and flipped out to a *G*. The alphabet was the one set of signs he was certain he knew, if the signer wasn't too fast in their movements.

"Hi, Airy," Simon said, trying to use the signs Adrian had just given him. Adrian corrected his hands once but didn't chastise or even comment, and Airy didn't seem put out about his lack of correct signage. "Hi, Teague." He again used the name sign he'd been shown. That time no one corrected him, so he assumed he'd gotten it right.

"Guys, this is Simon." Adrian spoke and signed as usual, but he noted that Adrian only signed the letters for Simon, no name sign—or he guessed that's what the signs were for—given for him. He would have to ask about that when they were alone. He didn't mind but was curious if it was something one earned or if there was a standard way names were signed.

"Cute," Airy signed but didn't speak. That was one of the signs Simon did know, and by the heat he suddenly felt on his cheeks, he knew he was blushing.

"Very. Now play nice and let's head in."

Adrian extended his hand to Simon but didn't take his; he just stood waiting. Simon beamed as he slipped his hand into Adrian's. He was still nervous about Adrian's friends and the event, but the feel of Adrian's slightly calloused fingers squeezing lightly as he turned and walked beside Simon helped calm him.

Stepping inside the mall was a bit bizarre. The cool but processed air hit him first, then the scents of all the competing fast food places huddled into the corner hall. But what stood out the most and drew his eye and attention immediately was the mass of people. He'd been there before, so it wasn't the numbers per se but rather the realization that most of the people he saw were signing. Some signed and spoke; a few clusters spoke only—most of those were giving the Deaf group odd looks.

Simon followed along, feeling suddenly a little panicky and a whole lot out of place. That was a feeling he wasn't used to—unless it was with his family, whom he never saw anymore, he reminded himself, pushing the depressing thoughts away. When Adrian let go to sign his hellos with others, Simon became increasingly confused and worried. He didn't mind that the others were Deaf, didn't think it weird like he heard a few people along the sides comment. No, what had him upset was the thought he was the outsider, the weird one who lacked basic communication skills. Everyone around him seemed to understand the others, but not him.

A hand fluttered in his vision for a moment. When he looked up, a tall, thin woman signed, "*Hi. My name is Anna.*"

Name… right. Um… "Hi, my name is Simon," he signed and mumbled, spelling out his name slowly. He concentrated and thought he got it all right.

Her long, thin face lit up. *"Simon's a good name. Are you new to ASL?"*

"Yes." He thought about it for a moment but couldn't remember the right signs. "I don't know much yet," he said, hoping she could read lips.

"Oh, you're brand-new, then." She spoke that time but still signed as well. It was worded as a question, but the tone was all statement. Thankfully she didn't seem upset or annoyed with him.

"Yes. I start classes next week and have been using ASLPro and HandSpeak.com, plus Adrian signs when he talks to help me learn." He signed what words he knew, spelling out the sites.

"You'll get there. Don't worry. Is this Adrian?" she asked, motioning to Adrian as he stepped up beside Simon again.

Simon leaned into Adrian's side a moment and smiled. "Yes. Adrian, this is Anna." This time he signed the whole thing, knowing he had it all right by how Adrian's face radiated approval.

"Hi, Anna. Thanks for helping Simon." Adrian touched his cheek, a delighted expression on his beatific face. "And Si, Anna will probably be one of your teachers. She teaches ASL at the community college and at the continuing education center."

"Oh!" Great, he'd already failed in front of a teacher. He'd never done anything but exceptionally well in school, whether as a child or once in university.

"Calm down," Anna said and signed. "It's good to see you trying. No one here is going to be upset if you have to spell most of the words or ask them to slow down and repeat, either. Everyone understands that most of the Hearing here are learners." She scowled at Adrian. "You, however, should have taught him such things as *slow down*, *again*, *don't understand*. It's not fair to him if he's not been taught yet."

"I…. You're right. He tries when we're alone. I didn't think about it overwhelming him." Adrian turned to face Simon more. "I am so sorry, Si. I wanted you to see my world, not make you feel bad. We can go if you'd rather."

Shaking his head before Adrian was through, he said and signed, "No. I want to learn. I want to see. I just wasn't prepared as well as I thought." He was pretty proud of himself. He'd made it to the last sentence before he lost the ability to sign anymore.

Anna laughed. "You'll do fine." She patted his shoulder. "I look forward to having you in class, Simon. We'll have you signing in no time." With that, she said her good-byes and wandered off to start signing with others.

"I really am sorry, Si. I wanted you to see what it's really like, to be certain you could handle being with someone Deaf. I didn't mean to—"

Simon held up a hand, pressing the tips of two fingers over Adrian's lips and clutching Adrian's hand with the other. When Adrian went still, Simon released him. "I don't want an apology, Adrian. I understand the logic, though I wish I was better at all this. But I don't mind learning, I promise. I want to learn for you but also for us and for myself."

"You sure?" Adrian finally asked, hands flying as he spoke. "We can go as soon as you want."

"No, I'm going to go get a drink and maybe see if I can't find someone else to have pity on me and let me practice what little I know. You want something?"

When Adrian suddenly grabbed him, Simon gulped, his hands fluttering, eventually coming to rest on Adrian's biceps. He found himself tilted back slightly and kissed so soundly Simon nearly forgot where they were and that there were probably fifty or more people staring at them.

Adrian pulled back, holding Simon a moment longer. Once they'd separated, Adrian gave Simon such a look of pride it made his chest hurt. "No, I have everything I need right here."

Simon stared at his feet a moment as he tried to get both his breathing and his face under control. He wanted to reply to Adrian's words, but the lump in his throat barely let him breathe. "I," he croaked. *"Thank you,"* he signed, hoping Adrian could read in his eyes how much those words meant. After another moment, Simon realized Teague had joined them. He waved to Adrian and Teague, then walked over to the Dairy Queen to get his favorite naughty treat, a Double Fudge Frozen Hot Chocolate, hoping to calm his nerves and cool his face before he returned.

Drink in hand, he headed back to the event, having to set down the cup every time someone signed with him. He didn't mind, though, now that he knew he could ask for *slow* or *again*. Knowing that finger-spelling words was acceptable in this setting, he was able to enjoy himself a great deal more.

By the time Adrian collected him, saying he wanted to wander the mall some—and honestly, most of the large group had dispersed already—Simon was still feeling a bit slow, but more hopeful than before. He'd proven to Adrian he could handle being around other Deaf people and that he wouldn't run or refuse to try. Shopping sounded like a great way to unwind after all that. He did wonder how Deaf people didn't wind up paralyzed from the shoulders out, though; his arms were sore from holding them up so much to sign.

ADRIAN'S INSIDES churned, and the knot in his stomach tightened when Simon walked away to get a drink. Anna was right, he should have better prepared Simon for today. He'd wanted to see Si's true reaction to the reality of being with a Deaf person. However, he hadn't thought about how far out of Si's communication ability the event would be. Simon had done wonderfully, trying to use what signs he knew and sticking it out. The perseverance warmed Adrian's heart and buoyed his hopes for them, for a future together. He knew he was probably getting ahead of himself, but he really didn't care.

Teague bumped his shoulder as Adrian continued to watch Simon, thrilled when he saw Si stop and try more conversation with random people as he wandered through the food court. Adrian turned back to Teague. *"What?"*

"You really like him?" Teague's ever-present smile was missing. Instead, his countenance held a seriousness Adrian was unaccustomed to from him.

He nodded and glanced back to where he'd last seen Simon. Adrian smiled when he saw Si sign *again* and *slow*. Turning to meet Teague's gaze he signed, *"Yes, I do. He's like no one before. I want this to work out for us."*

"I know. You look—" Teague cocked his head as he looked at Adrian carefully. *"—happy. Come on, let's go find Airy and keep him out of trouble. Let your boyfriend have time to learn and enjoy."*

Torn, Adrian started to protest, but when he looked around, he noticed Simon standing with a new person, smiling as he fumbled through signing. Simon didn't look distressed or unhappy. He looked…. Adrian observed as the guy Simon was signing with corrected a couple of signs. The joy on Simon's face as he redid them correctly, made him realize that Teague was right.

It took them nearly twenty minutes to track Airy down and corral him, letting the poor, shy boy he was hitting on escape.

"Why did you do that?" Airy's irritation was clear in both motion and body.

Teague's joyous mood turned sour as he stared at Airy. *"The poor kid was going to hyperventilate if you didn't back off. Why you do that?"*

"Do what? Flirt?"

"Aggression is not flirting. Be nice. What's with you?" Airy could be aggressive when he wanted someone, and he'd been more argumentative and over-the-top since he'd arrived at Adrian's that morning. This was simply one more case of Airy being "too much."

"Nothing."

Nothing my ass! *"Spill, now!"*

Adrian and Teague stood in front of Airy, blocking him from the view of the crowd, shoulder to shoulder, arms crossed. They waited, Airy fidgeting and shifting from foot to foot the longer they waited.

Eventually, Airy gave in. *"Sorry."*

"No... why are you being so...?" Adrian was unsure of how to explain it to Airy.

"Predator. You're not so pushy normally," Teague added.

"Not!"

"Yes," Adrian and Teague countered.

Shoulders drooping, Airy looked away. Finally he focused on them again, a deep frown marring his delicate features. *"One, he was cute. Two, I—"*

Adrian had no patience for Airy when he got like this. He cut his friend off, using his best scowl, the one he usually saved for particularly horrible students. *"You were being overbearing and sleazy. Let's go mingle."*

"OK," Airy replied, posture slumping, gaze cast down.

For the next little while, Adrian managed to enjoy himself. He spent more time watching Simon than paying attention to those around him. Simon stopped by a couple of times but didn't stay long as he continued to work on trying to sign with others. Simon's determination and happy mien when he got harder things right, even if he was shown a couple of times first, was truly something to behold.

As the crowd thinned, more and more people leaving, either out the exit or farther into the mall, Adrian moved to collect Simon. Before he managed to get there, though, Anna was back in front of him, her face pinched slightly. *"Adrian?"*

"Hi, Anna."

"Why did you do that to that sweet man with you? You trying to scare him off?"

"No. Yes."

The agitated moue became even more pronounced as she asked, *"Which, yes or no?"*

"No, I want to keep him. Yes, I wanted to see if he could handle my reality. Why?"

"Understand this is not the way to do that? You overwhelmed him. That's not fair to him or you. Many would have run just from fear and pressure."

"I know. I didn't think it out carefully enough. I want him to be sure."

Her attitude dropped, and in its place was sympathy. *"He seems very nice and determined. Give him a chance and stop painting him with the same brush as others. Not all Hearing people—"* She paused, smirking as she swatted his arm lightly. *"—are bad."*

He knew that! He did. He had many Hearing friends and associates, but his dating history had pushed him to test Simon, something he now knew he shouldn't have done. However, Simon had done amazingly well once he calmed down and took his time. *"Sorry?"* He knew it was a lame response, but he didn't have a better one.

"I know. Go get your sweetheart and go shopping or get some real food in him. That chocolate thing he had earlier was not food."

Chocolate thing? *"Yes and thank you."* Moments later he was across the hall, leading Simon toward the escalator and down the long hall toward the GameStop—knowing how much Si loved video games.

chapter eleven

BY THE time they left the mall, Simon had three new games, one of which was for Dale. Adrian seemed to be in even higher spirits than usual, though Simon wasn't certain if it was over his actions at the event or getting to hang out with his friends or some weird combination, but whatever it was, Simon was thrilled. He'd gone into the Silent Supper thing worried he'd fail Adrian, but the pride that had shone from Adrian's eyes and stance was as clear and bright as if he'd shouted at the top of his lungs.

It was a little depressing when they exited the mall and split up, though. He liked riding with Adrian, or the idea of Adrian riding with him, didn't really matter. He simply didn't want to stop being with Adrian yet. "Would you like to stop for dinner?"

Adrian smiled wide. "No."

"Oh," he mumbled.

Before he could get too maudlin, though, Adrian continued, signing as he spoke. "I have everything at home for dinner. I want to cook for you tonight."

"You want to cook for me?" Not as though others hadn't cooked for him, though not usually his dates. Still, the idea of having more time with Adrian and that Adrian had planned to spend the evening with him had Simon throwing his arms around Adrian and hugging him tight.

The vibration Adrian made confused Simon. He pulled back, trying to figure out what was wrong. What he saw, though, had him giggling. Adrian was laughing! "That was a yes, right?" Adrian managed to ask between the gasps as he calmed. A little.

"Yes," Simon signed and said. He figured if he was going to do this right, he should sign as much as he could with Adrian so he would learn faster. It was important to him, but Adrian's actions that day had shown him how concerned Adrian was about the hearing and language issues. Simon wanted to ask about his past lovers but bit his tongue. "What are we having? Should I pick anything up on my way over?"

Adrian shook his head. "No, I went shopping last night for everything we should need. Just need you." The look Adrian gave him was similar to the one he had earlier, when Adrian had said he thought he had what he needed, again making Simon's heart squeeze and his palms sweat.

"You have me," Simon whispered, knowing Adrian wouldn't realize he could barely get the word out. Once he managed to clear his throat and thought he could manage to speak and think at the same time, he asked, "Will your friends be joining us?" Looking around, he realized he no longer saw them. That was odd. They had been right there.

"No, they waved as they left when we stopped at my car."

They had? Simon had been so focused on Adrian, he hadn't even noticed. "I don't think Airy likes me, but Teague seems nice."

"Airy is just worried. He—" Adrian paused, his eyes going unfocused as he stared over Simon's shoulder a moment. "He's been hurt by others for being Deaf and knows the few times I've tried dating Hearing, haven't gone well. He'll come around. He just worries."

Simon could understand that. He and his close friends had worried when James started seeing Seth, but they all thought Seth was the perfect husband for James now. He just had to hope Airy would feel the same about Simon as Simon now felt about Seth. "Hope so."

"He will. Now go to your car and meet me at my house?"

When Simon agreed, Adrian again gave him the address and basic directions. Simon would put it into his GPS—that was why he had the noisy thing, after all. He was well aware of how bad he was at following directions while driving. He hated to stop and ask for directions, but unlike most men he knew, his reason was simply that he tended to phase out halfway through, even when he tried to focus. He didn't mean to, but his brain would start mapping out the next part for a story he was writing and only tune back in at the end. GPS made life much easier for him—he had even spent extra to have a self-updating system that told him of traffic issues in real time.

They hugged again, Adrian pressing his lips to Simon's in a chaste kiss, as he had when Simon first arrived, then stepped back. Simon took his bag from GameStop and walked to his car, still having a hard time believing Adrian wanted him as much as he claimed. As much as it was clear to Simon Adrian's words weren't just for show, Simon still worried how things would change when Adrian realized how rich he was or who his family was. Pushing the morose thoughts away, Simon unlocked the car and started the engine with his key fob before reaching the car. He hated being cold, and while it was no longer freezing out, as the evening got later, it was definitely getting chilly.

It didn't take long to reach Adrian's home. Well, he guessed it did because traffic was slow, but he was still floating on the high from seeing the pride and want in Adrian's eyes earlier, so even idiot drivers and red lights failed to get on his nerves.

Simon looked out the window at the duplex when his GPS informed him he had arrived. Adrian stood next to his Rogue, parked in the driveway on the left side, a soft smile on his face. Simon pulled in behind him, parked, and then turned off his car. After storing the games in his glove box, he exited, hitting the lock.

"Hi," Simon signed and said. "Are we going inside?" He used what signs he could remember, then looked from Adrian to the front door and back again.

"Yes. Just wanted to wait for you." Adrian slipped his hand into Simon's, then tugged, leading Simon up and inside. "Come in and make yourself at home."

When Simon stepped into the house, he found a simple layout where the living room, dining area, and kitchen seemed to flow from one to another. To his immediate right was a hallway with three doors. The only other doors were the sliding-glass ones that led out back and one on the far side of the kitchen that he guessed went either to a laundry area or possibly to a storeroom of some kind.

The walls were all a peculiar off-white—the same as most rental places he'd visited since he moved away from his über-stuck-up family—though the furnishings were unique. Heavy wood furniture that was obviously well made and comfortable-looking was scattered around the space with accent lamps, a few paintings, and a simple entertainment center. There was a large TV with a Blu-ray player, but where his had a stereo and video game systems, Adrian's had books and knickknacks displayed in the cabinets. It was a simple home but not uninteresting.

"Would you like a drink or to watch something while I cook?" Adrian signed and asked.

"I would rather hang out with you in the kitchen, if you don't mind." Sitting alone in the other room held no appeal for Simon. He could sit alone at home; here he wanted to be with Adrian.

The shy smile Adrian gave him encouraged Simon. He knew Adrian liked him, and he recognized his own hang-ups were causing their relationship to move so slowly; he simply didn't know how to fix the problem.

"Thank you."

Moments later Simon found himself seated at the long bar dividing the kitchen and dining space as Adrian prepared the various foods for their dinner. Watching how Adrian moved, how his slacks shifted and pulled as he bent or walked, entranced Simon. It had been a long time since such simple actions had brought him such comfort and peace.

Simon was pulled out of his musings when Adrian set a glass of beer in front of him. He'd been so caught up in his thoughts he'd missed what the man was actually doing.

"It's the peach beer you like." Adrian gently touched Simon's face before he returned to the stove.

Simon looked down at the drink, torn between amusement and wanting to go hug Adrian. No one but his closest friends would ever think to buy, much less bring him, his favorite beer. Most of the men he knew from his family circles would, maybe, think to have a servant bring him a drink, but then it would be wine or scotch, not the Pêche Mel'Scaldis he preferred. Simon liked wine, he even liked scotch, whiskey, bourbon, vodka…, but he couldn't get over how thoughtful Adrian was.

He took a sip of his drink, but instead of continuing to sit and watch, he stood, leaving his glass on the bar, and stepped behind Adrian. Swallowing hard, he lightly placed both hands on Adrian's shoulders. When Adrian stopped what he was doing but didn't pull away or move otherwise, Simon ran his hands down Adrian's arms, then back up, before repeating the motion. This time he left his hands at Adrian's wrists. He wanted to step up, so he pressed against Adrian but couldn't seem to make his legs move him any closer.

When Adrian moved back, pressing his back to Simon's chest, Simon closed his eyes and sighed. Moments later his fingers tangled with Adrian's, though he wasn't sure who reached first.

"Simon," Adrian said. His voice was always deep, but this time it seemed more so. Adrian's head turned against his, his lips brushing Simon's temple. "As much as I love having you hold me like this, the tuna steaks will overcook if I don't finish them now."

Simon let go and stepped back quickly. The heat spreading across his face only added to his embarrassment, but the depth of Adrian's voice and the combined warmth and scent of Adrian still surrounded him. He knew Adrian wasn't actually pushing him away, something he reminded the twisted knot in his stomach—not that it helped.

Adrian pulled the large skillet off the burner, then turned and grabbed Simon's hand. "Let's eat and clean up, then I would love to hold you, Si."

Simon looked down, not wishing to seem too eager, though he felt like a puppy. If he had a tail, he knew it would be wagging.

"Look at me, please."

"Sorry?" Simon said and signed once he managed to look up. He knew the sign extremely well for that one word.

"No sorrys. Let's eat, and then we can continue where we left off." When Simon nodded, Adrian gestured to the fridge and gave instructions for their salad.

Once they were seated, Simon finally noticed the food and smiled. It had been plated as beautifully as he would have expected at one of his preferred restaurants, only with better proportions. "It looks wonderful, Adrian. Thank you."

As usual, they didn't speak much as they ate, though in Simon's case it was a mixture of the wonderful food and his excitement for later. He wanted to hold Adrian more and have Adrian hold and kiss him as well.

Partway through the meal, Adrian reached over and took Simon's free hand. When Simon looked up, he was caught in the luminous green gaze. The heat there shot straight to his cock, which hardened almost immediately. "Y-yes?"

"Relax, Si. We don't have to do anything you don't want."

Huh? Why would he say that? "I know."

"Good." Adrian motioned to their mostly cleaned plates with his other hand. "Do you want dessert now or later?"

Excited at the thought of time with Adrian on the couch—his mind flashing back to the other night and how wonderful it had felt to touch and kiss Adrian, how strong his orgasm had been, made his answer immediate. "Later."

Adrian smirked as he pulled Simon up and into the living area. When they stopped in front of the couch, Adrian raised a hand and gently cupped Simon's face before he stepped back enough to sign as he spoke. "I want to spend more time with you, Si. I want you, but I do not want you to feel like I'm pushing faster than you want."

Simon groaned, his frustration warring with his amusement. He'd finally found a considerate lover, and all he could think about was how he wished Adrian would be a bit more demanding. He couldn't decide if he wanted to laugh or cry. Instead Simon tugged on Adrian until their bodies were flush together. He tipped his head back enough to make sure Adrian could see his lips and said, "Show me, please."

He watched as Adrian swallowed hard, enjoying how Adrian's throat worked and his Adam's apple bobbed. "I—"

"I want—" Simon gulped around his nerves. "—faster."

The sudden tension in the body Simon held startled him, but before he could voice his concern, Adrian continued. "I tend to be very—" His mouth snapped shut as his head tilted. "Toppy, I guess."

A groan slipped out, though he knew Adrian couldn't hear it. He wanted a guy that was sweet out of bed but who knew what he wanted and took it when the clothes came off. Could he be that lucky? "Please" was all he managed to push out.

Before Simon knew what was happening, Adrian pushed him down on the couch, settling his body into the V of Simon's. He took Simon's lips in a deep yet coaxing kiss, nipping and teasing them before sweeping in with his tongue. Simon had never felt so devoured or wanted as he did right then. His skin burned everywhere Adrian touched, sounds falling nonstop from his lips as Adrian continued to plunder and torment him.

Try as he might, Simon couldn't manage more than to moan and rock up into Adrian. The sensations were shorting out his brain as Adrian continued, his hands roaming across Simon's body. When the first pinches to his nipples came, Simon cried out, thrusting his chest into Adrian's hands. The only hands he'd felt in over a year were his own, something he had trouble reconciling at times. Right then, all he could do was react and revel in what Adrian did to him.

One hand continued to torment Simon's nipples, switching back and forth between them, as the other slid down, drawing shivers and more sounds from Simon. When Adrian pushed Simon's shirt up enough to trail his fingers around Simon's navel, his mind switched from "more" and "please" to "oh God, lower!" He knew he was saying the words but was unsure if Adrian realized how much he wanted from him.

When Adrian's hands suddenly pulled away, Simon cried out, not wanting the touching to stop. It took him a moment to focus on Adrian's words, as they were low and more slurred than normal. "I need to taste you, Si. Stay still and watch me," he instructed. Simon couldn't have torn his eyes away from the raw, open hunger in Adrian's eyes even if he'd wanted to.

Simon nodded, unable to form words, much less complete thoughts. He watched as Adrian slowly unbuttoned his slacks, and then even more slowly slid the zipper down, the sound bizarrely loud compared to their harsh breathing. Adrian's gaze shifted then from Simon's face to his groin. Just as carefully, he peeled back the material, leaned his head down, and mouthed Simon through his briefs. Simon trembled as both the pressure and the wet heat soaked through the thin cotton.

Adrian groaned and shifted down more until he knelt on the floor. He continued his teasing, his hands running up and down Simon's thighs. What seemed an eternity later, Adrian pulled back, then tugged down Simon's pants and briefs. Simon raised his ass up enough to allow them to slide down, but then his world again zeroed in on nothing but Adrian and his luscious mouth.

When Adrian swiped his tongue across the tip of Simon's cock, he yelled and shook, trying to stay still and let Adrian do as he wished. Adrian kissed up and down Simon's shaft, one hand teasing Simon's sac, the other pressed lightly to his abs—not teasing or even moving, just there, which made Simon curious, but he just filed it away to focus on Adrian's mouth as he finally took Simon in deep.

Adrian moved with mind-numbing pressure and suction as he bobbed up and down on Simon's length. His tongue teased and traced along Simon's various spots until he snapped and started thrusting into Adrian's mouth, hands in Adrian's soft, black hair. Fingers clutching, trying not to pull, Simon thrilled in the feelings and in how Adrian took all of him again and again.

The sounds from Adrian worked to make Simon crazier, the grunts and slurps adding to Simon's need. He fought his impending orgasm, not ready for it to be over, but Adrian seemed just as determined to make Simon lose all control. Adrian added tugs to Simon's sac before his fingers slipped down farther to tease along Simon's taint and around his hole.

Simon pushed at Adrian, trying to make him look up as he panted out, "Close."

Adrian ignored him, and when Adrian added more suction at the same time, he started tapping against Simon's needy opening, Simon lost the last thread of his restraint, screaming and arching off the couch as he pumped stream after stream into Adrian's hungry mouth.

It took what seemed to be forever for Simon to come back to himself, the feeling of bliss having shorted out his mind completely. When he could focus, Simon grasped Adrian's biceps and pulled, tugging him up until he again lay across Simon's body. He took Adrian's lips as he rocked his oversensitive body up against Adrian's, encouraging him to take his pleasure as well.

Not pausing more than a moment to look into Simon's eyes, Adrian thrust his hard cock along the juncture where Simon's groin and thigh met. Adrian's sounds of need growing louder, he rocked and pushed into the kiss, bruising Simon's lips—a fact he reveled in—until he finally arched up, Adrian's face twisting in a silent cry as Simon felt Adrian's seed spread between them, warm and wet.

Simon reveled in both what Adrian had given him and in the feeling of Adrian draped across him as they calmed. Simon caressed up and down Adrian's still-dressed back. Only then did he realize that at some point, Adrian had released his own cock from its confines. He idly hoped he'd finally get a peek before Adrian tucked himself away.

It was only fair, after all. Adrian had seen and tasted him.

chapter twelve

AS SIMON lay in bed later that night, he replayed their time on the couch, not just the blowjob, but the cuddling and companionship as they talked and watched a movie together. Simon loved kissing and cuddling so much that more than one ex had accused him of being a girl. Adrian seemed to enjoy it as much as he did. He prayed that was true and not simply his hopes bleeding over into reality.

He'd already gotten off to the memory twice, once in the shower, and he hoped his dreams were as filled with Adrian as his waking thoughts. Simon rolled over in his king-size bed, punching and rearranging his pillows until they suited him, then curled up, hoping sleep came quickly.

Instead, his cell rang.

Frowning, Simon unburied himself enough to retrieve his phone. "Hello?"

"Hey, Si," Dale said. "You want to hit the clubs with me?"

Simon glanced over at his alarm clock and sighed. It was almost midnight! "You realize what time it is, right? And that I had a date today?"

The long pause made Simon more curious than annoyed. When Dale finally replied, Simon rolled his eyes. "The clubs will still be open for a few more hours, Si, and so what? Are you still with Adrian?"

"I'm in bed, if you must know." The gasp through the line was less than amusing. "Alone," Simon ground out. "But no, not tonight. Not tomorrow night, either, as we both know you have work early Monday morning."

"Si," Dale whined—not a pleasant sound on the best of days, much less right then. "You have to come out with me. I hate going out by myself, and Chase is too much of a homebody now that he's with Rhys!"

He couldn't hold in his chuckle. Yeah, Chase and Rhys didn't go out much, more because Rhys didn't feel comfortable with how many guys try to hit on Chase than a lack of wanting to dance or go out together. "Since when do you need a wingman to go clubbing, Dale? Besides, I'm not getting up to go watch you get drooled over. Maybe another night, but not tonight."

"I don't need a wingman! I just—"

"You need to slow down on the man-candy, don't you think? I thought you were interested in Rhys's friend Grayson." Simon knew Dale liked the tall, quiet man; he'd seen the lust and want in Dale's eyes.

"I don't date, Simon." Dale's voice turned hard and low. "Grayson was fun for a night or two, but you know me better than that. It's nice James and Chase are happy with their partners, but that's so not me, and you know it."

Simon sighed. He couldn't help it. His friends all thought he was the scared one thanks to how his family and dating history had gone, but none of them were as messed up as Dale. Not that Dale would ever acknowledge that, of course. "You turned Rhys's friend into nothing more than a trick?" Even as he said it, he knew better. Of course Dale had, and he knew they would all hear about it soon enough. Rhys didn't play when it came to his friends, any more than Simon's circle did about their own. "Please tell me you didn't."

"He's yummy, Si, but he's too serious for me. I don't want a long-term thing with anyone. Now, if you won't come out tonight, what about next Thursday night? I have Friday off," Dale singsonged, the grin evident even over the phone.

"Well, I guess that would work. Adrian is usually busy most of the week thanks to his job, so I only get to see him Wednesday night and then over the weekend." He wished he could take Adrian out to the clubs with them, but he knew it would all be lost on his…. *Boyfriend?* Well, he hoped that's what they were moving toward, especially after their activities recently.

"Yay! I'll catch ya later in the week and then we'll go out Thursday!"

"If Rhys hasn't killed you by then," Simon qualified. "I'll go, but no pushing me to trick. I'm with Adrian now." They hadn't discussed exclusivity, but that's simply how Simon was made. He wanted long-term and expected monogamy from his partner and himself.

"I'm not scared of Rhys," Dale huffed.

"Maybe not." Though Simon couldn't imagine willingly getting on the man's wrong side. "But pissing Chase off is never a good idea, and he likes Grayson too. Now be a good boy and remember, condom, condom, condom."

They both laughed as Dale said good-bye and hung up. Yeah, they all knew Dale was the slut of the group, but he was also the one of them most obsessed with "safe sex." Hell, as far as he knew, Dale even used condoms for oral, something few men he knew insisted on. That thought brought him back to what he and Adrian had done earlier. Adrian never even asked his status. True, they hadn't done much yet, but still, had their positions been reversed, he knew he would have asked.

Simon sent a quick text to James and Chase, then snuggled down in his huge bed again. He fell asleep before either man replied to his question. *Is it poor form to give a possible partner your test results in hope they will return the favor before things go any farther?*

ADRIAN TOOK a sip of his tea as he continued to read over his most recent batch of security scans on his computer. He knew how many people out there liked to screw around with other people's systems and didn't feel like being another statistic on their list. He smiled when he got the results he expected: that everything was as it should be.

He drank more of his tea, then picked up his cell and texted Chase.

»Any suggestions on how to push Simon forward? «

The reply was almost immediate. »Two. 1-stop pussyfooting about what you want. 2-make sure you show him you want him, but don't need him (money). Oh, and 3-in case his being a romance author doesn't tell you enough, he's a romantic at heart. «

Yeah, he'd figured all that out. Adrian thought about it, wondering how to apply Chase's suggestions. Having already found out about Simon's family and wealth, though he still wasn't certain how wealthy Simon was himself, he understood the need to show Simon he didn't care about the money. The pussyfooting thing was harder.

After considering for a bit, he sent another message. »What do you mean by #1? I don't want to push too hard, Chase. I can see how scared he is. «

»True, but he's not just a dedicated bottom, he likes a top that takes control. «

Takes control? Hmm…. Adrian had noticed how well Simon reacted when he'd pushed for more, and Adrian did prefer to have control during sex and lovemaking; he just simply wasn't sold on the idea that pushing Simon was the best thing. He'd never tried to date someone who was both certain at times and skittish at others.

»We're talking kinky vanilla, not D/s like your friends James and Seth, right? I'm no Dom. «

Adrian was pretty certain, actually, that he couldn't be that. Not even for Simon, who he knew stole a little more of his heart every time they spoke, much less spent time together.

Thinking of Simon, he sent a separate text to him. »Off this Friday. You want to come over Thurs night? «

Chase's reply came first and thrilled him. »Kinky vanilla? Sounds yummy ;) but yes, that's what I mean. I didn't even know he knew what BDSM was until recently, lol. «

»Thank God! «

Oh, but the ideas that started swirling through his mind. He was half-hard when his cell vibrated and flashed again. Simon. »Can't. Going to club with Dale Thurs. Lunch on Fri instead? «

Club? Adrian thought about it a moment before sending back »Sure. Looking forward to it. «

He knew Simon and his friends like to go clubbing, dancing, but as that wasn't something he could share, he pushed aside the twinge of jealousy. He just hoped Simon wasn't like a lot of guys when they went out like that. Adrian didn't share well and had no intentions of changing that about himself.

He was so lost in thought he nearly missed Chase's next text. »LOL. When do you see him again? «

»Fri. He's going dancing with Dale. « After Adrian hit Send, he wondered if Chase would read his trepidation or not. He doubted any Hearing person would.

»Don't worry. I'm going too. Simon would NEVER cheat. «

Adrian appreciated the words but was mildly annoyed with them at the same time. It wouldn't be fair not to expect Simon to go dancing at the clubs. He knew Simon, Dale, and Chase loved doing that, though their other friend James didn't—though he knew that was because of James's mobility issues, not a lack of loving music.

Shoving the worry away, again, Adrian sent one last message to Chase before he got down to the task of grading tests, a time-consuming responsibility that seemed never ending. »Hope you all enjoy your outing. Hugs. «

TEAGUE BOUNDED inside Adrian's home, a wide grin on his handsome face. *"Hi!"*

"Hi. Come in." Adrian held up a beer and three movies, brow raised in question. Because he didn't want to sit at home, alone, moping that Simon was out having fun without him, Adrian had decided to invite Teague over to hang out. Well, that and to see if he could pry into Teague and Airy's love life.

He knew Teague was in love with Airy, but Airy was oblivious and still sleeping with everything that moved that would stay still long enough to bed. Adrian had tried to convince Teague to just tell Airy, but his friend never listened. Honestly, he understood Teague's reasoning; Airy didn't believe in love. Or that's what he claimed. Love was for other people, Airy said; he wasn't *ready* to settle down. Blah!

"Movies?" Teague snagged the beer from Adrian's hand, his smile never dimming.

"You have a better idea?" Adrian didn't. He wanted something to help him keep his mind off Simon. And clubs. And Simon out at the clubs. Probably wearing something too sexy for public consumption.

Teague stared at Adrian a moment but then nodded. *"Yes. Tell me what has you nervous. Why isn't your sweetheart here instead of me?"*

Dammit! That wasn't what he wanted to focus on. *"Simon is out with Dale and Chase at a dance club. No, I don't know the name. Now,"* Adrian signed and then pointed to the movies he'd chosen. *"Blow shit up, kill everybody, or save the world?"*

Ignoring Adrian, Teague raised one brow and stared at him. After a moment he signed, *"Did you tell him his going out would bother you? And why are you upset? He's Hearing and likes to dance. That's normal as far as I know."*

Adrian glowered at Teague, not appreciating the questions or statements. He knew it was normal for Simon to want to go dancing with his friends. Honestly, he was glad to know Simon was going out with his friends again, having learned how much Simon had retreated into himself after his last bad breakup. None of that was the problem, though, not that Adrian believed for even a moment that he had a right to say anything to Simon about his going out. He wasn't even certain why it bothered him, honestly. Simon wasn't the kind to sleep around while they were dating.

"No, I did not. He has every right to hang out with his friends, and while I don't know that I trust Dale, I know Chase will watch out for Simon."

Now if he could get his heart to listen to his head.

He didn't like the way Teague looked him over, as if he was trying to solve a Rubik's Cube or something. Eventually Teague gave a tight nod. *"Have you told him you know about his family and money yet?"*

He should have invited Airy over instead. *"No. I've only seen him a couple of times since you and Airy bullied me into snooping."*

"Keeping secrets is never a good thing."

"Like you not telling Airy how you feel?" At the hurt that flashed across Teague's face, Adrian's gut twisted. He shouldn't have signed that. He knew how much Teague wanted things to be different with Airy, and that Airy wouldn't take the news well if he knew. Not until Airy grew up more, at least. *"Sorry! Sorry, Tea."*

"OK. Maybe one day Airy will change, but my situation is not the same as yours. You are dating the man you want. You need to be honest with him or you will lose him."

Yeah, he knew that. Really. It didn't change the reality that he didn't know how to bring the matter up without upsetting Simon. That was the same reason he hadn't said a thing about Simon's clubbing. *"How do I tell Simon I feel uncomfortable with him going out like this without sounding like a controlling or jealous asshole?"*

"Don't know." Teague shrugged. *"You can feel the vibration of the music and watch the dancing. You could ask to go so you can see what they're like at the club? Simon would take you, I bet, if you asked."*

Simon might, but how weird would it be for Simon to take his *Deaf* boyfriend to a gay dance club? He'd have to think on that one, as he wasn't sure seeing Simon shimmying his sexy body with all the other guys, all sweaty and fluid, would help him feel any better. *"Maybe."*

After that, Simon got Teague on task with movie time, and before he knew it, they'd finished off four beers each and were on their second movie. He knew a lot of their friends thought it weird to watch movies, as they couldn't hear all the actors' inflections and the little nuances of sound, but Teague was just as into movies, especially action ones, as Adrian.

He'd set his cell on the coffee table when he'd retrieved the last round of drinks, but when he felt the vibration through his socked feet, which were crossed on top of the low table, he sat forward and scooped it up. The screen flashed as he slid his thumb across it, and a moment later, he nearly dropped his phone. There, in full color, was a picture of Simon grinding on the dance floor with Dale, head back, shirt off, dark pants sitting so low on his hips Adrian wasn't sure why they were even still up. He looked completely sinful and delicious.

Adrian's grip tightened as his heart sped. Simon was breathtaking!

When Teague nudged him a minute or two later, he barely managed to tear his eyes away from the pic. *"What?"*

"What's on the phone that has you so upset?"

Instead of answering, Adrian handed it over, letting Teague see the image. Maybe Teague could take the sting out of what he was seeing. Why would anyone send him something like that? Why would they rub in his face the fact that he couldn't do that with Simon?

"Wow, H-O-T!" Teague signed, a leer on his face. *"Who's the sexy punk boy dancing with your Simon?"*

It took a minute for the words to make sense, but the look on Teague's face as he asked, then waited, was simple curiosity. Adrian looked at the image again and frowned. Right, Teague hadn't met any of Simon's friends yet. Well, except Chase. *"That's Dale. I don't know his last name, but he's part of the group Simon hangs out with. Chase, James, Dale, and Simon, plus various partners and husbands. Oh, and Dal and Alex, but they're in Chicago."*

"Dale is yum, but if that's a friend, why do you seem so upset?"

Upset? No, *jealous* was a much better word. But why was he? He knew Dale and Simon were only friends, knew Simon wanted their budding relationship to continue and was coming over the next day to spend it with Adrian. Instead of answering, Adrian shrugged and frowned.

"Who sent the pic?" Teague asked when Adrian continued to stare.

Good question. Adrian checked to see the sender and grimaced. It wasn't a number, exactly. It was from Anontext. *Well hell!* That wasn't trackable. Well, it was but only to an open hub, not to a specific person.

"Anonymous. Why would someone send me this and not attach a note to it? Why send it at all?"

Confusion rioted through Adrian as he fought with himself about responding to the text. Yes, he wanted to know who sent it and why. Yes, he wanted to know why Simon had to rub up against Dale so completely. It looked more like upright sex than anything else. And yes, he hated seeing his Simon being that close and sexy with another guy!

"Don't know. How did they get your number? Your business cards only have your office number."

Adrian shook his head. He had no idea, as only his friends and family had his cell number. He'd never had any crank texts before, much less texts meant to cause trouble. That was the only reason he could think for someone to send the picture the way they had. *"No clue."*

Clicking the Plus Sign to call up a fresh text screen, he typed a quick message to Chase. Adrian knew his friend was supposed to be there, but with how loud a club would be, or so he assumed, he wasn't sure how long it would take Chase to see his message. Still, he felt the need to try.

»Any reason someone would send me a pic of Simon and Dale dancing? «

To his surprise, Chase answered back while he and Teague were still debating if there was any hope of actually finding out who sent the message.

»Not that I know of. Why? «

Instead of answering, Adrian forwarded the image to Chase and waited. While he did, Teague collected their bottles and headed to the kitchen. Just as the cell vibrated again, Teague returned, two fresh beers in hand.

»Um… creepy! Great pic but I have no idea why you got it :(I didn't send it and no one else with us has your number. «

Yeah, that's what he was afraid of.

Teague leaned over and peered at the screen. *"You think someone wants you two broken up? Trying to make you think he's cheating on you?"*

"Who would care that much? Not my exes. He's been single for over a year, so not his exes either." The whole thing made no sense. Of course, trying to figure it out when he hadn't eaten dinner and was now working on his fifth beer probably wasn't helping.

"Don't know. Finish the movie and your drink, then we should both get some sleep."

Adrian agreed, then sent one last message to Chase, telling him not to worry about the picture and that he hoped they all had fun out. He then settled in to watch the TV and try to do what he'd told Chase: not to worry. Yeah, easier said than done.

He startled when Teague asked, *"You mind if I crash here?"*

Like Adrian ever minded? He shook his head and smiled, feeling a little loopy from the alcohol. *"The guest room is made up. Just remember to set your alarm for the morning."*

Other than his family, Adrian had never had a Hearing person stay over, so everything was set for him. Even Adrian's guest room was set up to be Deaf-friendly with a shaker alarm.

By the time the movie was over and they'd cleaned up the rest of their snack and drink mess, Adrian was beyond tired. He still hadn't made any sense of the anonymous text but decided to push that confusion away for when he was sober and alert. And for when he could actually talk to Simon.

That settled, he waved to Teague as he passed him in the hall and went to his room. He quickly stripped down to his boxers and sprawled across his bed, sleep claiming him almost immediately. Unfortunately his jumbled thoughts managed to find him even in his dreams.

chapter thirteen

SIMON PACED across the living room, annoyed that Chase insisted on a shower before they discussed whatever it was that'd had Chase acting twitchy for the last hour or two before they'd left the club the night before. Actually, he wouldn't be quite so frustrated if Rhys hadn't woken them up that morning by beating on the door before the sun was even fully up.

A glance toward his kitchen showed Rhys leaning against Simon's counter where the coffeemaker was. "Why are you here again?" Simon grumbled.

Rhys shrugged with one shoulder as he blew across the top of his mug. After he took a sip, he replied, "Dunno exactly. Chase messaged me that he was crashing here and to be here in the morning. All I know is something is worrying him. I wanted to come over last night, but he insisted I wait." Rhys continued to stare at Simon as he drank more.

"Why didn't he tell you? Better yet, why didn't he tell me? Is something wrong between you two?" Simon didn't think so, not with how Chase talked about Rhys and his life now. Unfortunately, he couldn't think of any reasons for Chase to act odd, well, more so than normal.

"Nope."

Yeah, that was helpful. Not! "I'd tell you to go hurry him up, but somehow I don't think putting you in the same room as a wet, naked Chase would help any."

A deep chuckle rumbled from Rhys, only serving to irritate Simon more. "Think you're right on that one. Don't worry, Chase will come out in a minute and explain to us both what's going on."

Rhys's reassurances, sadly, didn't help much right then. "Fine, but he'd better hurry. I refuse to let whatever this nonsense is make me late for my lunch date with Adrian. As much as I loved going out with Dale and Chase last night, I want to be back with Adrian now."

"I'm glad to hear you talk like that again, Si," Chase said from behind him. "There for a while, I worried you'd never let yourself get that attached again. But really, the reason for Rhys being here so early—though you could have waited a little, hon—is Adrian. Or well, a text Adrian received last night while we were out dancing."

Simon frowned. *A text Adrian got? How would Chase even know what texts Adrian got the night before?* "Uh, I'm not following. What text, and why do you know instead of me?"

"Good question," Rhys added, sauntering over to Chase with a second cup of coffee.

"I know because he texted me about a message, a picture message, he received last night. One showing you and Dale grinding out on the dance floor. If it were a picture of Rhys out dancing like that once we were a couple, I'd have shown up then and there, and *someone* would have had trouble walking away, honestly. However, Adrian decided to ask me instead of accusing you of anything. What I don't get is why someone sent the text, much less how they got his number."

"Wait," Simon squeaked, not happy with anything Chase said or how his voice sounded right then. "Someone took a picture of Dale and me dancing? Did you tell Adrian that I'm not with Dale?" Simon ran out of the room, into his bedroom, to snatch up his cell. He started tapping out a message to Adrian.

»You OK? Chase just told me about the pic. I wasn't cheating on you with Dale, I SWEAR! «

Almost immediately, his cell chimed with a new message. »I didn't think you were. You want me to come over? «

»Thought I was going to your place at noon, but why don't you come here so we can all talk about whatever is going on. Chase called Rhys over because of the text. «

»Not dressed yet. Give me 30—45 mins? «

Not dressed yet? Simon groaned. He still hadn't seen all of Adrian, though he really wanted to—if he could just get past his stupid hang-ups thanks to his crappy exes. »I'll have coffee waiting. «

100

"You didn't have to run away," Chase commented from the doorway. "I have the pic on my cell, so you can see what started all this. Is Adrian coming over now?"

"Yeah, he is." He looked up as he slipped his phone into his pocket. "Um, did you say you have the picture? Do I get to see it?"

"Yeah, come on out here again. I know how you feel about people being in your bedroom unless they're your current boyfriend." That said, Chase turned and walked back to the living room, where Rhys now sat. Simon followed, wishing Adrian were here already.

"Now that you two are back out here again, someone want to let me see the text that started this mess?" Rhys's voice didn't raise, but his annoyance was still crystal clear.

"I'd like to see it as well," Simon added.

Chase flopped down on the couch beside Rhys and then messed with his cell a moment. When he turned it around, Simon saw an image of exactly what Chase had described: Dale and him dancing, grinding, and writhing on the dance floor. It didn't prove anything other than he'd gone out clubbing with Dale, just as he'd told Adrian he would. Still, he could see why the image might upset Adrian if he didn't realize that Simon and Dale had *never* been more than friends.

"Yeah, I can see why that would bother Simon's new boyfriend, but why would Adrian go to you instead of Simon? And who would send it to Adrian in the first place?"

"How many people even know we're dating yet? I mean, I guess anyone who's seen us out, but who would care? I haven't dated in well over a year, so it's not like I left someone that might be jealous about being 'replaced' so fast or anything else insane." The fact the text had been sent at all was the part that concerned Simon, especially the anonymous part.

"All good questions, Simon," Rhys rumbled. "Maybe once he's here, Chase can dig through his phone and find something about the sender?"

"Actually, the text came from Anontext, so no, that won't really help any. Adrian is in IT too, remember? He was one of my professors for the computer forensics courses I took thanks in part to your pushing, Rhys, so I seriously doubt I'll be able to find anything Adrian couldn't."

Simon didn't like the idea that neither Adrian nor Chase would be able to find out the source. "Oh-kaaay, but I don't understand the reason for sending it."

"Neither do I, hon. If I did, I promise I'd tell you."

"Anyone been snooping around lately, Si?" Rhys continued to stare at the image. "Any of Adrian's friends not approve of you?"

"Well, sort of," Simon explained. "Adrian's friend Airy doesn't seem to overly like me much. Adrian said it's just that he's worried I won't treat Adrian well or that I'll see him as disabled because he's Deaf. I don't and I won't, but his other friend... um... Teague seemed to like me, and by the time we left the Silent Supper thing the other day, Airy seemed to have decided I was okay."

"Well, that's one place to start, but I don't see a Deaf guy sneaking into a club to take a picture of his friend's boyfriend and then sending it anonymously. That's more a jilted-lover move than a friend one." Rhys rubbed his fingers over his permanent five-o'clock stubble as he finally handed the cell back to Chase.

The doorbell going off drew Simon's attention from Rhys and Chase as they debated different reasons someone might want to cause trouble for Simon and Adrian's relationship. When he opened the door, he smiled despite his worries. Adrian's hair was still wet. He wore low-rise jeans, a tight emerald-green T-shirt, and black Nikes.

"Hi." Simon smiled at the open joy on Adrian's face.

"Hi." Adrian leaned in and pecked Simon on the lips before gesturing to the door. "May I come in?" he both signed and said.

Simon stepped back, remembering to sign as much as he could as he spoke. "Of course. Chase and Rhys are in the living room, debating who might have sent the image."

"Then let's go talk to them." Adrian stepped inside, slipped his hand into Simon's, and tugged.

Chase and Rhys stopped talking as soon as Simon and Adrian entered the room. Chase grinned up at Adrian. "Hey! Glad to see you, though I wish it were for a happier reason. Come sit."

Adrian sat in one of the overstuffed chairs, but instead of taking the other, Simon sat on the arm of the chair, not wanting to be away from Adrian right then.

"Si? As much as I like you close, I won't be able to see what you say like this." Adrian tugged Simon down and briefly took his lips. Warmth spread through Simon quickly before Adrian pulled back. "Could you sit a little farther out from me so I don't have to guess what you're saying?"

"Sorry." Simon squeezed Adrian's fingers a moment before he moved to the other chair and turned to make sure Adrian had a clear view of his face. "Better?"

"Thank you." Adrian looked over at Chase. "You said you had an idea why I got the text? I mean, I would never tell Simon he can't go dancing, though I'd rather it not be quite so...." He rolled one hand as he seemed to search for a word. "Sexual, I guess. But that's not the point. Why is someone trying to cause trouble? The fact it came in the way it did tells me it's not an innocent thing."

"I agree, and that's why it's bothering me so much." Chase looked between Adrian and Simon before settling on Simon again. "Si, I wondered if it might be your parents or maybe your sister. You said Zoey contacted you recently and demanded you rejoin the family and stop being you. Would they try to break you and Adrian up? Maybe they're thinking if you're alone you might be easier to bully or con into playing their 'normal family' game?"

"Zoey?" Simon mumbled, shaking his head slowly. He couldn't imagine her going to all this trouble to mess with him. His family tried to pretend he didn't exist for the most part, him being the evil pink sheep of the family and all. "I can't imagine her bothering. Father hates me. However, he'd be more likely to finally try to legally disown me then send anonymous texts to Adrian."

"Well, if crazy, bigoted people made sense, Chase wouldn't have been hurt last year," Rhys rumbled, arms folded across his broad chest. "And if families did the right thing, then James's brother wouldn't have stalked and terrorized him, and his parents would have sided with James, not his abusers, both when he was a teen and when his brother tried to set his house on fire."

The look of shock on Adrian's face worried Simon. "Adrian?" he asked, making sure Adrian could see him. "You knew about what happened to Chase. That was after you two met."

Adrian nodded, hands flying, motions sharp, as he signed and spoke. "I did, and I still don't understand how that monster got away with it so long, but he, Rhys, meant James, the James you're all friends with. The sweet guy with the funky crutches I met not that long ago, right?"

"Yeah, that James. His family is vile. Well, his biological family is. We, his real family, love him for him and think he's fine just the way he is.

However, I don't believe you're in any danger by being around us—me. My family would never risk sullying themselves by harming you."

"Sullying?" Adrian asked, brows furrowed, voice so low Simon had to strain to hear it.

"I know who your family is, and I'm not so sure I agree," Rhys countered. "They have called for reforms to imprison gays, force all homosexuals to go to those camps to be *cured*, and for all LGBT families to have their kids taken 'for the good of the children.'"

Simon scrambled to find a way to both shut Rhys up and to take the power out of the words he said. Adrian didn't know about his family yet. Now wasn't the time to change that. "Rhys! Stop it. You're going to scare Adrian."

"I'm telling the truth, and if he's going to be involved with you, he ought to know what he's getting into, don't you think? You really want him hurt? You want them to be able to attack him, at his work or in other ways, without knowing the risks?"

No, no he didn't, but he also didn't want to lose Adrian! "No, but—"

"Si?" Adrian said, cutting off his return rant at Rhys.

Simon turned back to Adrian, hoping to mitigate some of the power of Rhys's words. "They wouldn't hurt you. I wouldn't let them, I promise."

"It's not that. I know who your family is, Si. It's not like your name isn't out there in the society pages and that your family isn't prominent in many of the hate groups." Simon's shoulders slumped. He should have known Adrian would check him out. He would if their situation was reversed. "Being the kind of wealthy they are makes it hard not to notice, and while you don't participate in the same circles, every event, social gathering, charity thing, etcetera that they do, the ones you do help with and support are very happy to point out your donation."

"You know about all that?" Simon couldn't make it all fit. Was Adrian only involved with Simon because of the money and social standing he might receive? Most of his exes fell into that category.

"Of course, but it means little to me other than how it affects you and us. Would they care about us dating? I know they're rabidly homophobic, but they didn't disown you, as you said already. So why bother us now?"

Simon wasn't certain he believed his family and money meant as little to Adrian as it seemed, but he pushed those thoughts and fears aside, focusing on the current issues instead. "I don't know, but I doubt it. If they had tried to pay you off to go away, that would make more sense than sending you a text of me dancing."

"I would agree." Adrian turned back to Chase and frowned. "What about an ex?"

Chase shook his head and signed no. "Si's been single for well over a year, so that makes no sense. Could it be someone that likes you? A friend that doesn't approve of you dating Simon?"

Adrian opened his mouth but then shut it again. Simon had had that thought earlier but didn't want to believe it would be one of Adrian's friends, but who else could be responsible? And was it really as huge an issue as Chase seemed to believe? "Chase, are you sure it's even a real problem? It could be someone thought it would be funny to be a brat."

"I might agree if it weren't for *how* it was sent, Si," Chase said and signed. Chase's signs were much more fluid and faster than anything Simon could manage. He hoped to get that good, for Adrian's sake. "It's the forethought to send from Anontext that bugs me. Why hide who you are if you aren't trying to cause trouble?"

"Airy might, if he really thought Simon was cheating on me. He would have told Teague and tried to get him to help intervene on my behalf, though. Teague was with me last night when I got the text and was upset about it too, so that leaves Airy out of it."

"Would Airy have done something like that? Really?" Simon asked, worried Adrian's friend might dislike him that much. Best friends tended to trump new boyfriends.

"Go to a dance club to protect me? He might. Send a picture like that anonymously to try to make me jealous and break up with you? No. That I can't see him doing. And like I said, Teague knew nothing about it, so there's no way Airy had anything to do with this."

"Look," Rhys said, his deep voice cutting through the room, "I have to agree with Simon and Adrian at the moment. Yes, it's weird and might spell trouble, but I don't think it's Simon's family or Adrian's friends. The method doesn't ring true to me. How about if we do a little digging," he continued, gesturing to Chase and himself. "And *if* we find any reason to suspect either Simon's family or Adrian's friend, we revisit this discussion. If not, we let it go, as there's no reason to borrow trouble."

"It's not borrowing trouble, Rhys!" Chase snapped.

Rhys tugged Chase into his lap and put one huge hand over Chase's lips. "It is if it's just someone being stupid. It could be someone that likes either Simon or Adrian and wants them available. It could be someone that knows Adrian and is worried for his heart. It could be nothing to get upset over. Let's make sure there's even a reason to worry before we all freak out."

Chase moved Rhys's hand to his cheek and said, "Fine, hon, but if there's any reason to worry, you promise to do a full investigation and help them. Right?"

"Of course, *Cariadon*."

"Um, guys?" Simon loved seeing Chase so happy, and he'd even learned to really like and appreciate Rhys, but he had no interest in turning Chase's panic about the text into a make-out session for the two. "If you're done worrying for now, why don't you go on home and continue the cuddle time?"

Chase pouted, but the twitching at the edges of his lips gave him away. "No free porn?"

Simon laughed. "As cute as you are and as beefy and hot as Rhys is…. No. I'd rather cuddle with Adrian, sorry."

"As I would you," Adrian added, his deep voice sliding over Simon's nerves, making him think all kinds of naughty things.

Ten minutes later Simon and Adrian were alone in Simon's house, and Simon was settled across Adrian's lap, lips busy. They spent the rest of the day in various similar positions, and the two men only came up for air to eat dinner. Simon had never enjoyed kissing so much in his life and was thankful Adrian didn't mind how much Simon loved to just kiss and cuddle; there was nothing more delicious than Adrian's lips on his.

chapter fourteen

"*IT'S BEEN two more weeks, Chase. What do I need to do to make Simon relax? Other than kissing, he withdraws if I try to push any further in the physical intimacy department since the incident with the picture. We've gone out, and hung out some at each other's homes, but he's more nervous than before. I don't understand.*" Adrian hated how Simon seemed to have retreated from their relationship.

"*I asked James to go talk to Simon about this. He's there now, and if anyone can get through to him, it's James.*"

"*Thanks, but I need some guidance, I think. I don't like needing your friend sent in to help.*" He really didn't like asking for help either, but something was going on in Simon's head, and Simon refused to discuss it. Simon had managed thoroughly to derail Adrian with kisses every time he'd tried.

That was another issue altogether. Adrian wondered more and more if Simon really wanted to kiss as much as they did, or if it was more a self-defense tactic. Adrian loved to kiss, loved to snuggle, and could do so for hours, but it seemed that even as they kissed more, their relationship was faltering, which made no sense at all to him.

"*Simon is probably the most complicated one of our group in some ways. He's been burned because of his family, his money, his work. He writes romance but doesn't believe he is lovable.*" Even as Chase signed with him, the words made more and yet less sense than he hoped. Adrian knew all of that, though he hated being reminded of the sad past of *his* Simon.

"*I don't care about all that, but if family or money is brought up, he retreats from me, from us, faster than I know how to counter. I asked him to meet my father. Instead of giving me a yes or no answer, Simon sat on the other side of the couch from me until he left to go home."*

"Meet your dad? Cool!" Chase paused, staring off at nothing as far as Adrian could tell. *"Invite your dad over, and don't tell Si. He'll love getting to know your dad if he's as nice and accepting as you say."*

Invite but don't let Simon know? *"Won't he get upset?"*

"Maybe, but he needs it, so do it for him. I told you, you have to be toppy outside the bedroom too with Si, or you will never move forward."

Adrian could do that. He'd honestly been trying to rein in his normal pushy self because of how shy and timid Simon seemed to be most of the time. *"And the money issue? I don't care about his money. I don't want his money."*

"Easy. Pay your way. Don't let him pick up the tab all the time. If he invites you to a function—he has to go to some, though he hates it—go but buy your own suit or tuxedo. Don't ask him to introduce you to people. That kind of thing."

"Thanks." He could do all that. Hell, he was doing those things already, other than the "going to a function" thing, but he figured that wouldn't be too hard. He rarely attended such things. Being Deaf bothered a lot of people, and he got tired of being ignored or treated as though he was stupid.

Adrian shifted gears after that and simply hung out with his friend, enjoying their time and Chase's antics. By the time Chase left, Adrian felt more at ease and hopeful than he had in weeks. Now, to plot how to get his boyfriend to become more at ease with them as a couple and with having a future together.

"SI, YOU need to stop pacing," James said, cutting into Simon's internal freak-out. He didn't know what to do to fix things with Adrian. Even if he hadn't known there was a problem, the fact James had shown up first thing that morning to "talk" would have clued him in fast.

Simon stopped and turned back to his friend. "Adrian wants me to meet his dad."

James stared at him a moment, then smiled. "And that's a bad thing, why? Meeting the family is a positive step, and at least you get to meet his family with warning, unlike when I met Seth's parents."

"You love your in-laws." It wasn't the same thing! What if the man hated him? What if him being Hearing caused issues? Though Simon knew Adrian's parents were both Hearing, they might think Adrian should date another Deaf person. And while Simon had started the ASL classes, he was nowhere near even Chase's level of proficient, much less like Adrian and his friends.

"I do, but I didn't love meeting them when they just *poof*, appeared at my door, with me in my normal painting attire." James grinned and Simon laughed. He'd have loved to have seen that first meeting. Seth's parents were rich, powerful, down-to-earth, and loving. However, having them just show up while James and Seth were still trying to work out their relationship and while dealing with being sudden fathers? Yeah, he could see how that would have been rough.

"Paint-spattered jeans, a T-shirt, and crutches are not a bad way to meet someone if you're an artist. Which you are," Simon added pointedly. "But you were living with Seth and Danni by then, not still trying to start a relationship, as Adrian and I are."

"So going from alone with a total of three people I trusted to a ready-made family I didn't even know I was getting until Danni's mom died doesn't seem a bit much to you? Weren't you one of the ones that thought Seth should have told me he had a daughter sooner? But," James continued, wiping away the argument with a flick of one long-fingered hand. "That has nothing to do with your issues with Adrian. I understand worrying if he's too good to be true. Of any of us, it would be me that understands that fear, but I think you're seeing monsters where there aren't any."

"You didn't trust Seth's interest in you at first." Simon knew he was being stupid, but he couldn't help it. He was afraid Adrian held more of his heart than he could get back if—when—he decided to leave.

"And look how that turned out. I do believe you were one of my groomsmen at my wedding. You're going to be for Dal soon, and if we can ever get Chase and Rhys to do the whole 'walk down the aisle' thing, you'll be a groomsman for Chase as well."

"Arguing with you is frustrating!" James was supposed to be on his side! Why didn't any of them understand why he was worried? Well, Dale sort of did, but mostly he was about not being tied down by any man. Period. Ever.

"Then stop arguing and do the right thing for you *and* for Adrian. Give the relationship a chance. You helped sabotage Chase's attempts at dating when he tried running from Rhys. Do you really think any of us will be any less stubborn in supporting you, even against your wishes?"

No, no he didn't. James was right, dammit! "I have to sit down and talk to him about the family and homophobia thing, don't I?" Simon really didn't want to, but he knew he had to do it sometime. Obviously soon was the right time.

James simply cocked his head to one side, brows raised, and stared at Simon.

"Fine. He's coming over to dinner tonight; actually, he should be here soon. Wow, didn't realize how late it was getting. I promise to talk, even if I have no want to do so."

"You do want to, Si. You're just scared of the answers you'll get. It's not the same thing, and I think you'll find Adrian isn't like most of your exes. I don't believe he cares how much money you have or how phobic your family is. The only person he's here for is you. Now do you need help making dinner? You obviously haven't been cooking."

Simon stuck his tongue out and gave James his best pout. "But I don't have to cook."

"And why not? You invited him over for dinner but plan *not* to feed him? Didn't anyone tell you that the way to a man's heart is his stomach? Starving the poor man is so not going to win you good-boyfriend points."

"But he's the one winning points tonight," Simon said and winked, thrilled when James grinned. "He said not to cook, that he was bringing everything for dinner."

"Ahhh, so he's trying the wine-and-dine method of wooing the infamous Simon 'Fussy Brat' Tyler. Good for him."

"Yeah, he is. He's a great cook, not like you or Chase, but still good, and I love watching him in the kitchen. He's not like me. He doesn't look out of place and like he doesn't know what he's doing."

"You know how to cook, Si." James and Chase had spent many a night teaching him to cook when he'd first left home to attend college and met them. He'd grown up with servants and had never even been allowed in the kitchen until he moved away from home, so he'd had no clue what to do. He'd found out quick that it was, in fact, possible to burn water.

"Yeah, but it's no fun to watch me. Especially for me," he quipped, feeling better than he had since the night Dale and Chase had dragged him to the club. He wasn't looking forward to the coming talk, but maybe, if he was lucky and Adrian was patient, he would still have a boyfriend after the discussion. Even better would be if they could move past kissing.

ADRIAN DROVE carefully through the streets, maneuvering past parked cars and dogs that seemed to run free, as he approached Simon's home. He didn't want to spill any of the food. When he finally arrived—he knew the drive over hadn't taken any longer than normal, but right then it seemed to have—he smiled at seeing the curtain move. A moment later Simon stood on the front stoop, a wide smile on his handsome face.

He parked and got out of the car, but before he reached the other side, Simon was there, hugging him. Adrian hugged him back, confused as to why Simon was so excitable all of a sudden, not that he minded. When Simon stepped back, Adrian said and signed, "Hi. You that hungry?"

"No. Missed you."

Simon signed without talking? Wait? Did he say he missed me?

"Missed you too." Adrian pressed his lips to Simon's for a brief moment but then released him. He turned and opened the passenger-side door to retrieve the large black Crock-Pot. It took two trips, but then everything he'd brought over was sitting in Simon's kitchen.

"What did you bring? It smells wonderful!" Simon said, signing most of the words. Adrian had been thrilled when Simon revealed he was to take ASL classes, but he hadn't expected Simon to pick it up quite as well as he seemed to be. The attempt alone warmed Adrian's heart, and Simon's determination and dedication to conversing in Adrian's language made him fall just a little more each time they spoke.

"Beef stew with onions, baby 'bellas, baby carrots, small red and yellow potatoes, cut parsnips and turnips, and gravy. Plus biscuits and strawberry-pistachio tarts for dessert."

"Wow! You made all that?" The wonder on Simon's face startled him. Simon's best friends, well, two of them at least, could have been chefs had they chosen to be. He also knew the friend of theirs named Alex in Chicago was a personal chef, so Adrian didn't see his homey meal as being anywhere near the same.

Adrian shrugged. "It's still cool out at night, and stew is always yum."

"Thank you." Simon leaned in and pressed his lips to Adrian's. "I love that you're trying to be so…." He rolled his hand in a circle as he trailed off, staring at the Crock-Pot. "That you want to take care of me. I don't want you to think you have to, though."

Huh? "I don't think I have to take care of you, Si. I figured we would take turns doing things like cooking or taking the other out."

"I've never had a boyfriend say something like that before."

Adrian nodded. "I assumed as much. The way you act about money and your family—" He shrugged, not wanting to upset Simon already. "But I don't care about all that. Only you."

Simon swallowed hard, eyes wide. "You know who my family is, I know that, but—" Instead of signing along as he spoke, Simon's hands twisted around one another. "—you really don't care?"

"I really don't. Simon, look at me." Adrian waited until Simon's gaze met his. "I don't need your money, and your family doesn't scare me. I'm more worried about my mother than yours. What I care about is you and us."

The way Simon stared at Adrian made him worry that maybe Simon wasn't understanding—or perhaps not believing him. When Simon did finally speak up, Adrian started at the movement of Si's hands. "You want me for me, only, right?"

"Yes!" he said and signed emphatically.

"My family loves to cause trouble for me and are very public about their anti-gay-rights stance."

Adrian shrugged, not understanding why Simon was insisting on making sure he knew about the hate within the Tyler family. "And I'm very pro, obviously. I don't understand your point."

The dumbfounded look on Si's face almost made Adrian smile. The only reason he didn't was concern for how his—boyfriend? Lover?—his Si would take the motion. "They have nothing to do with us, Si. They can't control our lives or relationship unless you let them."

That seemed to finally snap Simon out of his daze. "They have *no* control over my life, money, career, or choice of lover!"

"Good. So instead of worrying about how I see them, let's focus on how we see us," Adrian signed and said, giving Si another smile and a wink. "Though, maybe we should eat too."

Nodding, Simon grinned before stepping away to collect bowls, plates, and silverware. "Let's eat and then maybe we can talk more or watch a movie?"

That decided, they set about serving up the stew, setting out the bread and butter, and pouring drinks. In only a short time, Simon and Adrian were happily devouring their meal, sharing small touches every chance they got, and feeding each other by the time dessert came around.

When dinner was over, Adrian was about out of his mind with wanting Simon. He just hoped Simon was finally on the same page as he was.

chapter fifteen

FULL, HORNY, and *happy* were the words Simon thought of as he rinsed and put the last dish into the dishwasher. Adrian never ceased to surprise him, both with his thoughtfulness and his determination in their relationship. He couldn't remember the last time a boyfriend had cooked for him and then helped clean up without drama or guilt. The fact Adrian acted as if it was a normal behavior thrilled Simon all the more.

"Hey," Adrian said and signed. "You're thinking awfully hard for someone just putting up dishes."

Unsure how to express his gratitude and joy over Adrian being so different, he instead leaned in and took Adrian's mouth in a soft press of lips. Moments later he wound his arms around Adrian, pulling him in as he deepened the now-ravaging kiss.

When his back hit the wall, Simon groaned, clutching at Adrian as his lover devoured him. Hands pulling and holding tight, bodies dragging against each other, friction pushing Simon's excitement higher. Simon started when one of Adrian's hands made it to his groin and rubbed firmly across his cockhead even as it strained against the layers of clothing in its way.

"Please." Simon whimpered. "Need you."

Adrian pulled back, his brows scrunched up in confusion. "What?"

Instead of answering Adrian, Simon grabbed his hand and pulled Adrian along with him as he exited the kitchen. Adrian tried to ask what was going on, but Simon shook his head and kept going, not stopping until he stood next to the couch. With a slight shove, he pushed Adrian down until he was sitting on the sofa, legs spread wide.

"What are you doing, Si?"

Meeting Adrian's gaze, Simon answered, "Letting my heart and body decide instead of my fears." Not waiting for Adrian to respond, Simon grasped Adrian's waistband and tugged until his lover's ass was barely on the cushion. Simon knelt between Adrian's legs and looked up through his lashes at the man he knew was inches away from owning his heart. "Tell me no, now, or let me taste you. Please," he begged. That Adrian couldn't hear the whine in his voice didn't matter to Simon; only the man's answer did.

"Oh God, yes," Adrian rumbled in that deep, muted voice of his, spiking Simon's need even higher.

Not taking the time to consider his actions, Simon slid his hands up Adrian's thighs, loving how the muscles jumped at his touch. The low groan from Adrian only served to spur Simon on, especially as he knew the sound was honest want. Focusing on what he was doing, Simon leaned down and nuzzled Adrian's cock through the pants and briefs trapping it.

Making quick work of Adrian's belt, Simon unbuttoned Adrian's pants, and then slowly slid his zipper down. Simon paused to take a deep breath as he stared at the clear outline of Adrian's need. When Adrian's hand gently touched Simon's hair, Simon looked up. "You don't have to, if you're not ready."

"I do. I...." Simon had no idea how to express his want, fears, need, or hope. He wanted to taste Adrian, but he also wanted Adrian to take him, fill him, want him so much he wouldn't settle for a mere blowjob.

Before he knew it, Adrian had both his wrists in his hands. When Simon looked up, he was startled to see the level of heat in Adrian's gaze. "Wha—?"

Adrian released him, then signed, *"I want you. All of you. Now!"*

Simon focused, trying to make sure he understood it all, the concentration helping to calm his passion and help him think things through a little better. *All of me? Does that mean...? "Bed?"* was all he could think to ask.

A nod was all he got for an answer, but then Adrian stood and kicked off his slacks before he pulled Simon back into a kiss so hard he knew he'd have bruises later, a thought that made him thrilled, not worried as he thought it should.

Adrian didn't allow his mind to shift too far away, continuing the kiss, hands roving over Simon's body, as he nudged Simon toward the bedroom.

Simon led the way, never releasing Adrian, and in just a few moments, they were next to Simon's king-size bed.

They grinned at each other as they kicked off shoes and toed off socks. The next thing he knew, Adrian was sprawled on top of him, nibbling along his jaw, making those deep groans Simon was already addicted to. Lifting up, rubbing his trapped cock against Adrian's abdomen was bliss, but when Adrian pulled back and signed something, he had no clue what, as it was a sign he was certain he'd never seen before. He froze, confused and frustrated.

"I don't understand."

Adrian ducked his head a moment, his face flushing even more than the kissing had done. "Sorry. Um, condom? I want you so bad it hurts, Si."

The words sent a jolt through Simon. *Condom? Oh God... he's going to....* "Yes and there," Simon mouthed, pointing to the nightstand on his side of the bed. Even though no one had slept with him in well over a year—unless you counted his best friends, but that was never anything but comfort and had never been sexual—he still only slept on the one side, never able to hog the whole space for himself.

A moment later Adrian was hovering over Simon, a condom and the bottle of slick next to him on the bed. "Ready?" Adrian husked out, speaking seemingly harder for him than normal—something that secretly thrilled Simon more than a bit.

He nodded as he reached up and started unbuttoning Adrian's shirt, leaning up to lick and kiss the skin as it was revealed, teasing it with his fingers when he got too low to kiss. When he reached for Adrian again, Adrian shifted and pinned his hands to the bed.

Confused, Simon looked up at Adrian's face, hoping for some clue as to what was wrong. The hunger there nearly undid him. Adrian moved Simon's hands to above his head and pushed down slightly before moving away. "Stay" was all he said.

Adrian then slowly, so slowly Simon thought he'd burst from the anticipation of it, unbuttoned each button of Simon's shirt, licking and nipping the skin, making the most indecent sounds as he tasted each new bit of Simon's chest and abs. Simon nearly lost it when Adrian used his lips to tug on Simon's light brown treasure trail until he reached the waistband of his slacks.

Simon couldn't tear his gaze away from each little thing Adrian did, and when Adrian raised his head, a question clear on his face, Simon nodded. He sucked in a huge gulp of air when Adrian immediately bent to the task of unbuckling, then unbuttoning and unzipping Simon's pants. Adrian peeled the material away from Simon's aching cock, then nuzzled him through his tight briefs. He gasped, barely holding on, not wanting to come yet!

A tap to his hip refocused Simon, and he raised his butt so Adrian could slide the pants and briefs off him, leaving him naked while Adrian was still mostly dressed. Simon shivered slightly, not cold but rather too excited to be still. He loved Adrian being so commanding and in control, even if it was without words mostly. Or maybe because of that. He wasn't sure which and truly didn't care.

Adrian slipped off his shirt, finally, having lost his pants earlier, frustrating Simon. He wanted to see all of Adrian! But before he could protest, Adrian was back to teasing him. He kissed Simon but only for a moment. He then dropped down to kiss, lick, nip, and nuzzle every bit of flesh, starting from behind Simon's ear all the way to the tops of his feet, and damn near every spot between. However, Adrian avoided touching Simon's cock, making him writhe on the bed, a litany of "please," "more," and "oh God!" falling from his lips nonstop. That Adrian couldn't hear him wasn't even a consideration at that point.

About the time Simon was going to scream and flip Adrian over to move things along, Adrian pulled back a moment and signed, *"Want you!"* He then stood and quickly divested himself of his remaining clothing.

The undignified whimper Simon let out was the only sound he could make. Adrian was… beautiful. *Long* and *lean* described more than his body type, making Simon's mouth water. He took in the black curls on Adrian's chest that tapered down his abdomen to a thin trail from the little indent of a belly button to a thick nest of curls around the cock he'd felt but not gotten to really see yet. The tip leaked steadily, the head near purple. Just the sight of it made Simon's muscles clench and his body shake.

Simon sat up fast and reached for Adrian, thrilling when Adrian moved closer and allowed Simon to touch. The feel, the heat, the scent of his lover made his head spin. He focused enough to look up, even as he wrapped his hand around Adrian's cock and started a slow stroke, and mouthed "Please."

Adrian laid Simon back again, then hovered over him a moment before lowering himself so they touched from chest to toes. Unable to stay still, Simon trembled under Adrian, overwhelmed with how Adrian touched him. The whole time was unrushed except by Simon, which he vaguely knew meant something, but right then, all he could focus on was getting Adrian inside him. *Now!*

Taking his time, Adrian kissed down Simon's body again, but by then Simon could tell he had a real goal, though Adrian did nip and tease his nipples until Simon writhed and cried out again. Adrian kept one hand on Simon's stomach as he moved down and took just the tip of Simon's cock into his mouth, licking and stabbing his tongue into the slit, sucking until the whole cockhead was inside the perfect wet heat of Adrian's mouth.

Trembling, Simon tugged at Adrian's hair, but Adrian ignored him, licking and mouthing down Simon's length before licking across and around Simon's sac, making him buck up at the touch. Adrian continued to tease and lick, sucking in first one ball then the other, before pulling both in and tugging them away from Simon's body even as he continued to suck and lick.

His cock had been leaking since before they'd moved from the kitchen, and the slight pain mixed with the immense pleasure had precome flowing nonstop. Adrian pushed Simon's legs up and out, exposing him even more, and before Simon could process the pleasure already rocking his body, Adrian released his sac. He then licked along Simon's taint, across his hole and down, then followed the same path back up, making the circuit again before zeroing in on his aching entrance.

Adrian alternated wide licks with pointed stabs with his tongue, adding a finger after a few moments, teasing his need higher. When the finger disappeared, Simon cried out, but when it returned, slick, he continued his whimpers and begged Adrian to go faster.

Raising his head, Adrian continued to tease, slowly pressing in and pulling back out. When he added a second finger, Simon nearly came, his need so high. "Soon," Adrian rumbled, his speech slurring heavily, but Simon could still understand him.

"Now," Simon begged, rocking on Adrian's fingers.

Instead of pulling them out and replacing the fingers with his cock, Adrian moved the one hand that had been on his abdomen and wrapped it around his cock even as he added another finger to Simon's ass. The bite of pain as his body was stretched was bliss, as was the hand stroking him. Even as good as it all felt, what he wanted, no, needed, was Adrian to push inside and fill him. He needed it so badly he thought he'd die if Adrian didn't hurry the hell up.

Just when he thought he'd come, Adrian stopped, both hands stilling as he looked Simon over. Confused, Simon started to reach for Adrian, but then Adrian shifted back. Simon watched as Adrian quickly donned the condom and slicked himself, adding another dollop of slick to his fingers and kneading it inside Simon before shifting to line himself up to Simon's clenching hole.

Finally Adrian pushed forward until the head of his cock entered Simon. Then he set up a slow, sensual, and totally frustrating rocking as he inched his way inside Simon's body as Simon cried out. Once Adrian hit bottom, he again placed one hand on Simon's abdomen, holding himself up with the other, as he began the slow slide in and out, in and out, making Simon writhe and moan nonstop. He'd never had a lover like Adrian, and right then he hoped to never need another. Even as Adrian breached his body, he seemed to invade Simon's soul as well, making him giddy and terrified at the same time.

At that moment, though, all he could really focus on was how wonderful Adrian felt and how fast the sizzling in his balls built. It pissed him off that he knew he wouldn't last long, but as Adrian sped up, his thrusts becoming harder and sharper, Simon let go of his worry and simply enjoyed the pounding bliss he felt with each movement.

He rocked up into Adrian's thrusts, clutching Adrian with his hands and legs, trying to drive himself up harder, to impale himself deeper. His mind shorted out about the time he lost the war and his orgasm ripped through him, along with bliss, joy, *and oh my fucking god what the hell is he doing* ripped through him. Moments later Adrian roared out his own release, his thrusts erratic, his one hand not releasing Simon's ball sac even as he trembled.

When Adrian finally freed him, Simon was both thankful and saddened. He'd never thought he'd like a little pain with his pleasure, but if Adrian wanted to do whatever that was again, soon, Simon was all for it.

They panted and held each other as they rode out the high, the hot come smearing between them. Finally, when Simon thought he could function again, he nuzzled Adrian's temple, smiling against the skin as he luxuriated in the slight aftershocks caused by Adrian's cock slowly slipping from his body.

Adrian rolled off and tended to the condom, then returned and pulled Simon into his arms, holding him tight. Eventually Simon pulled back, the drying come itching and annoying him enough to release his hold on Adrian for a moment or two. He thought hard, then signed, *"Shower with me?"*

When Adrian nodded and smiled, Simon reveled in the pleased look Adrian gave him. He knew his ASL was still very slow and he didn't know nearly as many signs as he needed to, obviously, but the fact his using sign made Adrian happy made learning it all worthwhile.

Simon stood and pulled Adrian up with him and then led him to the en suite bathroom, thrilled with the wide-eyed gaze Adrian gave his large freestanding shower. It would hold eight people if you were all very close. He knew this thanks to too much vodka and his friends drinking just as much as he had. Shaking off the memory, Simon turned the water on and fidgeted with the temperature control.

Moments later the two men were in the shower, kissing and touching, exploring even as their bodies were, for the time being, sated. Simon took the time to wash Adrian's hair, massaging his scalp as he rinsed the inky-black strands, then lathered Adrian up, making sure to wash every bit of him from the top of his head to the soles of his feet. When he was done, Adrian took the time and care to return the favor, exciting Simon in ways he didn't think possible. By the time they were clean, Adrian had sucked him off again, and Simon had managed to return the favor, finally tasting his lover—something he swore he would do more of and soon.

Clean and dry, Adrian took Simon's hand as they reentered the bedroom. Simon turned and smiled, though he knew it was brittle. He swallowed and released Adrian's hand, then raised his own trembling hands to sign, *"Stay tonight? Don't go home."*

Adrian grinned and nodded. *"Happily."*

Simon offered a pair of sleep pants to Adrian, and in a short time, they were curled together in bed, Simon on the side closer to the bathroom. Adrian toyed with Simon's damp hair as they both drifted off to sleep. Simon couldn't remember the last time he felt so safe with a partner. He hoped Adrian would turn out to be all he seemed, as Simon wanted nothing more at that moment than to keep Adrian, as his friend, lover, and eventual partner.

chapter sixteen

ADRIAN WOKE in small bursts, slowly becoming aware of the furnace he was currently curled around. When he managed to open his eyes, the night before flooded back, stealing his breath. He couldn't believe how uninhibited Simon had been. The way he'd writhed. For once, Adrian had truly wished he could hear, certain the sounds coming from Simon would have been wondrous.

Not ready to move, Adrian curled tighter against Simon and nuzzled against his nape, loving how the man in his arms tasted and smelled. When Simon shifted, his chest vibrating even as he snuggled back so his ass pressed against Adrian's already-hard cock, Adrian closed his eyes, praying for calm and patience. He didn't want to do anything to spook his lover, and he wasn't positive Simon would still think their actions the night before had been the right ones.

Before his worry could get too far out of control, Simon turned over in his arms, a soft smile on his handsome face. Without thinking about it, Adrian reached up to trace a small line left on Simon's face from the sheets. The simple image of his lover sleep-tousled and soft-skinned made his heart ache. He wanted so much to make Simon his, long-term; now he just had to figure out how to make that hope reality.

"Good morning," Simon said, a sweet smile following the words.

Elated, Adrian returned the look and pulled Simon into his arms. He kissed him gently but thoroughly. Adrian couldn't believe his luck at winning Simon from his fears. Now if he could keep Simon as he was now, not how he'd been before. "Morning, love."

Simon swallowed hard, his smile slipping slightly, confusing Adrian. "Love?"

Oh, maybe Simon doesn't like endearments? That made no sense, though, so he asked, "You don't mind, do you?"

The quick head shake had him releasing the huge breath he hadn't realized he'd been holding until then. "Then yes, Si, love." Adrian caressed Simon's cheek, slipping his hand into Simon's hair and tugging lightly. "I like calling you Si, like your close friends do, but 'love' is just between us."

"I…. Thank you." The sudden frown that crossed Simon's face confused Adrian, but then Simon continued. "But I don't have a pet name for you. I mean, you're always Adrian. I don't even know a good nickname version of Adrian, and I call my friends 'hon' half the time, so…."

Adrian couldn't help it, he started chuckling at the annoyed face Simon made as he continued fretting over names, even as he worked to keep up with Simon's rambling—first thing in the morning wasn't the best time to make him lip read, but he thought he got it all. The scowl Simon then turned on him only served to make Adrian laugh harder. "Love, you don't have to have a pet name for me that's unique, if you don't want." He continued to sign as he spoke, having promised to do so to help Simon learn.

"But…." The frown didn't lighten, but it didn't deepen, either.

"For now, how about breakfast? Then maybe we can hang out; go to the park or something?"

"Food and nature?" Simon grinned. "That sounds doable," he said, bouncing slightly.

Adrian loved watching Simon, especially when he was happy, or horny, or better yet, happy and horny. "Good. Let's see what your cabinets have to eat, as I didn't bring morning food with me."

Simon hopped off the bed after giving Adrian a quick peck on the cheek. "Breakfast I can do. But more importantly, coffee!"

In a short time, Adrian and Simon were dressed and in the kitchen, each with a mug of coffee and plated omelets before them. By the time they had eaten and finished their drinks, Simon was nibbling his bottom lip and fidgeting again.

He didn't like how hard Simon was abusing that sweet bit of flesh. Adrian reached out and traced his thumb along Simon's bottom lip, freeing it gently. "You okay?"

"You want to go for a walk or talk here?" Simon asked instead of answering.

"Talk, I think, and then a walk?" Adrian smiled and laced his fingers with Simon's as they walked to the living room again. "I'd like to know what's going on in your head, why you're so nervous."

Simon didn't answer right away, instead settling on the long couch sideways. He stared down at his hands instead of looking at Adrian, which annoyed him immensely. He hated not being able to read Simon's face. "Si?" He didn't want to think Simon might regret the night before, but he wasn't sure why else Simon would be so nervous. "What's wrong?"

After taking a deep breath, Simon looked up, though his gaze skittered away almost immediately, Adrian could at least see Simon's lips to know what was said. "Nothing, exactly. I-I don't know how to discuss certain things with you, but you, Chase, and James all insist I need to."

"Okay, so what are you needing to discuss with me?"

"You asked me to meet your dad and have brought up my family a few times. I—it's not that I don't want to meet your family, but I can never return the introduction. Not that you would want to meet them even if I could take you to their home. They hate what I am. They would be horrible to you and—" Simon sat straighter, shoulders back, finally making proper eye contact. "—I will never allow that to happen."

"I know who your family is, and they don't scare me, Si. I want you to meet my father, to include you in my life more. I'd even like to have Airy and Teague over, to spend more time with us, not just with me."

"They scare me half the time, so I have a hard time believing they don't worry you."

Confused, Adrian asked, "Your parents or my friends?"

A small smile flitted across Simon's face. "My parents. Your friends seemed nice." The frown reappeared, deeper than before. "But…."

Adrian sighed, frustrated. "Love, it will be all right," he said and signed, then tugged Simon into his arms again and caressed his hands up and down Simon's back until he finally relaxed some. After a moment he shifted back so he could see Simon's face again. "I don't know all the history between you and them, but I know all about their efforts to undermine gay rights, to re-criminalize homosexuality, and more. But I don't care about them. Only you. You are an amazing man who needs to learn to see himself separate from his family. Besides," he continued, cradling Simon's face gently. "Your real family is Chase, James, Dale, Rhys, um… your friend Vaughn that I've only been told of but never met. Do I need to keep going?"

Simon shook his head, though Adrian didn't release him. "Vaughn is away on some teacher-exchange thing. But no. I know. It's just—"

"That you're scared and don't want to lose anyone else in your life. I know, but, love, I'm not going anywhere. Now can we move past your biological parents and focus on us?"

"Yes," Simon said with a tight nod.

"Good. Will you meet my dad now? I won't subject you to my mom yet, as she can be a bit much. However, I would love to have you and Dad meet."

"I would like that. I think spending more time with your friends would be good too," Simon added, his cheeks flushing pink. "I'd like you to get to know more than just Chase out of my friends too."

Adrian grinned, thrilled Simon had agreed and wanted to include him with his chosen family more. He hoped that meant Simon was seeing them as being long-term, but wasn't about to push it. Yet. "Thank you."

Simon nodded. "Can we have that walk now?"

"Sure."

While Simon made a call, Adrian pulled out his cell and texted his father to let him know Simon had finally agreed to meet and asked when would be a good time. When he looked up, he couldn't help but grin at how open Simon seemed, the cloud of fear and sadness not so apparent.

"Ready?" he asked and signed.

"Almost." Simon disappeared into his office, then returned, a messenger bag thrown over one shoulder. "Now I am."

Adrian looked down at the bag, then shrugged. Si had never done that before, but okay. Instead of commenting, he simply took Simon's hand and led him out of the house. He didn't know Simon's neighborhood well but knew there was a nice park nearby, so he turned and led the way. Curious how Simon would act around his home—wondering if he would be more open or reserved around the people he lived near—he watched Simon as much as he did where he was going.

He should have known better than to worry, as every time Adrian looked over, he caught the soft smile on Simon's face as he strolled along. He tightened his hold on Adrian's hand in a squeeze every time he noticed Adrian watching, which made Adrian's heart give a squeeze in return.

"Thank you." Adrian wasn't certain what he was being thanked for. His face must have shown his confusion because Simon added, "For wanting to do simple things with me. Outside."

Puzzling the odd comment over, Adrian tugged Simon closer and pressed a kiss to his temple. "You're welcome," he said, not wanting to give up his hold on Simon to sign.

They wandered the park, watching the ducks as they played in the water. Simon didn't speak or sign as they simply walked along together. When they stopped at a bench and sat, Simon turned to face Adrian. "I know what we did last night, and what we've done before, but—" Simon's gaze averted from Adrian's again, his body rigid as he paused. "You know I don't share?" Simon asked and signed, most of his signs correct—though Adrian did correct *share*, though without comment.

Adrian nodded, hoping to encourage him to continue.

"If we're going to continue, meet the family and everything, I need a promise." Simon bit his lip hard enough Adrian worried he might draw blood, but he didn't interfere this time, hoping Simon would spit out whatever was eating at him. "I'm the only one in your bed for as long as we're together."

Well, that's what he thought Simon said. It was more a jumble of motions, though reading his lips was usually easier than that. "You went too fast. You asked for us to be exclusive. Right?" He thought Simon understood that, especially with what they'd discussed before. Still he'd wanted Simon to stake a claim on him, so he didn't mind the mumbled demand.

"Yes."

Signing and speaking as clearly as possible, he replied, "I told you before, I want to date you. Only you. So yes—" He couldn't promise to love Simon yet, though he knew he was losing his heart fast. Regardless, Simon would never believe him. Not yet anyway. But this he could do. "You are the only one I'm going to kiss, hold hands with, make out with, and sleep with. I don't share either, love."

Adrian found his arms suddenly full of Simon as he practically climbed into Adrian's lap, his lips taken in a hard kiss. He returned the kiss, trying to calm Simon down before they wound up arrested for indecency—besides, it was too cool out for exposed bits, his mind helpfully added.

When he managed to extricate himself from his octopus-like boyfriend, both men grinning at each other, he hugged Simon tight before shifting Simon to sit beside him, instead of on him.

"Thank you," Simon signed and said, a cross between excitement and disbelief on his handsome face.

"For wanting you?" Adrian shook his head, torn between wanting to hug Simon again and hunting down his exes to beat to death, and he wasn't a violent guy! "You're perfect just as you are, Si."

Simon shook his head. "No, I'm not, but thank you for saying so anyway. So how long do I get to keep you for?"

Adrian tilted his head and stared at his boyfriend, hoping that was a joke. Or maybe that he hadn't understood correctly. "How long? Well, I hope things work out and we stay together, personally. What do you mean, 'how long'?"

The sudden flush on Simon's cheeks along with the obvious laughter only served to make Adrian more unsure and confused. "What?"

It took a minute or two for Simon to calm, but when he did, he grinned wide. "I mean how long today, hon. As in, do you have to get home soon to do professory things, or do you want to head over to one of the restaurants on the other side of the park and stay a little longer? I know you have to get home at some point, but—" Simon looked down, then back up, not quite meeting Adrian's gaze. "—I don't want to let you go yet."

The words from Simon thrilled Adrian more than he would have admitted to any but his closest friends, maybe. As he didn't want to go yet, either, he decided to take Simon up on his late-lunch idea.

"Eating would be good, love." Adrian wound his fingers with Simon's as they sat together a little longer, then walked, holding hands the rest of the way to the restaurant. The knowledge that Simon was being so open about their relationship thrilled Adrian and reassured him all at the same time.

BY THE time Adrian left that night, Simon had enjoyed being pounded into his mattress again. An event he hoped to repeat often. He still worried about how long Adrian would stay interested, but the longer they were together, the more optimistic Simon became. Most men he'd dated would have dropped him a long time ago over nothing more than how long it took for them to have sex. Not Adrian, though.

He tidied up the house, not that they'd been messy anywhere but in bed—a thought that made him grin—but he still hated leaving dishes out or glasses half-full. Part of it, he knew, was how he'd been raised, but he also just liked living in a clean place. Well, other than in his office. In there he could collect a huge number of dirty dishes, coffee mugs, and more without even realizing it, but that was the writer in him. Then the story was more important!

His phone ringing pulled him out of his thoughts. Simon set the last of the cups in the sink, then pulled out his cell. *Chase?*

"Hello."

"Hey, hon. Your date done yet?" Chase teased, his voice light and happy.

"Yes, thank you." Simon knew he was grinning into the phone and refused to acknowledge how rare his smiling had been until recently.

"Happy still? You seemed it when we saw you out earlier. The hand-holding was too sweet, by the way."

Hand-holding? "You saw us out today?"

"Uh-huh. Rhys and I were out and about. He noticed you before I did, you two being all cute and sweet."

Yeah, sweet was right. Adrian is the sweetest man! "That had to be on our way to or from the park. He didn't act weird about it or try to pull away."

"Oh, hon, of course he didn't. Unlike your usual picks, Adrian is a real man. You should want a partner that is proud to be with you, not one that wants to hide you away. I still don't get how you can write such wonderful romances but not know these things should apply to you, not just your friends or characters."

He'd heard that argument off and on over the years from all his friends, but for once, he was glad for them to be right. Adrian was what he always aspired to write as the love interest in his stories, except he was real and warm and *ohmygod* hot! "Well, I think I finally managed to get it right."

"If the happy little sigh is anything to go by, I think you just might. Does that mean you…?" Chase led off suggestively. Simon could just imagine how Chase's brows would waggle as he grinned.

"I do *not* kiss and tell," he countered.

The loud squeal through the cell made him pull it away and frown. He loved his friend but truly hated that sound—especially at that decibel level. "Done yet?" he asked from a short distance away.

"Yes!" Chase said, this time at a little more of a non-ear-splitting level. "I'm so happy for you."

They spent a little time talking and discussing Adrian and dating, though Simon did redirect Chase the few times he tried to be nosy about sex. He wanted to keep that between him and Adrian, nosy friends be damned.

chapter seventeen

SIMON SIGHED, again, and turned up the radio. His wish right then was for the music to drown out his worry and fears about going to Adrian's. Having been raised always to be "on," Simon was no stranger to meeting new people. However, the other man waiting for him at Adrian's wasn't just anyone. No, this was Adrian's father. Simon knew it shouldn't be such a big event—even if only so in his head—but it was.

Things had been going well; their relationship deepened daily. Simon's feelings for Adrian had done the same. Unfortunately he couldn't convince his head or heart that Adrian's father would like him and approve. Parents always liked him, especially if they knew who he was, or rather what his financial status was. He'd managed to get Airy and Teague to like him, and friends often trumped what family thought, yet Simon had been unable to eat all day, and even the thought of food made him queasy.

Much to Simon's frustration, he arrived at Adrian's home only a few short minutes later. He pulled in next to Adrian's car and parked but didn't immediately turn off the engine or get out. Adrian was Deaf, so he wouldn't notice if Simon sat outside and tried to calm down, right? That was the hope, anyway.

The front door opened before he was ready. The sight of his lover as he stepped out onto the stoop calmed him more than all the pep talks he'd tried. Adrian stood there in low-rise jeans with a tight light green long-sleeved T-shirt that brought out the vibrant green of his eyes. Adrian's wide smile flashed, and Simon was able to breathe easier and finally turn off the car.

Moments later Adrian pulled Simon's door open and motioned for him to hurry up. "Come on, Dad's been here half the day," Adrian signed and said. As soon as Simon stood, Adrian wrapped his arms around Simon and held him tight. "It will be fine, promise," he added before stepping back.

Simon did his best to paste on a convincing smile, then threaded his fingers with Adrian's and let his boyfriend pull him up and inside the small house.

Once inside, Simon couldn't help but look around. It took a moment, but his gaze finally landed on a man who looked a great deal like Adrian, though a bit bulkier and older. Simon swallowed hard but kept his smile in place. He released Adrian's hand, then lifted his to sign as he spoke, not wanting to leave Adrian out or make Adrian's father question his resolve to be a proper partner for Adrian. "Hello. I'm Simon." Technically, he signed *Hello, my name is Simon*, but he'd learned how to translate what he signed versus what he said, mostly. Occasionally it still threw him, and his vocabulary was still limited, but Adrian was worth the effort.

"Hi, Simon. I'm Leland, Adrian's father. I don't bite, so relax," Leland signed and said, a small but welcoming smile on his face.

Once they shook hands, Adrian pulled Simon down onto the couch beside him. "Dad's here to meet you, not investigate or question you. Oh, and to eat."

"Yes, but hopefully you won't mind if I ask a few things as we go. It's easier to get to know someone that way." Leland winked. "But come, now that you're here, we can eat, and then I promise to let you two have a nice evening together. Without me in the way."

Simon looked from Leland to Adrian, more confused than anything, though he was still nervous too. "He's only here for dinner and then leaving?" It didn't make sense to him. Not if Leland really wanted to find out more about Simon and about them as a couple.

"Yes. Come help me in the kitchen?" Adrian asked.

Of course he'd help, but the fact Leland wasn't asking him anything, rather simply watching him as he followed Adrian into the kitchen, unnerved Simon. Before he could come to any conclusions or even ideas about Leland, Adrian directed him to pull the pot roast out of the oven. While Simon did as he was bid, Adrian unwrapped and sliced a large loaf of what smelled like sourdough bread. Simon's mouth watered when he opened the oven's glass door, the scents of roast, onions, carrots, and more managing finally to wake his hunger.

For a few minutes, things felt like they normally did when he was over there. They worked together to make dinner and set the table, though the knowledge that there was a third place setting stood out and reminded Simon of Leland's presence, even if he wasn't being intrusive.

Doing his best to remain calm, Simon reveled in the near-constant touches they shared as they worked around each other. When Adrian spoke again, Simon almost jumped in surprise. He'd grown used to how quiet their evenings tended to be—well, when not engaged in exploring the uses of the bed, couch, wall, etcetera.

"Go sit with Dad at the table. I'll be right in with the food."

Simon leaned in and pressed his lips gently against Adrian's, just for a moment, but he needed the connection. Normally Adrian welcomed him with a kiss, and they would have done more kissing after he arrived, but with Leland there, even Adrian seemed a little more reserved. Not that Simon could blame him. If he could introduce Adrian to his family, he wouldn't kiss or even hold hands with Adrian—that simply wasn't done in *polite company*.

"Okay. Just don't be long." Simon stole another kiss, then turned and walked to the dining room.

Leland already sat on one side, leaving both ends of the table open. Simon took his usual spot.

"So what do you write? Adrian said you are an author, but I couldn't find you on Amazon by your name."

Simon took a gulp of the tea he'd placed there earlier while setting the table. "Um, I'm a homoerotic author. You wouldn't find anything there under my legal name; I use a pen name instead. Though I'm public about what my pen name is, so if you google me, you'll find my site and such."

"Homoerotic?" Leland asked, his face scrunching just like Adrian's when he was confused. The fact he reminded Simon so much of his son helped to relax him a little more. "Thought it was called M/M romance or gay romance."

"For most authors, that's true. I don't like that term because I write more than gay romance." Simon paused to think of how best to explain it to someone that didn't read the genre, much less his stories. "Yes, all my main characters have been physically male, but that doesn't mean the same thing to me. I have bi characters. I just started a story with a gender fluid main character, and I'm planning one with a trans man as an MC. So it's not just gay, or even male-male as some would define it, but it's all love and all falls under the LGBTQ-plus umbrella."

Leland nodded as Simon spoke, a soft smile on his lips. "So even though you're gay, you don't define your stories that way?"

"No. I'm not of the belief that bisexuality isn't real or anything like that. People love, period. I just only tend to write male characters as that's what I find sexy, but that doesn't mean I have any issues with other couplings. Well, as long as you don't expect me to participate, at least," he added with a slight grin.

"Don't worry, son. I'm not trying to pick apart what you write. I was honestly curious. I don't read romance but had thought it might be interesting to see what kind of romance you write, being you're trying to live it with my son."

"Dad," Adrian said, his voice deeper and a bit sterner than Simon was used to.

"What?" Leland signed and asked, his face the picture of innocence—not that Simon or Adrian bought into the look.

"Be nice." Adrian set the platter with the sliced roast and the roasted veggies scattered around it, in the center of the table. "Si, you feel free to ignore the nosy busybody if he gets too fussy."

Simon giggled. The contrast of the pout on Leland's face and the wink from Adrian made him feel a lightness he didn't expect or control well. Once he calmed and Adrian sat at the head of the table, Simon replied, "He's fine, love. We were just talking about what I write."

"Oh, that's okay, then," he said and signed.

"You really love my son, just the way he is?" Leland said, drawing Simon's attention back to him.

Unsure what Leland meant, Simon cocked his head and stared at Leland as he thought about what he might mean. "The way he is? I don't understand, or at least, I hope I don't. Adrian's perfect just as he is."

"I would agree, but I know many Hearing people don't see him as normal, his mother included. His lack of hearing doesn't bother you? I mean, I know you're learning to sign and you seem to do well enough, especially if you've only been learning for a few months, not years as he and I have, but…." Leland looked lost for a moment.

"Sir, respectfully, I think your wife is an idiot. Ad—"

Leland barked out a laugh and nodded but motioned for Simon to continue. "Sorry."

"Adrian is not disabled in any way that counts. He doesn't hear, but he sees more than most anyone I know, and if you knew my friends, you'd understand just how serious that statement is. As far as I'm concerned, it's the same as if I was dating someone for whom English wasn't their native tongue." Simon paused a moment to order his thoughts. "Well, that's what it is, really. The only difference is that Adrian can speak English already, but it's not fair to expect him to only read lips and speak for me. I should learn his language as well."

That said, Leland relaxed completely, and they were able to eat in peace. The food was wonderful, but that was to be expected from Adrian. He wasn't a gourmet cook, but Simon loved that Adrian cooked for him, not just expected Simon to take him out all the time.

Actually, as he thought about things more during and after dinner, it occurred to him that he was rarely expected to pay for things when out with Adrian. His lover never pushed for gifts, outings on Simon's dime, or, well, anything other than his time and care.

By the time dinner was over and Leland was gathering his things to leave, Simon could barely restrain himself. He wanted Adrian all the time, but the little things Leland said and the realizations Simon had come to by himself had Simon torn between wanting to kiss Adrian breathless or drop to his knees and worship his body to show how much Adrian's actions meant.

"Don't forget, you promised to come over for a family dinner sometime soon," Leland said, cutting into Simon's internal debate. "Should help shake things up a bit, though you might want to bring your battle armor, Simon."

"Armor?" *Um....* "Why?"

"Adrian's mother never thinks anyone is good enough or will be willing to do everything needed for her baby." The eye roll that accompanied Leland's words made Simon chuckle. "But then, I'm not sure Jane realizes that Adrian is a grown man and that he has a perfectly normal life."

"Nor has she learned ASL," Adrian added, his voice sounding tired suddenly.

"Well, I look forward to seeing you again, and don't worry, mothers love me," Simon teased and grinned.

"That she may, son." Leland hugged Adrian, then proceeded to startle Simon by pulling him into one as well. By the time Simon's shock wore off, Leland was gone and Adrian stood beside him, smiling wide.

"Told you Dad would like you." Adrian bent and took Simon's lips in a soft, yet heated kiss. Gentle lips teased his until he parted his own, allowing Adrian inside.

The sigh he released as he sank into the feeling of Adrian normally would have embarrassed him, but he was too happy right then to care. Why it took meeting Adrian's father for it to click with him that Adrian really didn't care about the money and that he never took advantage, he didn't know. He was just thrilled with the knowledge.

When they pulled back, Adrian cupped Simon's face, then signed, *"Thank you."*

Simon didn't give himself a chance to chicken out. He straightened up and smoothed his hands down his pants before saying and signing, "I love you."

He wasn't sure what he expected of his impromptu declaration, but Adrian gaping at him wasn't it.

Adrian swallowed then and signed, *"You what?"*

Saying it once was hard enough, but having to repeat it? Yeah, that about killed him with nerves bordering on fear. "I love you." That his voice was barely loud enough for him to hear didn't matter, as he knew Adrian could read his lips and see his signing. "I just… thought…." Unable to continue, Simon looked away.

Before he could decide where to run to hide from his stupidity—*Why did I have to go off and say that!*—Adrian pulled him back into his arms and smothered him in kisses. It took a moment, but he eventually returned the kisses and touches, though he was still confused and embarrassed.

"I love you too," Adrian said and signed, using his whole body to emphasize each word.

It took a moment for the words to sink in, but eventually they did, and Simon was certain his heart stopped before it picked up and ran laps around his chest double time. "You do?" Damn! Did his voice really crack that bad? Yeah, it did. For once, he was glad Adrian couldn't hear him, as even when he cleared his throat and tried again, it didn't sound any better or louder. "You l-love me?"

The nod was sharp, but Adrian's voice was gentle and low as he signed and spoke, "Of course. I just didn't want to freak you out and say it too soon," he finished with a shrug.

Simon wanted to be annoyed at the "freak out" comment but couldn't. He was too busy trying to not act like a teenage girl and start squealing.

Adrian pulled him back into his arms, and this time when he took Simon's mouth, the kiss was devouring and demanding. The longer and deeper Adrian plundered, the more Simon wanted to give. When his back hit the wall, Simon came out of the drugging haze long enough to take note of how hard Adrian's cock was against his and that they were almost to Adrian's bedroom. Well, he was plastered against the wall just to the left of the doorway, and he'd never hated a wall more.

Taking a huge, gulping breath, Simon pushed Adrian back enough to shift away from the wall and into the room so they could get to the bed. As much as he'd loved each and every time they'd been together—couch, floor, bed, wall—Simon wanted this time to be in bed. Declarations, he was certain, deserved beds, not walls.

Eventually they made it to the bed and lost their clothes, though Simon couldn't remember when they'd stripped. Adrian lowered him slowly to the mattress, then stood back. Simon took that chance to look his fill as Adrian rummaged around in his nightstand. Adrian was still just as handsome and drool-worthy as always, but now that the words were said, Adrian seemed even more breathtaking. He knew it was all in his head, that Adrian hadn't actually changed how he looked just by saying special words, but that didn't change how Simon felt.

Adrian turned back to face Simon, the look on his face arresting Simon's thoughts. "What?"

He tossed a condom and the slick on the bed next to Simon, then prowled closer. When Adrian spoke again, his voice was more rumble than ever. "One day soon, Si, we're going to go to the clinic and get tested, but for now, scoot back and let me have you."

Simon did as Adrian bid, his mind reeling from all the happenings in the last few minutes. It would be a long time before they would come up for air, refueling, and maybe a shower or three, but in the moments he could think past *ohmygod* and *please!* his heart hurt from how happy he was. There were still fears and worries, but in Adrian's arms, filled with Adrian and love, he couldn't be made to care.

chapter eighteen

THE FLASH on Adrian's cell blinked, as did the light in his office. Curious who would be there so long after hours, he shifted his gaze from the next-to-last test he had to grade. Standing in the doorway, looking oddly from Adrian to the light and back was a woman he'd never thought to meet, though he knew who she was. Adrian had seen many images of Simon's biological family, though he was hard-pressed to think of the woman staring at him as Si's sister.

"Hello?" he said, not bothering with sign as he was certain it would be lost on his visitor.

Zoey smoothed her hands down her narrow pencil skirt and stepped into his office. Adrian took a moment to look her over, but the severe white button-up paired with the long skirt and prim little kitten heels—not to mention the pursed lips—made her stand out on the UW campus, not that she would care, he was certain.

"Can I help you?" he tried again, annoyed at her lack of response. She was at his door, not the other way around.

"You're Deaf?" she finally asked, a strange mixture of humor and disgust crossing her face.

"Last time I checked." He flashed a smirk her way as he decided to go ahead and pack up the last little bit and head out. Adrian was certain he'd be in no mood for staying once he knew why Simon's sister was there. "But I can read lips and body language just fine, thanks for asking."

"No need to be rude." Her pique was a waste, as he could neither hear her nor did he care. "I'm here to…." She tugged at the cuff of her long-sleeved blouse. "My name is Zoey Tyler Bringham, Simon's sister. What will it take to

make you leave Simon alone? He needs a normal life, not slumming with—"
She rolled one dainty hand as if looking for the right insult. More likely trying
to find the one most likely to hurt. "—a poor, handicapped fr—geek."

Adrian stood, papers forgotten in his hand as he gaped at the... he'd
call her a bitch, but he didn't want to insult all the lovely female dogs he'd
met. "I happen to be a well-respected professor, ethical hacker, expert in
criminal computer forensics, and your brother's lover. I am not, however,
poor, a freak, or handicapped." He would give her the geek part, but he was
proud of that, thank you so very much. "And you and your filthy money can
turn right around and leave. Now!"

He knew he'd been yelling by the last bit; his throat told him all about
how loud he must have been. He didn't care one bit, however. The thought
came to him suddenly, and he wondered how many times money had been
dangled in front of Simon's previous lovers.

Adrian also wondered if Zoey might have been the one behind the
picture text. Before he could pursue that thought, she withdrew a checkbook
and a pen from her small clutch. "Fifty thousand?"

"You're insane. I don't want your money." He finished gathering his
things and then hitched his laptop bag onto his shoulder.

"One hundred thousand, then?"

"I know I'm speaking in plain English, Ms. Bringham. I. Do. Not.
Want. Your. Money. Now leave, and don't come back." He pulled out his
cell long enough to send the campus cops a text, then stuffed it back in its
holder on his hip.

She waved the checkbook at him and tried again, much to his irritation
and confusion. "Fine, two hundred thousand. You have to leave him
immediately and have no further contact with him."

When Adrian saw the first officer turn the corner, he smiled. "Look,
lady—and I use that term very loosely here—there is nothing you have that
I want. Nothing that is worth more to me than Simon."

"Three hundred thousan—"

Adrian full-out grinned when the officer interrupted her. Bribery was
illegal, as was blackmail. He knew she'd have tons of high-priced legal sharks
to get her out of any trouble, but it was still satisfying to watch her be led away.
Just before he lost sight of her as the cops took her around a corner, he pulled
his cell out and snapped a picture to send to Simon.

As satisfied as he was to watch her turn red as she no doubt yelled and tried to wiggle out of things, he didn't want Simon blindsided when his family rallied against what he'd just done. Honestly, he wasn't sure campus cops could really do much to her other than escort her off campus, as he only had his word and whatever the cops overheard her say, but still, he was glad she was gone.

He sent a text letting Simon know about her visit but would wait to explain it all for when they were face-to-face. Adrian just hoped Simon wasn't too upset. Once he'd assured Simon he would be over soon, he texted Chase, knowing Simon would most likely need his friends, not just his lover, when he found out what his sister had tried to do and had, most likely, done before.

»The psycho harpy from hell did WHAT? «

Yeah, that's about what Adrian expected. »You read what I typed. The question is, once he knows, how he will he react? I know he doesn't get along with his family, but this was something straight out of some old movie. «

»I'll talk to Rhys and see what he thinks and I'll do some digging. «

»Thanks. Can you not mention to Si until I talk to him? «

It took a couple of minutes to get a reply that time. »I don't like hiding things from Simon. He needs to know what's going on. It's HIS sister. «

»Agreed, but I want to talk to him first, face-to-face. Please. «

»*grrrr* He's not going to take it well. He will see it as you trusting me more than him. «

Damn! He hadn't thought of it like that. »If he calls you, fine. But don't call him first? «

»That I can agree to. You want us to come over? «

Ha-ha. No, he didn't. Adrian wanted to spend the evening with his lover, not entertain all their friends. Thinking of that, he debated how long he could wait to tell Teague and Airy about Si's sister and her *request* but didn't think he could put it off too long. Pissing off friends was never a good start to a situation. »Let me text you later about that, but don't think so. Tomorrow? «

»*smirk* Fine, go "comfort" Si and I'll see what I can think up. Thanks for letting me know, hon. «

»Smart ass! And always. «

Adrian again thanked his luck or guardian angel or whatever it was that had brought Chase into his classroom all those months ago. He'd not only found Simon but a great new set of friends. Pushing off thoughts of anything but Simon, Adrian finally made his way to his car. He tossed his bag on the passenger seat and slid inside. Only moments later he was driving toward Simon, anxiety and excitement warring with his thoughts and body as he considered how the night might go.

By the time he'd arrived, he had ten text messages and Simon was sitting on the front steps of his house. Adrian ignored the texts in favor of getting to Simon's side faster. He'd check them once he was inside. Maybe.

TIME MOVED in bursts and lags for Simon as he wrote furiously and spent every spare moment he and Adrian could manage together. As spring moved into summer, Simon thrilled at how things were going in his personal life. His sister still called to spread her vitriol, but he did his best to ignore her, though she did work to make that hard. Honestly, he still couldn't figure out why she'd suddenly started calling him. It made no sense as she had to know by now there was no way she could guilt or harass him into the closet.

Closets were for clothes, not people.

With summer almost there, Simon looked forward to when Adrian's classes would get out. He knew it was greedy of him, but he hated not seeing Adrian every day. Not falling asleep with Adrian curled behind him. And, well, everything in between. He'd thought more than once about asking Adrian to move in with him, but even though they'd said their "I love yous," Simon still worried Adrian might get tired of him.

The ping of his laptop drew his attention from his thoughts and worries. He should be working on edits on his newest story, but the promise of more of his boyfriend never failed to distract him.

He clicked on his e-mail program, then scrolled through the newest batch of mail, unimpressed with how many were junk. No, he didn't want a larger anything! No, he wouldn't like to learn more about....

His attention was redirected when his cell chirped. Looking at it, he smiled, thrilled to see the message was from Adrian. Well, until he opened it and he saw the image attached. *What the hell is Zoey doing near Adrian?* No matter how he tried to rationalize it, he came back to nothing that made sense. Giving up, he scrolled to the bottom of the text.

»Hi, love. Thought I should warn you that I had a visitor. Your sister is… interesting. I'll tell you all about it later. You want me to pick up dinner? «

He could see Adrian had had a visitor! Simon wanted to know the whys and whats, not just that she'd been there. »Dinner sounds great, but I'll make us something. What did Zoey want? Are you okay? «

»I'm fine. I promise. We can discuss her visit when I get there. Should be about an hour. Don't worry! Love you. «

He promises? Why the hell wouldn't he be fine?

»Grrr…. Since I don't have a choice, I will await your arrival. :(I'll go make something for us to eat while I wait. «

Simon wanted to know what had happened *now*, but his only other option was to call his sister, and that wasn't high on his list of ways to torture and slowly kill himself. Instead, he stomped into his kitchen and slammed things around as he tried to come up with something to eat for dinner.

"Fish and veggies with rice," he mumbled to himself as he pulled out the needed items. It wouldn't take long, so he didn't want to start it yet, but he could prep it all and just flip the On button or slide the fish in when he knew Adrian was on his way.

Sadly, that only took about five minutes, total. As he paced around the house, he gave in and called Chase. He would've called James, but his friend didn't need the drama or worry. James had had enough of both for multiple lifetimes. And Dale…. He so didn't want to deal with Dale's "love 'em and leave 'em" attitude about his relationship. James and Chase had been thrilled for him when he'd revealed that he and Adrian had said "the words." When he'd gotten ahold of Vance, he'd been just as excited, though also put out as he hadn't ever met Adrian. Dale had rolled his eyes and asked, "Why bother?"

Chase answered on the third ring. "Hey, Si. What's up?"

"My blood pressure, I think." Simon groaned as his brain caught up to his mouth. He ran his fingers through his hair and tried to explain. "Sorry. I'm a bit fried and need to be talked down from the 'I want to kill my sister once and for all' ledge."

The laughter that rang through the line helped calm him a little. "So what's the psycho-prude done now? And where's Adrian?"

Something was off about Chase's tone, but he pressed on anyway. "Not entirely sure yet. All I know is she stopped by to see Adrian. He said he's fine, but he won't be here for close to an hour. I don't know any more than that." Simon paused to breathe, hoping to calm more, but failing. "Why's she have to want to mess up my life?"

"You don't know that she's doing any such thing to you. Maybe she's planning to take a class and wanted to meet the hot prof?"

Simon snorted. "Yeah, and I'm going to sprout wings and fly too. I'm pretty sure her kids are via artificial insemination, because there's no way I believe anyone, even her moron of a husband, has ever even gotten to first base with her, much less anything more. And I don't think I like you still thinking of Adrian as hot," he added with a pout. He had no issues with IVF, just with his sister. Also, the fact Chase couldn't see the pout didn't change a thing as far as Simon was concerned.

"Okay, so that was a bit of a stretch, but still. If Adrian told you about the visit, it can't have been too bad. She would have called to gloat otherwise."

There is that. "Solid logic and all, but still, we *are* discussing my sister."

"Eh." Simon was certain he could hear Chase's shrug. "Oh, and Si? You need to get over that little fit. He's hot, so are you. And I *so* don't want your man. I'm quite happy with the one I have."

Not wishing to be derailed with talk of hotness, he tried again. "I told you how Zoey's been calling since shortly after I first started seeing Adrian. I don't trust it."

Chase sighed. "I would ask if you really thought your sister was trying to sabotage your relationship with Adrian, but he texted me to ask for help."

"Your help? Wait, you know what's going on?"

"Listen to me before you jump to conclusions. He wanted the help and support of your friends. For you, not himself. I'm going to see what I can come up with, what might be pushing her current insanity, and we'll be over tomorrow morning."

"I don't trust her or my parents."

"I don't either, but I know she has no pull on Adrian."

"I hope not," he mumbled, not wanting to consider losing Adrian. "Dad's working on some 'take back America' thing, one of those 'gays are destroying the country' stupidities that starts every couple of years. He's pissed about all the wins for gay marriage."

"You keep up with him?" Chase asked, sounding aghast at the idea.

"Not by choice, I assure you. But between Zoey, the news, and that I get hit up for donations from these nutcase groups occasionally"—Well, until they got an earful from him—"I know a lot about what he's doing and up for. But what if she tries to convince Adrian to break it off with me? I mean, I don't want to sound like a child, but I really don't want to lose Adrian because of them."

"I wouldn't worry about that if I were you. There's no way they could convince him to leave you. He's almost as bad as James. They've both got it bad, though James for Seth and Adrian for you."

That Chase had actually clarified who went with whom made Simon laugh. "Yeah, yeah. You really think I'm overreacting?"

"Just a little. But no worries, I'm always here to talk you down. Just wait 'til he gets there and talk to him. Oh, there is one thing I need to talk to you about...." They spent the next bit discussing their plans for PrideFest in less than two weeks. The fact the Wisconsin Supreme Court decision on gay marriage should come down about the same time excited Simon more than he wanted to contemplate. He was sure thoughts of marriage were too far ahead even for himself, much less for Adrian. Moving in with him, however, was something he wanted more and more. Especially at the end of each evening with Adrian.

chapter nineteen

ADRIAN STEPPED out of his car and looked over to where Simon still sat, noticing how Simon twisted his fingers around each other, how he didn't look up, and how pale he appeared. "Si?" he called out.

Simon's head snapped up. "Adrian!" Simon was off the stairs and into Adrian's arms so fast Adrian staggered back into the side of the car under Simon's sudden weight. Si vibrated in his arms and wrapped himself around Adrian so tight he wondered if something else had happened in the time it took him to drive over.

"Baby, did something else happen?" Adrian smoothed his hands up and down Simon's back, hoping to calm Simon down some.

A shake of Si's head was all he got for a moment, but eventually Simon pulled back enough Adrian could see his face. "No. Just worried about you. She didn't do anything to hurt you, did she?"

To hurt him? She was all of five two, maybe, so he didn't think Simon meant physical hurt. "No. Though, she may reconsider that after I had her led away by campus security."

The small smile that spread across Simon's face made Adrian smirk. "Now that I would have loved to have seen. But what did she want? Chase said to wait for you to tell me."

He sighed, not wanting to hurt Simon with the truth of what his sister had done, but knowing he had to. "How about if we go inside and talk? It would be easier and more private. Just, Si?"

Simon looked back at Adrian after stepping away. "Yes?"

"Don't forget to look at me so I know what you're saying. Okay?" he signed and said, hoping to reinforce why he needed Simon to think a little more clearly.

"Oh God! I'm so sorry. I forgot," Simon said and signed, his face an interesting shade of red.

"It's okay. Let me get my stuff and we can go inside." Grabbing his bag didn't take long, so in no more than a minute he was inside Simon's home. He dropped his bag beside the couch and then followed Simon into the kitchen.

Simon turned the oven on preheat, but Adrian stilled his hand. "Why don't we talk first? That way we can both focus on what's said and then on eating together. I don't want her hanging over our meal."

"Aren't you hungry?" Simon asked, not quite meeting Adrian's gaze.

"Always. Food sounds good too."

Simon's head whipped around so fast he worried for Si's poor neck. "What?"

"I'm always hungry for you, but I could eat dinner too." He laughed at the dumbfounded look on Simon's handsome face. "One day you will learn just how much I want you, but for now, let's talk. Then we can eat because what you have prepped looks wonderful."

Adrian took Simon's hand in his, then led him back out to the living room and sat on the couch. Simon sat next to him but turned, one leg folded under him so they were facing.

Simon's shoulders drooped, but then he spoke. "I need to know what my sister said and why you had her led away." Simon stopped and frowned, then repeated himself, using both speech and signs that time. "What did Zoey want?"

"Thank you for signing, Si."

Simon smiled, more a curling of the edges of his lips than a true smile, but Adrian would take it.

"She wanted me to leave you. Offered me money, even. She was quite put out that I said you were worth more than her money to me."

"She…. Zoey tried to pay you off?"

Adrian nodded. "I don't know why now, or why me, but she wanted me away from you so you could have a 'normal life.' Her words, not mine. But I had her removed instead of staying and letting her continue to spew her hate and nonsense."

"How can she hate me so much that she would try to take you from me?" Simon asked, still signing, thankfully, as his head drooped in defeat. "I just don't understand."

He wished he knew, but since he didn't, Adrian pulled Simon into his lap and held him. It took time, but eventually Simon shook and wrapped his arms around Adrian tight. Si held on like that for a while, the shaking only subsiding after Adrian realized Simon was crying. He couldn't hear Simon, and with Simon's head against Adrian's neck, he couldn't see the tears, but he felt the wetness.

As he pushed Simon back enough to look at his face, Adrian's heart broke for his lover. He wiped Simon's tears and shushed him. "She can't take me from you, Si. I won't let her."

"But—"

Adrian put his fingers lightly over Simon's lips to still them. "No. I don't want her money and she doesn't scare me. I wanted you to know in case she or your parents tried anything else, that's all."

Simon turned his head enough to nip Adrian's fingers lightly. "They think money can fix everything."

"They're wrong. But there's nothing to fix here, is there?"

"No!" Simon lunged forward and crashed against Adrian before taking his lips in a deep, needy kiss. Normally Simon wasn't the aggressor, but Adrian kinda liked that Simon would seek comfort in him. Still, though, he indulged Simon, sweeping his tongue into Si's mouth, tangling and tasting, probing and thrusting. He missed nothing, but then neither did Simon. Somewhere during the kiss, Simon straddled Adrian and started thrusting against his abs, grinding down on Adrian's throbbing length.

"Si," Adrian gasped out, hoping it was loud enough for Simon to hear as he tore his mouth away and grasped Simon's hips to still them. "Baby?"

"You love me, right?" Simon demanded as he panted, staring so hard at Adrian he wanted to squirm under the power of Si's gaze.

Adrian nodded. "Yes. I said that already."

"You want us, more than just for a little while?"

Confused, Adrian nodded again. "You're my lover, partner, whatever term you want to use. I told you I was committed to us."

Si went from demanding to nervous in a blink. He fidgeted, staring at his hands, then to where Adrian still held him. Finally he looked up again, his posture tense and his face.... If Adrian had to describe how Simon

146

looked, he would have said terrified, though he had no clue why or what was with all the weird questions.

"Move in with me?"

"What?" That wasn't what he expected at all.

"Move in with me. Please?"

"Why, Si? I'm not against the idea," he quickly added when Simon started to pull away. "I just need to know why. Why now?"

"I was going to ask you anyway, well, when I got the courage up to, at least. But I want you with me, not going home all the time and—" He paused and swallowed hard a couple of times. "—I want a real partner, not just a boyfriend. I want you to be that with me."

Partner, not just boyfriend? Adrian rented, so giving up the house he lived it wouldn't be too hard, though he'd never lived with anyone after he'd graduated from college. The idea thrilled him but scared him a bit too. "*A* partner or you want me as *your* partner?"

He knew he was splitting hairs, but he wanted to move forward with Simon too much to not make sure he understood where he stood and that Simon really wanted him, not just anyone willing to stay. Simon hadn't even agreed for them to be tested so they could drop the use of condoms yet, so moving in seemed rushed to him.

"I'm not proposing or anything like that, but I—" Simon shifted off Adrian's lap and sat next to him, though Adrian did notice Si was still hard. "James told me a long time ago that family is those you chose and that chose you. Those that love you as you are. I knew that was true, for him. We all tried to help him find love and happiness, but I never thought I'd actually find someone that loved me, just for me. I want you in my life, in my home. Say you'll at least think about it?"

His nod was quick, but Adrian's mind and words were much slower to come. Could he give up his home and trust in Simon that much? If they didn't make it, he'd be at step one again, having to find a home and rebuild. But that was what everyone in a long-term relationship went through. Right?

"I have a couple of months left on my lease. If I move in, this has to be my home too, Si. It would need to be fitted with all the little conveniences I need, like the lights for the door and such."

"I know, and I already looked into that. There are local companies that do that kind of work, so that wouldn't be a problem. Does that mean yes?" The sheer hope and fear in Simon's eyes made Adrian tug him back into his arms.

"Will you accept us blending our homes for now?" The idea thrilled him but terrified him as well. Growing up, his father had supported him, but his mother and much of the family had treated him as broken. His mom still tried to baby him and often made him feel as if he were five again—if he was lucky. The thought of giving up his home… yeah, that was hard, but he did love Simon and wanted a life with him. "I'll move a few things in and we can work from there? Moving in means giving up my independence. I'll need to know how much to budget for my half of the mortgage and house expenses too."

Simon blinked at him a couple of times, then tilted his head to the side. "Mortgage?"

"Yes, you know, living together means I will share the costs with you. Partners?" *What the hell?* Adrian couldn't figure out the weird look Simon gave him then. Confusion, joy, confusion. Simon needed to pick one and stick with it before he gave Adrian a headache. "I'm not going to live off you."

"No, I know that. I do. Just, um, I don't have a mortgage or anything. I bought the house outright."

Adrian sighed and tried to figure out how to make Simon understand. "Okay, so no mortgage, but we will share expenses and such. Take turns buying groceries and all the normal living-together type things."

"But I don't need your money, love."

"Simon," he snapped, frustrated more than he thought he ought to be. "Partners share expenses, a home, responsibilities. If this conversation were between any of your friends, you'd expect them to share things, right? In your stories the couples pool resources and all. Don't they?"

Simon nodded, a look of pure wonder and joy crossing his face and staying, finally. "Of course! So that's a yes, right? If you want to be put on the deed and to share a home with me, our home, then you will move in."

"I agreed to that, though I won't move in all at once. I think you need time to adjust to having someone in your home like that, and I need to deal with giving up my home. Wait. Did you say you were putting me on the deed?" That couldn't be right. If he paid into the house, that would be one thing. If they bought it together.

"This will be our home. Now instead of worrying about money or houses, or even my psychotic family—who I still have to figure out how to deal with—come here and let's celebrate."

"Later, baby. For now, you really do need to eat, and the food's already prepped."

The excitement didn't clear from Simon's features as they worked to get dinner on the table. It was a simple meal, as Simon usually made, but it was delicious and filling. Adrian hoped to one day win Simon's complete trust, but then he still hoped to convince Simon he wasn't useless in the kitchen. When they went out, Simon always picked nice, often ritzy-slash-exclusive restaurants, so the home-cooking issue made little sense to Adrian. Well, it had until recently. If Zoey was a true representative of how Simon's family treated him, the lack of confidence started to make a lot more sense, sadly.

Food plated, they sat down to a nice meal of salmon, peppers, onions, and broccoli on a bed of brown-and-wild rice. The salad was delicious and the fish even better. The fact he had to prod Simon to eat, more than once, frustrated and worried him.

"You need to eat. I won't let your—that woman send you back to how you were when we first met. No starving yourself, please."

"I wasn't starving, Adrian." When Adrian continued to stare at Simon, his gaze occasionally flicking to the barely touched dinner, Simon finally picked up his fork and took a decent-sized bite. Once he chewed and swallowed, he waved his fork at the plate and said, "Happy?"

"Love you, Si. Let's hurry up? I want to show you how much."

Simon flushed all the way to his ears, but he nodded and ate. The realization he hadn't returned the words barely registered to Adrian. He was more concerned about getting Simon past this problem than anything.

Eventually they finished dinner. Adrian stood and tended to the dishes, rinsing them before placing them in the dishwasher. Once that was done, Simon dragged him back to the couch and straddled Adrian again. They picked up right where they'd left off, Simon grinding against Adrian, driving him insane. The sudden onslaught shorted out Adrian's already-muddled brain and left only lust.

Not liking how Simon took over, Adrian quickly lifted Si off of him and stood. He yanked Simon up, again kissing him, but this time, he used his slight height advantage and strength to devour his lover as he pushed him backward toward Si's—soon to be their—bedroom. They bumped into the coffee table and one of the chairs, but Adrian didn't pause in his plundering of Simon's mouth or in stripping Simon of his clothing as they moved.

When Simon suddenly stopped moving backward, Adrian realized he'd miscalculated and walked Si into the wall beside the door. Too into what he was doing, he instead pushed Simon against the wall harder, pinning Si's hands above his head with one hand, then dropping the other to tweak Simon's nipple.

Simon vibrated and thrust his dripping cock against Adrian's still fully clothed body. Simon vibrated nonstop, and Adrian knew Simon was making noise, probably begging, though he couldn't hear the words.

As far as Adrian could think, which wasn't much thanks to lust and the hot body thrusting against his, he didn't have condoms or lube close enough, so taking Simon against the wall was out—*dammit!* He quickly released Simon's wrists in exchange for grabbing Simon's butt and lifting, encouraging him to wrap his legs around Adrian. Simon weighed too much to go far like that, but he was certain he could at least get them to the bed.

He bumped Simon against the door before making it inside the room and to the large bed. Adrian pinned Simon beneath him, taking Si's lips again as he ground his clothed cock against Simon's. Eventually he managed to pull himself away. Clothed and without supplies was no way to celebrate anything, in his opinion.

Adrian moved back from Simon, then around the bed to get to the nightstand—and their supplies. "Si?"

"Huh?"

"If we're going to move in together, I want us to get tested." He held up, then tossed a condom and the bottle of slick beside Simon and quickly divested himself of his clothes. Simon reached out, his eyes glassy and his cock so hard it was near purple.

"I want that too. We can go soon."

Not wanting to delay any longer, Adrian prowled closer, climbing up onto the bed, then over to Simon, who grabbed ahold of him as soon as he was in reach.

Any thought of taking his time prepping Simon flew from his sex-addled mind when Simon grabbed the lube, squirted more than he should need into his hand, then spread his legs, reached between, and speared himself on two wet fingers. The sight of his lover impaling himself added an extra layer of need to Adrian, even more so when Simon withdrew his fingers. Simon snatched the condom from where it still sat beside him, ripped the package open with his teeth, and quickly rolled it down Adrian's length. The simple touches drove him crazier. Mere moments later, Si grasped Adrian's needy cock, using the rest of the lube to ease his hand down Adrian's now covered cock.

Before Adrian could come, he batted Simon's hand away. He took only the briefest of pauses before he thrust home, not stopping until he was fully seated. The way Simon arched against him, mouth open and using his legs to force Adrian deeper, made holding back near impossible.

Usually Adrian made sure Simon was ready, but right then that was impossible. Instead, he bent forward and took Simon's mouth again as he pounded Simon into the mattress. Push-pull. Thrust-withdraw. It seemed to take forever yet not nearly enough time when Simon stiffened, arched backward, and came, shooting hot and wet between them. The feel of Simon's already-tight hold clamping around Adrian, milking him, sent Adrian over the edge.

Screaming and thrusting, he spent himself inside Simon, his beloved, never taking his eyes off Simon's face.

When they both calmed and Adrian softened, he slipped out of Simon's body carefully. He then quickly tended to the condom before fetching a warm, damp washcloth and a dry towel. Simon watched him as Adrian took care of him, cleaning him, then drying him before tossing the soiled clothes into the hamper.

"Come here," Simon said and pulled on Adrian's hand.

Adrian climbed back onto the bed and settled himself, then curled his arm until Simon was partly on top of him. "We'll work on details tomorrow, Si. For now, sleep just where you are," Adrian murmured, hoping his words were loud enough to be heard but still soft.

Simon nodded against his chest. Adrian smoothed his free hand up and down Simon's shoulder and side until Si's breathing evened out. Adrian knew there were still issues to work out, many his own, but for that moment, he couldn't think of anything more than how he felt for Simon as sleep overtook him.

chapter twenty

SIMON STOOD in the kitchen, staring at his assembled items, and wished James or Chase was there to help. Since the whole issue was that he was making breakfast for not only his lover, but his closest friends as well, if either man was there, he'd be behind schedule already. Besides, he could do this without help, dammit.

Shaking off the circular thoughts, he flipped on his iPod and set it in the dock, smiling when Muse came blaring out of the small but powerful speakers. He chopped the various vegetables and put them into individual bowls to keep them all ordered. After receiving James's text earlier asking if he should bring anything and that he, Chase, Rhys, and Dale would be over soon, Simon decided build-your-own omelets sounded like a good idea.

He turned and pulled open the fridge again, shaking his head. Omelets needed eggs, he reminded himself as he pulled them out and set them on the counter to warm to room temperature. Simon wondered if he should text Airy and Teague but thought that better left up to Adrian.

The night before flitted through his mind, and the realization that this would soon be *their* house, not just his, thrilled him. The blending of homes, lives, and friends worried him a little, though. If Simon was being honest with himself, he was worried about a lot of things right then; however, their menagerie of friends wasn't actually high on the list. That he'd not only asked Adrian to move in but had agreed to get tested and possibly give up condoms was much higher on his list. Whatever was going on with his sister and parents was also high.

Simon still had trouble wrapping his mind around the idea that his sister had tried to buy off Adrian. How could she think so little of both of them? He knew she was rabidly homophobic, as were his parents, but still, it was insane. Simon hadn't completely decided if he was put out with Adrian for telling Chase what was going on before him or not. The fact his friends were coming over to brainstorm and rally around him and Adrian thrilled him, but he wished Adrian had told him first. Of course, knowing Adrian had his friends on call if Simon had needed them comforted him greatly.

The loud knock, accompanied by the doorbell ringing, effectively pulled him out of his questions and worry. He wiped his hands on the dishtowel, then tossed it on the counter next to his preparations and went to open the door. Simon grinned as he took in all of his closest friends—except Vaughn, and now Dal and Alex. He knew Seth had stayed home with Danni, Seth and James's daughter, so he didn't worry about his absence in the assembled group on his front steps.

"Come in, guys."

They all filed past, giving him their various *hi*s and hugs. Just as he closed the door, he heard a startled gasp and turned. Adrian stood in the bedroom doorway, mouth slightly open as he stared at the group settling in around the room. He'd only pulled on his slacks—zipped but not buttoned so the top band of his burgundy boxer-briefs was visible—and he wore no shirt or shoes, his hair still sexily mussed. His almond-shaped, vibrant green eyes widened as he looked from man to man. A slight flush tinted his lightly tanned cheeks before he quickly excused himself and fled back into the bedroom, the door closing immediately.

"Didn't you tell him we were coming over?" Chase asked, his shoulders shaking as he looked from the now-closed door to Simon.

"He knew. I just didn't realize he would be embarrassed like that. Most men don't think much of being half-dressed around others." That Adrian had been embarrassed made Simon curious about why.

"That's just because he was barely dressed," James teased from where he already sat on the couch. He looked around a moment, brows scrunching as he did. "Hey, thought we were eating, then brainstorming how to shove your sister off a tall building?"

"We are, greedy. I have everything prepped in the kitchen. I was going to get Adrian up and out here in just a moment, but you guys arrived before I could."

"That's okay," Chase said and bounced on his toes. "What's on the menu? You only said to bring eggs."

"I told *James* to bring more eggs, actually. And we're having omelets. Let me go drag Adrian out here, and then we can commence with the cooking and eating."

Before James had found Seth, they'd had a standing date at least every other Saturday to get together for breakfast. Often that was easy as they'd crashed at each other's apartments, but in the last while, they had had to resort to planning their "family" breakfasts. Even when they'd been dating others, they never failed to get together. Since the inclusion of partners and husbands, they still did, so it wasn't as if no one in the room hadn't been a regular in Simon's home.

"You go get him and I'll start the food. Just no undressing him to dress him." Chase giggled as he walked into the kitchen, Rhys not far behind, his head shaking as usual.

Just as Simon went to open the bedroom door, Adrian opened it and stepped out. He was dressed in jeans now with a hunter green long-sleeved T-shirt and a pair of black socks. His shoes were by the couch still, but neither one usually wore shoes inside, so Adrian wouldn't have had shoes in the bedroom to put on anyway. Of course, that made Simon think about having to set up the other master closet for Adrian—a thought that made him smile.

"Hi, love," Simon said and signed. "Let's go join them and eat."

Adrian bent and pressed his lips to Simon's in a barely there kiss and smiled. "Okay, but remember to have them speak so I can see what's being said."

"I will," Simon promised, then laced their fingers together. They walked to the living room, where most of the guys were sitting around on the various pieces of furniture. Adrian said hi before Simon and he tried to go help in the kitchen. Chase wouldn't let them, shooing them back out to the living room. He had, as usual, taken over the kitchen. As Adrian had done before, he insisted on taking the chair farthest from the others so he could see better. Simon wanted to sit with him but understood Adrian's need to see what was said.

They all chatted a bit, though everyone seemed to want to wait for breakfast before delving into the reason for the morning powwow. Simon wasn't sure if that was better or worse, as his stomach was twisted up again, though not nearly as bad as it had the night before as he knew where he stood with Adrian. He also knew his friends would stand by him, no matter what his sister or parents tried to do.

Dale rifled through Simon's games and movies, but otherwise everyone seemed fine to listen to music and just catch up on the week. Simon wished Adrian could hear the music with him. Honestly, he couldn't imagine a silent world, not with how important music was to him, but he knew the idea of sound had to be strange for Adrian.

"So everyone ready to eat?" Chase said from the kitchen doorway. "We've got omelets, fresh fruit, and cinnamon-raisin toast."

"Um, where'd the fruit and toast come from, hon?" Simon had fruit and bread, but not enough fruit for everyone and not that kind of bread.

"Brought it in with the eggs. Stop staring at Adrian long enough to notice the world around you, and you'd have seen the bags we brought in with us." Chase grinned and giggled when Simon pouted at him. "Now come on, you ingrates, it's food time."

Much grumbling followed but soon turned to sounds of happy men when they tasted Chase's cooking. Simon frowned at his omelet. His never tasted that good. "Thank you for cooking, Chase."

"Yes, thank you," Adrian added in that sexy, low voice of his. "It's very good."

"You're quite welcome, both of you," Chase replied with voice and hands. If Adrian was there, Chase always signed, even if Adrian couldn't see him. Simon thought it sweet, though he refused to say so.

"Now that we've mostly finished, is it okay to bring up *why* we're here this early?" Dale asked.

Adrian frowned and looked from Simon to Dale.

"Dale, you know Adrian's Deaf. Talk where he can see your lips," Simon chastised. He explained what Dale wanted to Adrian, then added, "But yeah, as soon as we're done, we can talk about the why."

Just for being rude to Adrian, Dale was stuck with dish duty—not that it was hard since he only had to rinse them off and load the dishwasher. In no time they settled back in the living room, coffee cups clutched in everyone's hands.

Simon made sure he was in Adrian's sight, then began. "Zoey stopped by Adrian's office last night to try to pay him to leave me. He, of course, told her no."

"Actually, I told her *no* more than once, then had her led away." Adrian grinned after his announcement.

"Really?" James asked. "Wish I could have seen that."

"That I can arrange." Simon dug out his cell, and once the image was on the screen, he passed it around the room. "I can't believe she'd do that. Well, if it were anyone but my family, I wouldn't believe it. But she's started this now, and I need to figure out how to stop it. Not that I don't have faith in Adrian—" He paused to smile at Adrian. "—but I don't want her trying to use her money or political friends to hurt his career or anything, either."

"I told you," Adrian countered and frowned. "She can't hurt me, and I don't want her money."

"No," Rhys rumbled. "We none think you would or I promise you, the guys here would have done everything they could to split you up. They don't play around with their friends' hearts or lives. However, that doesn't mean she couldn't try to hurt you in other ways. The university isn't likely to cave and let her start trouble. They have too much to lose, and a reputation of inclusively and honor they won't want tarnished. However, if you have loans, a landlord, even your family might become a target if his family is determined enough to push this."

"I won't allow that to happen to him or his family," Simon snapped. No way would he allow his insane family to hurt Adrian or his parents. *Not gonna happen!*

"No one said you would. None of us will, so chillax." Dale frowned at Simon. Hard. "I may not get why you want one partner instead of fun, but none of us will allow that. Besides, you have James—married to a man in the same league as your asshat of a family. James, whose art is sold by the wife of one of the top lawyers in the area. Rhys, a damn good PI, and who has a shit-ton of money, even if he never shows it. Me." He grinned. "Chase, who could delete them all from anything linked to a computer. And a soon-to-be hotshot lawyer. Well, once Dal gets through UC and all that."

Simon slow-panned from Dale's minispeech to his other friends, wondering if any of them were as shocked by Dale's outburst as he was. "Dale, hon, I appreciate all that, but since when do you care about my love life?"

"Since I met you, ya git." Dale crossed his arms and glared. "You're one of my best friends."

"Yeah," James interjected. "But you've never shown much concern about our love interests and such. I mean, you helped us keep Simon from being too alone and depressed after his last breakup, but...."

"I'm not heartless. I just don't get the monogamy thing. But instead of everyone looking at me like I grew a third head—two's enough, thanks—has anyone spoken to Zoey or Si's parents?"

Shaking his head, Simon replied, "No. Last night I was preoccupied, and this morning I worried about everyone coming over. Not that I'm sure what I want to say to them or even if my parents will take my call."

"Si," Adrian said, "maybe calling your parents wouldn't be such a bad idea. They can't want it known that one of theirs would stoop to bribery. Even if they are okay with what your sister did, they won't like it known about. Maybe go that route?"

"That's not a bad idea," Rhys added. "I did a lot of digging last night, as did Chase, and a couple of their closer buddies have been brought up on bribery and corruption charges recently. Another on blackmail. They will not like that idea. Also, I really don't think they would be behind this. They seem convinced homosexuality is a disease and perversion, but kidnapping you to force you into a conversion camp seems more their style than throwing money at your lover. Have they threatened to disinherit you or cut you out of any wills, trusts, et cetera?"

"No, and that really would be more their thing. They don't yet realize that even if they did, it wouldn't affect me financially. I have a trust fund I couldn't spend all of if I tried that my grandfathers set up together—my parents never could touch a cent of it, even when I was a kid. I make decent money as an author. In addition, my grandparents and an aunt that passed away in the last few years all left me tidy sums. However, they've never bothered to try. Just ignore me, refuse to acknowledge me, and such."

Simon noticed Adrian's eyes widen. They had never talked specifics of money, but once they were full partners, Adrian would understand all he had and owned. Adrian ignored his money usually, so the look didn't worry him too much. "Love?"

"Guess I didn't realize you had such money or connections. I don't care about the money, just didn't realize it."

"Money makes life easier, but it's not the key to happiness. My parents and sister are great examples of that. But I'll show you my financials later if you like."

"You ready to do that?" James asked, a soft smile on his face.

Simon nodded and grinned. "Adrian has agreed to move in with me, well, over a few months, but if we're going to be real partners and live together, he should know." He took in the wide eyes of some of his friends and added, "Right?"

Chase bounded up and over to Simon and threw his arms around his neck. "I'm so happy for you!"

Adrian chucked. "I can't even hear and I know that was damn loud, Chase."

Chase pulled away enough to pout at Adrian. "So? I'm thrilled for you both. Now aren't you glad we didn't work out?"

"Actually, I am. You're a great friend, and I love Simon very much."

"I'm glad too," Rhys added and laughed. "Since Simon was one of those that helped sabotage Chase's attempts to date anyone other than me, I'm glad he's found you. Now do you want to call your parents, Si, or do you want us to set this up as a lawyer-fueled intervention?"

"Let me try first. If that doesn't work, we'll sic the lawyers on Zoey." She'd learn to stay out of his relationship one way or another.

James asked with a totally innocent face that Simon knew was completely fake, "But would we call Mel or one of your lawyers?"

"Mel is one of my lawyers, James. Well, he is now, at least." Mel Holcomb was Seth Burns's best friend from university and the husband of the little spitfire who managed James's art career. He was also a top lawyer and ruthless as the day was long. No one survived against Mel, one of the reasons Simon liked him and his law firm so much. He'd not needed them much, but they never failed him.

"Oh really?" he asked, head cocked to the side.

"Yeah. I met him thanks to you dating Seth. I hired him and his firm before your wedding. That's not really the point, though. Yes, I will call. Yes, Adrian will be moving in. And yes, I'm ecstatic!"

"We'll have to throw you a housewarming party when it's final," Chase said, signing something else to Adrian than what he said. Simon couldn't read it all but knew that wasn't what he'd said.

"That's rude," Adrian said and signed. "Simon knows it too," he added, glaring at Chase. "Say what you signed or I will."

Chase gave a huge sigh but replied, "I asked Adrian if he was ready for that and if Simon was really moving forward that much. I didn't mean to be rude, I swear, but we all know how skittish Si is about lovers. I'm thrilled but also more than a bit shocked."

"Chase!" Rhys growled. "He didn't question you on your choice of lover, even came over with James and Dal to threaten me if I hurt you once. How could you question them like that?"

"I don't. I swear." Chase put his hands up in surrender. "I just wasn't sure Simon would ever move someone in. I'll call Alex and see about setting up a menu for the party, though."

"You don't have to do that, you know." Simon didn't like that Chase would ask Adrian that, much less do it in sign with him right there, but he also understood. Simon had never lived with a boyfriend, much less talked about showing his lover his financial standing. He wondered how his friends would react if he told about the testing but didn't want to share that bit. That was personal and private. Period.

"No, I know, but they will be thrilled for you too. You know that. Forgive me?"

He counted to twenty in his head before saying, "Of course. Like I could stay mad at any of you?"

Having to call his parents gnawed at him horribly, but knowing his friends were behind him *and* Adrian made all the difference. He could fully breathe again and focus on Adrian's yes instead of Zoey's bribe attempt.

They all hung out for most of the rest of the day. Simon planned to call his parents that evening when it was just him and Adrian again but didn't want to send his friends home yet. A little over an hour later, Airy and Teague joined them and were just as happy for Adrian and him as Simon's own friends had been. Airy was a little nervous about the idea Adrian would give up his home, but that passed quickly once he spent time with Simon and his friends.

Simon didn't talk as much as normal, happy to sit on Adrian's lap and lean against him for much of the day. The time to deal with stupid people would come soon enough, and basking in Adrian's love was far more important than anything else was for him.

chapter twenty-one

AFTER THEIR friends left, Simon did everything humanly possible not to call his parents, or so it seemed to Adrian. They had to eat, and then they needed couple time. Then he wanted to nibble on Adrian's neck. Then the knowledge that Simon was supposed to call flew out of Adrian's head. He didn't remember a thing about important calls until the next morning when he awoke with Simon curled against him so tight he thought Simon was trying to merge with him—and not in the fun way he had the night before.

Adrian wanted to wake his lover but worried Simon simply wasn't ready to deal with his family issues. The previous night had been fun, and he would never tire of how responsive and sensual Simon was, he was certain. However, he didn't think putting things off wouldn't help Si any. Still, the thought of the tense, brooding Simon returning didn't make him eager to wake Si and start the day. He had to, though; he had things to do that wouldn't allow him to sit at home with Simon all day.

The thought of this being his home made him smile. This would be their home. No more going home after a night with Simon to a cold, empty house. He just hoped Simon could really deal with sharing space with him like that.

Pushing his worries to the side, Adrian curled around Simon a little more and brushed his lips across Si's cheek, then ear, hoping to wake his love gently.

Simon sighed and snuggled into Adrian's side more, his nose scrunched. He watched, but Simon didn't stir again, so Adrian trailed the backs of his fingers up Simon's throat and neck to his ear, then traced the shell before bending to place a soft kiss there. When that didn't elicit the desired response, he sucked Si's lobe between his teeth and bit gently.

That got Si's attention. He opened his eyes and smiled up at Adrian. "Hi, love," Simon said, signing the "love" part.

"Morning." Adrian continued to trace Simon's skin, shifting to go down his arm instead of his neck. "How do you feel today?"

A light flush spread up Simon's face and down his neck. "A little sore, but good."

Adrian grinned. "Sore in a good way, right?"

Simon nodded. "Yes, a very good way."

"Good. You want breakfast soon? I have things I have to do today, so I can't lounge in here all day, though—" Adrian took Simon's lips in a light kiss, nipping his bottom lip before pulling back. "—staying would be much more fun."

"Right, work." Simon's lips turned down at the corners a moment. "Can you wait a little? Stay while I make a call or two?"

"Of course. I wouldn't leave you to do that alone. But it has to be in the next hour or so. Students get really upset when teachers don't show up."

"I'd have been thankful with most of mine. I swear, I had all the old, ugly, crotchety ones that hated anyone under about sixty. But I guess that means we have to get up, huh?"

He hated to make Simon get out of bed, but yeah, he had to. "Sorry, Si. You can stay in bed and we can eat breakfast in bed together, but then I have to go."

Simon shook his head. "No. Let's get up. Delaying would be nice but won't help any. Besides, I have edits waiting on me that I should have done two days ago but got a little distracted."

"Okay. Let me go grab a shower, and then we can make breakfast." He curled one hand behind Simon's head and held him still, then swept in and delved inside Simon's sweet lips. He tasted and teased for a moment but pulled away rather than start another round of sex. The previous night had been fun, as always, but they didn't have time right then. "I'll be right out," Adrian added, then kissed the tip of Si's nose before stretching and getting out of bed.

Simon's gaze didn't leave Adrian as he left the room. Adrian put a little extra wiggle into his walk as he entered the bathroom to shower, shave, and get dressed. He'd have to stop by his house and change properly, as he hadn't intended to spend both nights when he grabbed clothes the other night. He turned and gave Simon a wink before he closed the door and dropped his smile.

Adrian didn't linger, not wanting to waste the limited time he'd have with Simon that day. His mind spun the whole time as he worried about how the call with Simon's parents would go. They might have been in on Zoey's visit. They might not know. They might approve. They might not. She might have been behind the text. She might not. When he flipped the shower off, he worked to shut off his worries, knowing Simon didn't need to see his concerns. Simon needed his support only.

As he dried off, the scent of bacon tickled his nose, making him hurry to get out to Si and breakfast. He took the time to be careful shaving as he used a straight razor, not an electric or Bic-like one and didn't feel like bleeding just for some fried piggy.

Once dressed and ready, Adrian left the bathroom, having hung up the towel and mat. He looked, but Simon had made the bed already. *Guess that means the call won't be made while in here.* Shrugging, he left the room and walked directly to the kitchen. Adrian stopped in the doorway and leaned against the jam, watching Simon dancing around as he cooked. He was certain he'd never get tired of watching Simon, no matter what he was doing, but someday he wanted to take Simon somewhere Si could dance while he watched. Only problem was, everyone else would want Si too, something that didn't thrill Adrian. The picture sent to his phone flashed through his mind, as it often did, and he resolved to find somewhere to take Simon.

Simon turned and grinned. He put the spatula down and signed, *"Hi, love. Hungry?"*

That's interesting. No speaking? Just sign. *"Yes! Need help?"*

"No." Simon then pointed to the table and quirked one side of his lips, eyes dancing.

"I'll set the table."

In no time, it seemed, they sat down to bacon, eggs, and hash browns. Juice and coffee were both at the ready as well. *"Thank you, Si."* Adrian speared a bit of egg, the yolk thick and gooey and tasty. *"Yum!"*

Adrian tucked in and enjoyed the time with Simon. Si reached out to touch Adrian's hand every so often as they ate. He smiled at Simon every time, knowing Simon needed the support he was building between them for after breakfast. He loved how touchy Simon was, how he never fussed about the lack of talking while eating, and well, he simply loved Simon.

FOOD GONE, dishes done, Simon sat next to Adrian on the couch and stared at his cell. It was just a little bit of plastic and electronic parts, but the thought of talking to his parents made him nauseous. Nothing new there, but this time Adrian would see and feel Simon's reaction. At least he wouldn't be able to hear if Simon's voice raised or went out on him.

"Si, it will be okay," Adrian said and signed. "Just get it over with. Fretting is likely to be far worse than the call itself."

Yeah, he knew that. He did, but telling the tornado in his stomach that didn't help any. Still, Adrian was right, and he wanted to do this while Adrian was still here so if it went bad, at least he wouldn't be alone. The thought made him feel like a teen, but he didn't care. "Okay. Here goes."

Simon picked his phone up and hit the button for "parental units—do not answer." *Ring. Ring. Ring.* On the fourth ring, it was answered. "Hello, Simon," Betty's smooth voice said. "You don't usually call the main number. What's wrong, baby?"

Yeah, he didn't. Betty was the housekeeper and only one of two people in his parents' house who he missed. She always had a kind word and a smile for him, even as a child. Simon smiled at the memories. "I know I don't, but then no one usually answers it if it's me."

"I do, if I'm closer. But that's not an answer. You wouldn't call the house without a good reason. You'd have called me direct if I was why you're calling."

"Too true." He sighed and worked hard to stay calm—ish. "Are my parents home? I need to speak with one, or possibly both about a situation with Zoey." There, that didn't sound too bad. Right?

"What's she done now?"

"It's a strange story but one I'm not up to explaining more than once. If the units aren't in on it, I'm sure you'll hear all about it soon. I'll call you later and explain it all, but…." Simon took a deep breath and let it out slowly. "Are they home?"

"All right, but I'll hold you to that talk. They are both home, actually, though not in the same parts of the house. Would your father or mother be preferable?"

The edge of worry in her voice was both soothing and worrisome at the same time. She'd always been his favorite. "Father, probably. Don't want to talk to either, but...."

"I know, but it's obviously important. Let me announce you. Anything you wish me to tell him, to maybe get him to actually pick up?"

He found it sad that the housekeeper knew how bad his parents were. He also knew the biggest reason she stayed. Money. His parents were lousy people, but they paid very well and provided health insurance, vacation pay, and bonuses to their household employees. "That it's about Zoey and possible legal problems for her. That should get his attention and is true."

Betty gasped but agreed to his request. He thanked her and then waited.

"What are you threatening your sister over, boy?" his father, Theodore Francis Tyler, demanded.

"I've not yet threatened her, but if she tries to buy my partner off again, she may find out that I may be a Tyler on the outside, but not one without powerful friends. Father," he added as an afterthought. Coming off weak would only have his father ignoring him, he knew that all too well. He hated to attack, it not being in his nature, but he wasn't going to put up with her or their meddling.

"Excuse me?" Theo roared. "How dare you threaten your sister? She's a decent and upstanding woman."

"No, she's someone that would stoop to the level of trying to bribe my partner with money to leave me. She may also have been responsible for having me followed and photographed a few months ago. Is that what you've taught her?" He fought the urge to yell or throw the phone. *Upstanding my ass!* "That throwing money at people will fix it all? I will not have Adrian treated that way."

"I don't want to hear about your perversions."

"I said *bribery* and possible attempted *blackmail*, and there's nothing about me that's perverted, thank you very much." Well, nothing he'd admit to the asshat who spawned him. "She was even overheard, so there's no hope it was 'a misunderstanding,' Father."

"Bribery? Blackmail? I would never condone that. I don't approve of your choices, but why throw money away on your life? That makes no sense."

"Being gay isn't a choice. It's who I am." Simon glanced at Adrian, who'd been running his hand up and down Simon's back. He gave a slight smile and linked their free hands together. "But what she did was a choice, and a very poor one. I want her stopped and to have no further contact with Adrian. He doesn't deserve being insulted like that. Neither do I."

"Wait," Theo said quieter. "You think I put her up to that? You know me better than that. I refuse to condone what you are, but I've never denied you your right to live as you chose."

"Actually, you do. Every time you call for a reversal of gay rights, you try to deny me basic rights based on who I am. Every time you call me sick or perverted, you try to deny me the right to live, love, and be happy in life. However, I'm not calling to rehash things with you. You have no interest in my life, but I'm sure you don't want a scandal if your beloved daughter is brought up on charges. Or it's leaked to the news how she harassed a Deaf man and tried to buy him off. That won't look good on her or you."

Simon didn't care if it looked good or not, just that it stopped.

"Deaf? You're involved—" The word seemed to choke his father a moment. "—with a Deaf man?"

"Yes, not that his deafness matters in the least, but I'm certain she insulted him for that as well. He wouldn't admit it, but he wouldn't deny it, either." The fact she'd belittled Adrian for being Deaf had hurt more than knowing she'd gone after Adrian in the first place. But then he'd seen her belittle others for perceived disabilities when they were kids. She hadn't changed, sadly.

The sigh that came through the phone gave Simon hope. His father never made that sound unless he was either disappointed or giving in on something.

"We didn't raise either of you to belittle those less fortunate than yourselves."

"He's not less," Simon said forcefully, though managed to not yell, barely. "Simply Deaf. He's smart, kind, caring, a professor, concerned with others, not only himself. Nevertheless, even if he wasn't, she had no right, and I won't allow him to be treated that way again. He had her led off the campus a couple of nights ago, so I'm surprised you haven't heard from her already."

"Bet she was in a right state," his father said, then chuckled slightly. "Look, you know how I feel about your lifestyle, but I would not condone that kind of behavior. Besides, bribe once and you have to continue or it would come out later and then bite you in the ass. That's not logical. I'll talk to her. But...."

"But what?" Don't stop there!

"But I'm glad he said no to her. That shows good character on his part. I can't be happy you are with a man, but I can be happy you picked someone that is better than that."

Simon swallowed. That was the nicest thing his father had said to him since he was a young teen. When he thought he could get the words out without choking on them, he replied, "Thank you. Adrian is very special and.... Thank you, Father."

"Was that all?"

Yeah, that was more the man he expected, clipped tone and impatience. "Yes, it was. I'm glad it was only Zoey doing this. Um, did you and Mom get the gifts I sent for your anniversary?"

"We did. Would have been nice to have you at the party, though."

"With my partner on my arm?"

"You could have come alone."

"No, Father, I couldn't have. I won't hide who I am or whom I love. Adrian deserves more than to be hidden just so I can seem respectable to you and your friends. Pops and Gramps would have killed me, were they still alive, if I'd tried." His maternal and paternal grandfathers both had known he was gay and didn't give a care. Sadly, both their children gave enough cares and fucks for the whole family.

"Perhaps. Well, you have books to write, and I have a corporate world to conquer. I will talk to Zoey. Would-would you like me to tell your mother anything?"

Maybe the man was thawing? Could that happen? "Yes, sir. Could you tell her I hope she had a great anniversary and that I love her?"

"I will tell her, son. I wish you'd make other choices and come home, though, so you could tell her yourself."

"I won't lie about who I am or apologize for who I love, but that doesn't mean I don't care. Thank you for telling her and for speaking with me."

"Bye, son."

"Bye."

Simon hung up and swallowed, repeatedly, trying to make sense of the conversation. That was the most civil talk they'd had in a decade, at least. What the hell? He wanted to be happy but still hated that he wasn't welcome in his own family.

He was brought out of his musings when Adrian tapped him on the shoulder. "You okay, Si?" he asked.

Simon nodded, then looked up and said, "Yeah. He claims he didn't okay her doing that to you. I actually believe him. I also insinuated that she may have been behind the photo text. I don't know if she was, but I think Chase might have been right about it being about driving you away from me." He took a couple of deep breaths before he continued speaking and signing. "But the call wasn't as bad as usual. He was almost nice. Still against me being gay but not rabidly spouting like normal."

"So it was just your sister doing that? That's good, right?"

"Yes. He said he'd talk to her, which should stop her. No way she wants him mad at her. She knows if he turns on her, it's likely to be permanent. She saw how fast they dropped me when they learned I'm gay."

"Well, they may drop you, but I'll be here to catch you, babe. Always." Adrian pulled Simon into his arms and peppered his face with barely there kisses until Simon squirmed, laughing.

"Love you," Simon said, then curled against Adrian and held him until it was time to leave. Simon hated watching Adrian leave, but this time he knew Adrian would be back later and that soon, this would truly be *their* home.

chapter twenty-two

SIMON WAS on cloud nine. The last couple of weeks had been better than he'd have imagined. He'd set up the other walk-in closet for Adrian, had already gotten the house set up for Adrian's needs, and Adrian had even brought some of his things over. Not a lot, but enough to make the "yes" real to Simon.

The only part that wasn't good right then was that Chase and Rhys were missing. They were all to meet just inside the gates of PrideFest in Milwaukee, and everyone else was there, even Dal, Alex—sporting the most adorable little spring dress and low heels, his hair piled up high with little curling wisps framing his face—and Vaughn. Vaughn showing up at Simon's the night before had been a complete shock. He wasn't supposed to be back for another couple of weeks, or so he'd told everyone.

He'd nearly tackle-hugged Simon and then demanded to meet Adrian. When the two got along great, Simon had given a silent sigh of relief and said a quiet prayer of thanks to anyone listening. That all his friends liked Adrian thrilled him, not that he would have walked away if they hadn't, but it was much better this way.

Still, that two of their numbers were missing was not making any of them happy. Chase not answering any of their calls only worried them more. Chase always answered, no matter the time or what else was going on around him... or to him.

Simon loved going to PrideFest. It was huge, had tons of stuff to do, lots of people to see, drag queen and drag king shows, and music. He'd always stayed late with his friends, drinking and dancing all night at the "club" areas. He wasn't sure what he'd do that year as Adrian wouldn't want to just sit and watch him dance. Simon wouldn't ask him to, either.

But where the hell was Chase?

"Dal? Nothing from Rhys, either?" he asked, hoping Rhys's little brother would know what was going on.

"Nope. All I got was a text that said 'Not right now.' That's it. If it was something bad, he would have called or texted that he needed us." Dal's words were meant to relax them all, but the slight waver to his voice and the tightness around his eyes belied the confident words. The time Chase had been kidnapped probably ran through Dal's head, as he knew it did the rest of the group's.

"Simon, you know Chase and Rhys. If it was important, they would let us know," Seth said from behind James. The fact James had arrived in low-slung jeans, sneakers, a tight, blue, V-neck T-shirt, his rainbow forearm crutches, and his collar proudly on display thrilled Simon. James had bowed out the previous year. The platinum collar was still such a strange sight to Simon, and he knew it was for the rest of the group too.

"I do, but I also know how Chase is about the phone."

"Agreed," Vaughn said. "But making ourselves sick over whatever those two are up to won't do anyone any good. Why don't we look around some while we wait for them to show? The crowd is already a bit wild thanks to the gay marriage ban being overturned. I'm betting it will only get more so as the day wears on."

Dale snorted. "The 'love wins' stuff everywhere is a little much. Let's go party. When they get here, they can catch up."

"Seriously, Dale. You need to get over this commitment phobia you have." Dal didn't seem to like Dale's anticouple attitude, either. "But he's right about us not waiting. They can call or text when they arrive. They probably got *busy* and don't want to tell us that's why they're late," he added, then chuckled.

Adrian's hands slipped around Simon's hips as he stepped up behind him. He settled against Adrian's chest and smiled. Life was good. "Fine. We can do that, but if anyone hears from them, text the others. I want to—" Just then Simon saw Rhys and Grayson walking toward their group. He couldn't see Chase yet, but since Rhys was smiling and obviously being pulled along, he knew Chase was there and fine. "Speak of the devils, and it looks like they brought Grayson with them."

Simon waved, as did the others. When they got closer, and enough people moved out of the way, Simon finally saw Chase and stopped short of calling out. What the hell were they wearing? Both men were in suits, though with each man's signature style to them. Chase's showed how thin and fit he was, tailored to a tee. Rhys's was all elegance yet still carried the military crispness and edge Rhys always seemed to have, even this long after getting out of the Marines. Grayson wasn't dressed up as they were, thankfully, but his gaze, when he looked at the other two, was both soft and amused.

When they got close enough, Simon called out, "What's with the outfits? And where the *hell* have you been?" The chorus around him asked the same things, just with various wordings and tones and curiosity levels.

"Downtown getting this!" Chase exclaimed and showed off a... a marriage license?

James gasped, then yelled, "You fucking did not get married without us!"

"Of course not, you ninny. The ban was lifted. You know we'd said if it ever were, we'd get married. Well, big man woke me this morning with a proposal and all the paperwork needed already ready to go. We've been getting this all morning. The line was insane but...."

"We wanted to have it done here, with all of you," Rhys finished for Chase. His grin was just as out of control as Chase's. "Mark will be here in just a minute."

"I didn't know what was going on until Rhys woke me up yelling that if I'm coming, I need to get my ass in gear. Like I'd miss his wedding!" Grayson added, a look of humor and indulgence on his handsome face as he looked at his friend.

It suddenly dawned on Simon that there was no way Adrian could have understood all that. He shifted and signed everything to Adrian, who smiled wide and hurried over to Chase to hug him.

"So happy for you!" Adrian said, a huge grin on his face. He then stepped back and took Simon's hand.

After that it was a round robin of hugs for Chase and Rhys. To Simon's dismay, Dale kept his distance from Grayson after the hugs and congratulations were done. Dale still looked at Grayson with hunger and longing, but Simon also knew Dale was still refusing to acknowledge that he wanted Grayson.

"So where now?" James asked.

"To find someone who can do the legal part. I heard there were some clergy here willing to do weddings on the spot." Chase beamed, barely touching the ground as he walked. "So let's go hunt us a clergyman or woman and get hitched!"

They all laughed at Chase but dutifully headed out to find someone to perform the wedding. It didn't take long. Just walking down the horseshoe-shaped row of booths led them to more than one booth belonging to churches in town. One of the Lutheran ones even had a man in a cassock and collar.

By that point Mark—Rhys's business partner and other best friend—had joined them. They then walked down to the end of the festival grounds near the area where they found the priest. It was close to the lake and felt a little separated from the festival, yet not. They were still at PrideFest, but they were also a tight group nestled on the lake. They gathered in the area around their friends and waited as the priest began the short service. Chase and Rhys exchanged simple but sweet—and a little odd, but it wouldn't be them otherwise—vows.

When the priest presented them as Mr. Chase Manning-Sayer and Mr. Rhys Manning-Sayer, Chase lost control over his composure and tears slipped down his cheeks.

"I don't have a wedding present for you yet, guys." Pop a wedding on him like that! "But we'll do a huge reception for you. Though," Simon continued, frowning, "your parents are going to string you both up for this."

"No, they won't," Rhys defended. "We talked to them and promised to do something small for them later. Mom demanded we allow her to throw us a reception next week for us, but they understood why we wanted to do this here, now. Especially with no guarantee that the governor won't try to have a stop put to the licenses while the state appeals."

"He already said he'll try," Chase explained. "But Rhys wasn't going to let him spoil our day, so we're now legal," he added, squealing at the end. He stared down at his hand with the ring he and Rhys had exchanged at Christmas. Above that ring was another, thin band. They looked good together, as did the two men.

"Well, I'm thrilled for you. You going to go change or stay dressed up all night?" Simon asked.

"Oh, puh-lese. I have a bag in the car with our clothes. I can't dance in the pavilion like this!" Chase exclaimed, gesturing at his suit. "No way I'm ruining this or not dancing. I'll catch up in a few. I'm gonna go change and be right back." He looked down at his hand again and sighed, smiling.

Grayson stayed with Simon and the group, letting Rhys and Chase run off to change. They wandered the area, looking at all the booths. He stopped at one for the LGBT Center. They were doing photos with superhero capes and masks, so of course their group all had to have pics taken. Simon also hit the used-book-sale area also for the Center. As an author, he always loved supporting literacy, and the sale of the books went for the Center's library fund. They owned a copy of all his books, as he'd donated them along with books by other authors he liked and thought would be enjoyed by others.

Adrian stayed with him the whole time. They signed together, and Simon helped to make sure Adrian always knew what those around him were saying. His ASL still wasn't fluent by any measure, but he was improving and determined. No way was he going to let Adrian be left out of things!

"Simon?" Adrian asked, getting his attention as they hunted for food a short while later while walking past the area where music and beer would flow late into the night.

"Yes?" Simon asked and signed.

"You going to dance later? I know Chase said he was."

"I don't have to, love. We can go whenever you want." Simon wanted to go dance. He'd only been a couple of times since the incident with the anonymous photo, and he missed it. He wasn't about to make Adrian feel left out, though.

"No, we can go to the dance pavilion. I'll have a beer and watch you be all sexy. That picture sent to me was hot," Adrian said, the word *hot* low and growly. "I'd love to see you dance for real. Just...."

Adrian's gaze moved from Simon's to the ground.

"Just what, love?" Simon asked once he got Adrian to look up again.

"Just don't be too sexy with anyone but your friends. Please."

Don't be...? "Love, you're the only one I want to be sexy with. You know that, right?"

Adrian nodded but still seemed worried in Simon's opinion, though he couldn't put a finger on why he felt that way.

"Adrian. I know you saw me dancing with my friends that night in the picture you were sent." He'd still love to have confirmation that Zoey was behind the pic or to know who was. "But I never dance wild unless it's with my partner. You," he added, to make the point. "Or with my friends, whom I have never, ever, been involved with. We don't play together, and I don't play with anyone but you."

"Thank you," Adrian said and signed after swallowing a couple of times. "I really do want you to dance and have fun. I want to watch, and with how much vibration the music and dance area is putting out, I can feel the bass."

He knew that! Simon had learned a lot in his classes, but simple things like that often seemed to miss him completely. Adrian couldn't hear the music, but he could feel it; he couldn't dance, but if his leer was anything to go by, Simon was certain Adrian wanted to watch him dance.

Once he'd agreed to dance for Adrian, they hurried to catch up to their friends and pig out on oversized pretzels, then ice cream twists that resembled boats in Simon's opinion. He and Adrian split one and still had some left. It was the first time they'd done anything like that before.

They'd gone out, of course, but not with so many people around, the sounds, smells, and distractions a lot to deal with at times. And the outfits? One guy walked by wearing nothing but a thong with a tail attached and little fox ears on his head. Others in full drag with stark white faces with wild makeup, in interesting modifications of nun's habits. The first he didn't know, the second he did. That person was one of the Sisters of Perpetual Indulgence running around the PrideFest grounds. There were people of every class, type, race, orientation, presentation, and then some. He loved his community!

People-watching was beyond a blast at the annual event, but this year he had someone to share it all with who was more to him than a friend. Simon was so thankful he didn't have to deal with his date spending more time drooling over other guys than over him. Adrian never made him feel inferior.

Adrian slipped his hand in Simon's opposite back pocket and squeezed lightly as they enjoyed the day. When the music got to them all and they decided to go dance, Simon asked Adrian if he was certain about watching. Adrian pulled him into a deep, possessive kiss before sending him out to dance. Simon watched as Adrian settled with a beer at one of the tables with a clear view of the dance area.

Deciding to stop second-guessing Adrian, Simon allowed himself to be pulled onto the dance floor and let the music wash across his skin and into him. He always felt free when dancing, and knowing Adrian watched him thrilled him more than he thought it should. He didn't care about anything right then but Adrian and the music.

He threw himself into the beat, letting it move him as it would, dancing with his friends. Anyone else who approached was shut down—even just dancing, he didn't want some stranger's hands on him. The longer he danced, the freer he felt, until the worries and fears of the last few months ceased to exist, only happiness and sound filling him.

After a few songs, Simon decided to go see how Adrian was and to maybe get another of his drugging kisses. He danced and shimmied until he could reach Adrian and smiled when he saw how Adrian looked at him. His eyes were hooded, his lips slightly parted, and his legs spread to show off the prominent bulge there. *Damn!* He'd have to remember dancing turned Adrian on and give him a private performance later.

Adrian didn't try to talk, for which Simon was thankful. No way would he have been able to hear him over the music and people. *"H. O. T. You move—"* He paused and cocked his head. *"—as if you have no bones. Sexy."*

The compliment sent a thrill through Simon. To know how turned-on he could make Adrian made him hard in return. His jeans were a little too tight for that to be comfortable. Simon decided instead of sitting beside Adrian to plop down in his lap.

"You sit like that too long and I'm going to take you home and strip you out of those indecent pants and put that cute little ass of yours to better use."

Oh, damn! Simon was certain he whimpered, though the sound would be lost in the noise around them. *"Let me tell the guys bye."*

"You can stay, Si."

"No, want you. Now!"

Before Simon could register what was happening, he was on his feet again and Adrian was standing as well. He whipped out his cell and typed furiously, then looked up and grinned.

"Let's go. I sent everyone a text." Adrian turned his cell around, and sure enough, there was a message saying he was taking his sexy lover home and they could call Simon in the morning. Late.

Simon grinned, and once Adrian put his cell away, he linked hands with Adrian and hurried from the pavilion and back out to the street and

174

to the car. He'd driven and parked in the closest parking lot open, so they didn't have too far to walk. Walking to his car late at night downtown had never thrilled him. With the news of the ban lifted, he'd also worried there would be people picketing and the like. He'd seen some out trying to preach at those attending, but nothing major, and they were easily ignored.

It was hard, but he behaved driving home, not wishing to run into any cops. The only thing he was interested in was whatever Adrian had in mind for once they were home. By the time he pulled into the driveway, he was so hard and eager his jeans hurt and his body vibrated. Thankfully Adrian didn't waste time. As soon as they were inside the house, he reminded Simon of how it felt to be taken against the wall. They had stashed lube around the house, and so the wall, the floor, the couch, and eventually the bed were reintroduced to Simon as Adrian filled him again and again. He didn't even remember cleaning up that last time, just pleasure then nothing as sleep claimed him.

epilogue

ADRIAN COULDN'T believe he'd let his partner talk him into going to the UWM Drag Ball put on by the university there in Milwaukee. It was all about music and, well, he couldn't hear the music, and he didn't think it would be turned up loud enough in the theater to allow him to feel it, so other than admiring the queens and kings on stage, he was at a loss for why he was going.

No, he knew why. Simon had given his best puppy-dog eyes when he asked Adrian to go with him. And, well, it was for a good cause. He always gave money to the local community programs for the LGBT+ kids, teens, and disadvantaged people. This would simply be the first time he did so to music.

"Come on, lazy bug," Simon said and signed. His signing had improved so much since his first early attempts, though he still searched for words at times. That he'd even tried to learn was enough for Adrian, but the reality of how hard Si worked to improve was more than amazing to him.

Lazy? Yeah, that was pushing it. "Whatever!" Adrian replied, putting as much attitude and whole-body movement into the sign as he could physically manage.

He looked at his outfit in the full-length mirror in his walk-in closet. They'd been living together for four months, and he loved sharing his space and life with Simon. Still, he peeked at the mirror again and sighed. He had no idea what others were going dressed like, but Simon looked amazing. Adrian felt a bit lackluster next to him. The tight black jeans paired with his best cashmere, hunter green sweater and the black-and-green Chucks on his feet were nice.

As he looked over at Simon again, Adrian glared. Simon stood there looking as yummy as he had their first date. Actually, he was wearing the same funky pea coat he had that night. Simon had paired it with a chocolate-colored silk T-shirt that brought out his eyes and sinfully low black pants that defied gravity to stay up. It was freezing outside, but Simon looked like he was going clubbing, not to a show in winter.

Adrian blinked again and realized that, yes, Simon had the new makeup he'd recently started wearing on, including some sort of dark eyeliner. It made him wince even to think of a pencil near his eyes, but on Simon, it looked *so* good. It had been another growth point for Simon, to dress and act how he wanted to when he went places other than to his friends' homes or to the clubs. Keeping his admiration off his face was harder than it ought to be, but Adrian worked at it—otherwise, Simon would run all over him, as he was totally and completely addicted to Simon as it was.

"Fine. Not lazy. Actually, you look pretty hot. Nevertheless, you will not tempt me into missing tonight. I love going to this and have gone for years. Tonight, you will be there with me, which will make the whole thing even better."

Well.... "I'm glad you're so excited. You're sure there will be an interpreter there?" Honestly, he knew there would be, he'd checked, but he was still nervous.

"Oh yeah. In fact, they're often nearly as fun to watch, though I never understood what all went into what they did." Simon's smile widened. "And you have not lived until you've seen one of the drag queens that always attends. You'll wonder where she tucks it all for the next year! And so hot you'll wonder if you might like to try playing for the other side at least once."

Adrian wasn't sure that was a good thing, but he guessed he'd just have to go and find out. "Well, that sure would make things interesting," he teased, loving the hot look Simon gave him.

Yeah, Si would always have a jealous streak, but as Adrian was just as possessive of Simon, that suited him just fine.

"Ready?" he asked before Simon could get too obsessed.

"Always for you."

Dammit! Simon always said the sappiest things and got to Adrian so fast. He always had, and he hoped Simon always would. He reached to take Simon's hand as they left to drive downtown and was again caught by the thrill seeing Simon's ring on his finger always gave him. The same night as the reception for Chase and Rhys, Simon had pulled him aside and presented him with what Simon called a promise ring. The ring was platinum, the design a sort of Greek meander around the band, and it was studded with little diamonds and chips of jade all the way around. It was Simon's promise to love and cherish Adrian. They weren't ready for marriage then, but Simon had wanted to give him a ring anyway.

It took forever, or so it seemed, to maneuver through downtown Milwaukee, especially on a Saturday night, but eventually they made it to the theater and even managed to find parking in the large garage across the way. They wound up parking on the top level, though that didn't seem to faze Simon, so Adrian shrugged and followed along like a good partner.

The wait for the doors to open took longer than navigating the streets, but he'd always enjoyed people-watching, and this was no different. The added benefit of his and Simon's friends joining them after a few minutes made it a bit more fun. Some people were dressed up, others were in beat-up jeans, torn sneakers, and threadbare jackets—though that may have been a style choice instead of a money one.

By the time they made it inside, he was nearly as excited as Simon seemed to be. Simon bounced on the balls of his feet and smiled at everyone as they passed. It was hard to tear his eyes away from Simon, but as soon as they made it inside the main theater itself, Adrian immediately went in search of the interpreter. Once found, he grasped Simon's hand and led him to the right side of the room, then picked two seats close to the front.

He was a little surprised when James, Chase, Teague, and the rest of the group followed them to the same area and sat with them. He'd noticed that James even had his rainbow forearm crutches with him and a T-shirt with what looked like the poster for the show printed on it. Knowing James as much as he did now, Adrian figured James had probably made it himself. Dal and Alex had even come up from Chicago for the evening, and it had taken Adrian a moment to remember that the stunning woman on Dal's arm was his husband.

Simon sat beside him, and at the announcement that the show was about to begin, he pulled out his wallet and retrieved a large bundle of bills. Adrian had a similar stack in his pocket—as did all the others in their little group. Simon had explained that all the tips the acts got went to a group in town that helped youth in need through a shelter, drop-in center, and outreach and coordination programs.

Adrian pulled out part of his money, knowing he wanted to spread it out throughout the show. All the money went to the same place, but the different queens and kings deserved their own tips.

The deep vibrations through the floor and seats heralded the start of the show. He watched the signers—there were three, and all were wonderful interpreters and very engaging to watch—and the performers, loving each act more and more. The hosts were funny and the outfits blinding.

Watching Simon and their friends run up and hold out their tips was funny, especially when Chase got a kiss from one of the ladies. The smile when he returned to their group of seats was almost as dazzling as the glitter pasties the next lady wore.

Adrian had never given much thought to drag shows, or music really, but he quickly changed his mind as act after act lit up the stage and the music reverberated through him. He swore to himself that he would start doing more things like this, especially if Simon would go with him. Watching Simon seat-dance and clap distracted Adrian more than once, but he figured the performers would forgive his distraction, especially if they saw his hot partner.

The acts danced up the aisles, as well as across the stage, engaging the audience even more. The little kids who took tips up melted his heart, and by the end of the show, he wished it would start all over again. He'd never enjoyed a group outing like he had that one.

Well, no. Going to PrideFest and watching two of his new friends get married on the spot trumped the charity drag show, but still. As they left, he signed with Simon and Chase about how much he'd loved the show and showed them he'd even input the date for the next year's show into his phone's calendar already. And watching as Airy and Teague hung out with his new friends made the night perfect.

On their way through the open hall between the different areas of the theater, Simon stopped at one of the tables and picked up some cards. When Adrian went to ask about them, Simon handed one over. He blinked hard as he looked it over. It was a list of various forms of gender-neutral pronouns. Adrian read them, pleased to see the cards there. He knew of them, of course. He'd seen them at the LGBT Resource Center on campus, which he visited regularly. But seeing the cards and watching as others picked them up warmed him inside. The more that people understood how to embrace those not like themselves and the more those who felt left out by their own community found ways to be understood, the better life would be.

When they reached the front doors, Adrian noticed a couple walking along with a woman in a wheelchair. They were having trouble getting through the crowd. He turned and touched Rhys's arm to get his attention.

"Yes?"

"Want to use your size and presence for some good?" Adrian asked, then pointed to the threesome in question. Without another word, Rhys quickly moved over and got people to move, then he opened the door and held it so the three could all go out more easily.

It was one of Adrian's pet peeves; like Hearing people ignoring him or treating him as something lesser for not hearing. He tended to get indignant for others who were different—be they in a wheelchair like the woman was, on crutches like James, or any of a million other reasons that someone was looked on as disabled instead of as differently abled.

The touch to his own arm drew him out of his thoughts. Adrian turned and smiled when he saw James and Seth. "That was nice of you," James said, nodding to where Adrian had pointed Rhys. "I wish more people were like you and our friends."

Adrian was never sure how to respond when others praised him for things he considered simple manners and courtesy. "Thanks but—"

Seth held his hand up to shush Adrian. "No, there is no *but* to this. It was nice of you, and considering how James has been treated before due to his sticks—" Adrian loved how even the proper Mr. Seth Burns called the forearm crutches "sticks." "—it's nice to see others willing to help."

"Thank you." He smiled at them both but didn't see that he'd done anything worth their attention.

Simon leaned in and kissed Adrian on the cheek before he motioned them all to keep moving. They were a large group after all and sort of blocking the path for others.

As they spilled out into the cold night with the snow slowly drifting down, Adrian looked around at his friends and lover and wondered at how much his life had changed in less than a year. He'd gone from single and quiet, to being in love, committed to his partner, and out doing all the things he'd ignored because he thought they were for Hearing people or that he wouldn't fit in. He'd been surprised when Teague and Airy joined them, even more so when he learned they'd been going all that time.

He was still surprised how that one dinner outing could have led to all these changes. But not a day went by that Adrian didn't thank Chase—even if only in his own mind—for conning him into dinner with "the guys." Adrian once again took Simon's hand as they crossed the street, thrilled Simon was beside him.

A place he hoped Simon would be always.

TEMPESTE O'RILEY

DESIGNS of DESIRE

Desires Entwined: Book One

Artist James Bryant has forearm crutches in every color from rainbow for fun to sleek black for business. He even has a pair with more paint splatters than metal. After his family's rejection and abuse from a man he thought loved him, James only just gets through the day by painting. He lives in constant fear that he's not worthy of anything, let alone love.

As CEO of his company, Carrington Enterprises, Seth Burns is a take-charge kind of guy, and he is instantly smitten by the artist helping with his newest project. When he witnesses James suffer a panic attack, a protective instinct he never knew he had kicks in. He truly believes nothing is unobtainable—including James—if he's willing to put in the time and effort.

James is shy and confused by Seth's interest in him as a person. With Seth's support, can he work through his fears to finally find the true love he deserves, or will someone finally land the crushing blow he won't survive?

www.dreamspinnerpress.com

TEMPESTE O'RILEY

BOUND by DESIRE

DESIRES ENTWINED SERIES

A Spin-off of *Designs of Desire*
Desires Entwined: Book 1.75

Despite his past abuse, James has come to terms with his relationship with his Dom and lover Seth. Seth treats James with all the trust and love his sub desires. There is only one thing left to do to make it all complete: Seth needs to put a collar on James.

www.dreamspinnerpress.com

TEMPESTE O'RILEY

DESIRES' GUARDIAN

DESIRES ENTWINED SERIES

Desires Entwined: Book Two

Most people see Chase Manning as the party-boy twink he seems on the surface. Only James, Chase's BFF, knows the depth of his loyalty and the extent of the wounds Chase carries inside. When Chase meets Rhys Sayer, things don't go well, but he can't shake his attraction to the huge, sexy man.

Rhys is a man of contradictions and fear—a strange combination for a PI and bodyguard. He's in a bad place emotionally when he sets eyes on Chase for the first time. When Chase puts the moves on him, Rhys insults him, thwarting any possibility of a relationship. Rhys doesn't see himself as a complicated man, but he dreads the very kind of connection he desires.

Just as they're trying to overcome their uncertainties, Chase is put in harm's way. Luckily Rhys and their friends have all the right talents to help Rhys save the man of his dreams.

www.dreamspinnerpress.com

TEMPESTE O'RILEY

TEMPTATIONS *of* DESIRE

DESIRES ENTWINED SERIES

Desires Entwined: Book Three

Alexander James Noble is a gender fluid gay man who gave up on finding Mister Right a long time ago. He's not asking for much, though. He just wants a guy who loves all of him and appreciates his feminine form too.

At the local LGBTQ center where Alex regularly volunteers, he meets Dal Sayer, an officer of the Milwaukee PD. Because he's been rejected one too many times, Alex doesn't trust the huge cop and the interest he shows in him, but once Dal sets his mind on something, he goes all out. Pushing aside his preconceived notions, Alex opens up just a little and soon caves.

From their first date—while dealing with his father's failing health and his parents' demands for him to settle down and have children—Dal never takes his eyes off his goal of making Alex his. But proving to Alex he isn't like all the men who couldn't see him for who he truly was and only wanted to hide him away is harder than he thought.

www.dreamspinnerpress.com

TEMPESTE O'RILEY

TRUTH in LACE

DESIRES ENTWINED SERIES

A spin-off of *Temptations of Desire*
Desires Entwined: Book 3.5

When Alexander James Noble looks in the mirror, he sees a freak looking back at him. Despite his high grades and plans for culinary arts school after graduation, his parents would hate him if they really knew him.

Forced on a shopping trip with his twin sister, Lyric, and her friends, Alex eyes the girls jealously, longing to be able to dress like them—to be them. The constant struggle of being "gender fluid," wrestling with an identity that seems to change daily, begins to wear on Alex. But all those questions and fears seem more manageable when his sister gives him his first skirt and lace panties.

www.dreamspinnerpress.com

TEMPESTE O'RILEY

DESIRES' PRIDE

DESIRES ENTWINED SERIES

A Companion to Desires' Guardian

When Chase Manning wakes up on the first morning of PrideFest, the last thing he expects to find is his lover and life partner, Rhys Sayer, on bended knee. But the news that marriage has been legalized in the state is a game changer for both of them.

After a mad dash to the courts, all they want is to find their friends at PrideFest to celebrate. However, what happens when they arrive will bond them together forever—if their friends don't have a collective meltdown about their sudden disappearance first.

www.dreamspinnerpress.com

Tempeste O'Riley is an out and proud pansexual genderfluid whose best friend growing up had the courage to do what they couldn't—defy the hate and come out. He has been their hero ever since.

Tempe is a hopeless romantic who loves strong relationships and happily ever afters. Though new to writing M/M, they have done many things in their life, yet writing has always drawn them back—no matter what else life has thrown their way. They count their friends, family, and Muse as their greatest blessings in life. They live in Wisconsin with their children, reading, writing, and enjoying life.

Tempe is also a proud PAN member of Romance Writers of America®, WisRWA, and Rainbow Romance Writers. Tempe's preferred pronouns are they/them/their/theirs/themselves. To learn more about Tempeste and their writing, visit tempesteoriley.com.

Kaden Thorn, a dental surgeon who lives a quiet life, has no hope of finding the love he craves. A vicious gay bashing cost him the use of his legs and confined him to a wheelchair. He has given up hope of finding a Dom or even a nonkink partner to love him. When his best friend practically forces him to attend a dinner party, the last thing he expects is a strong Dom who can see beyond his wheels.

Deacon James is an architect and a demanding Dom, but he has spent the past couple of years without a sub or partner. When an employee invites him to a dinner party to meet his girlfriend, Deacon smells a setup but agrees anyway. He prides himself on being an excellent judge of character, and when he meets the younger dentist, he sees past the chair and finds a sweet submissive man who more than piques his interest.

Kade's fears and demons continue to haunt him, challenging Deacon to use everything he's learned as a Dom to earn Kade's trust and submission. Deacon's determined, though, willing to battle all of it to have Kade by his side and at his feet.

www.dreamspinnerpress.com

Jason Grant runs his own IT business from home, owns his own home, and has the best friend he could imagine. What he doesn't have, or believe he will ever have, is love. When Jason catches a glimpse of his new neighbor on moving day, his libido ignites and his fascination in piqued. He even manages to concoct an excuse to go over and meet the man who makes him hope and want for more than he has in years.

Keith Skyler is a shifter in a world where his kind is known only to a few, but they don't often mix and they never mate. Keith has been hoping for a mate since before he can remember, but gay lynx don't have true mates. As far as he knows, they don't have mates at all. However, while moving his little family across Seattle—and away from their tribe—his reality tips and spins more than he thought possible.

When these two men meet over a dish of five-cheese broccoli-noodle casserole, sparks fly. Who knew a welcome-to-the-neighborhood gift could give both of them their chance at love?

www.dreamspinnerpress.com

www.ingramcontent.com/pod-product-compliance
Lightning Source LLC
Chambersburg PA
CBHW060102260626
47160CB00005B/1758